**He knew that investigating a crime could be danger-
ous, but he hadn't expected trouble on a night like
this...**

Suddenly all the lights in and around the house began
to flicker—once, then again, then total darkness in the
entire neighborhood. A high-pitched sound suddenly
pierced the thumping of the wipers. It startled Sidney,
and then he heard it again. He peered through the rain
streaked windshield. Lightning flashed, and he saw the
shadow in the den move quickly toward the entry hall.
Then he heard a definite shout.

He turned the headlights back on. The lights from the
car picked out Cal starting up the stairway. Sidney
pushed open his door. The rain and wind hit his face, and
he struggled to get out of his seat. He still had his seat
belt on. The door slammed back at him in another gust of
wind. Finally getting unhooked and outside the car, he
had difficulty seeing anything in front of him as he headed to the house, but he knew something was very wrong.
The rain and the wind pounded him as he finally reached
the front door and opened it. He stopped momentarily,
surveying the scene in front of him.

Cal lay motionless at the foot of the stairs and Sidney
saw Becky at the top, trying to pick herself up with the
aid of Tillie. The contents of one of the overnight bags
littered the stairway.

Midsummer in the lowcountry of South Carolina is a dreamy, quiet time. Professor Sidney Lake uses this respite for literary research and planning his next semester, but his Gullah housekeeper, Tillie James, has other plans for him. She needs his help in dealing with a touchy subject: the death of George Reed and the suspicions it aroused that his wife Becky was involved, even though the coroner and the police chief declared Reed's death an unfortunate accident. As the police are in the business of catching the guilty and have no interest in proving someone innocent, it's up to Lake and Tillie—along with his graduate assistant, the local minister, and a retired policeman—to save Becky Reed's reputation. The proof of her innocence seems to rest on the quirks of the rising and falling tide in the marsh where George died. But the search for the truth turns out to be more than Sidney bargained for—and suddenly, his life and those of his friends are on the line...

it wasn't an accident, it must have been murder. And the most obvious suspect, of course, is George's long-suffering wife Becky. This is where Sidney Lake, a professor at a local college, comes in. Convinced by his housekeeper that Becky is innocent, Sidney sets out to prove it, setting in motion a chain of events that will put several people's lives in danger. *The Rising Tide* is both an intriguing mystery and a treatise on human behavior. Holland's character development is superb, creating a host of interesting characters, from down-to-earth local fishermen—who don't need forensics, only their knowledge of the tides, to know that this accident was murder—to charming, if somewhat clueless, graduate students, to interfering busybodies eager for any snippet of gossip they can spread to willing ears. Between his characters' fascinating idiosyncrasies, to his in-depth descriptions, Holland gives his story a ring of truth that's a rare treat. ~ *Regan Murphy, The Review Team of Taylor Jones & Regan Murphy*

ACKNOWLEDGMENTS

Writing about the lowcountry is a true pleasure, as the beauty and calmness of its vistas lend themselves to quiet thoughts and contemplation, although they can also lend themselves to daydreaming and excessive descriptions of the rising and ebbing tides of the salt-water marsh. Luckily, I had some very good people to keep me on track. Carol Kent Holland has always been my chief critic and editor, whether writing fiction or non-fiction. She has the sharpest pencil around and has great instincts for characterization and word sense. After all these years, she knows me better than anyone else and is fearless in her opinions and suggestions. I guess those early journalism courses had more of an effect than she originally thought. Thank you for your patience, love. and criticism.

My first readers of *The Rising Tide* were Pete Palmer of Beaufort, South Carolina, and Kevin Holland of Arlington, Virginia. Pete understood the lowcountry of South Carolina while Kevin did not and kept confusing it with Beaufort, North Carolina, a world apart. They made me write for both worlds so the familiar and unfamiliar reader could understand the images being presented.

Never underestimate the value of a good professional critique group. Other writers can be harsh critics and truly test your writing skills. The Silver Quill Writers Group of Williamsburg, Virginia, challenged me at every turn. Much thanks is owed to Elizabeth Brown (E. Compton Lee), Cynthia Fridgen, Pat Ryther, and Peter Stipe and their blue, red, green, and even purple pencils that, at times, cut and slashed unmercifully. However, I must admit I gave as much as I received when it came to their novels. The five of us tucked away in a small conference room every other week for three hours filled with criticisms, arguments, concerns, learning, and laughter made all of us better writers—and, hopefully, made our editors lives a good deal easier. Five story tellers crafting tall tales of murder, love, sadness and heartbreak—what great fun. Thank you all.

Black Opal Books tag line to its logo reads *Because some stories just have to be told*, and I am truly thankful for their support. Bravo to you all from Lauri to Faith, Jack, Arwen, and J.P. Sidney Lake and Tillie James thank you as well. You allowed them to be born and continue to thrive.

One other acknowledgement is especially needed and that's to Cassie—Cassandra's Chocolate Kisses—our chocolate Labrador retriever. She was my model for Mickey (Mrs. Micawber) and my constant companion while writing, walking, thinking, and planning. Although now gone, she continues as Sidney Lake's companion serving him well in the Sidney Lake Mystery Series.

Tim Holland

The

Rising

Tide

A Sidney Lake Lowcountry Mystery

Tim Holland

A Black Opal Books Publication

GENRE: MYSTERY/DETECTIVE/CRIME THRILLER

THE RISING TIDE
Copyright © 2017 by Tim Holland
Cover Design by Jackson Cover Designs
All cover art copyright © 2017
All Rights Reserved
Print ISBN: 978-1-6269436-73-6

First Publication: MAY 2017

Published by Black Opal Books **http://www.blackopalbooks.com**

DEDICATION

For Mary Frances Broderick Holland, who taught me to read, write, and love a good mystery just as she did—this one is for you.

Chapter 1

The skiff drifted quietly in the still water—barely moving. George Reed stood up slowly, not wanting to make a sudden motion that would attract attention. The small boat wiggled in the water and sent tiny ripples out from its sides as he looked straight ahead over the bow and focused on the forested shoreline ahead of him.

"You're sure about this?"

"Absolutely," answered Warren, sitting behind him with a paddle lying across his lap. The long pole he used to push them out into the secluded spot in the middle of the open area with the best view rested along the left side of the boat, as it could no longer reach the deep, soft bottom.

George, now using the binoculars, carefully searched the shoreline of the small marsh island nestled in the remote reaches of the Morgan River. The tall marsh grass, that extended out from the island and surrounded the area from which they watched, made the small boat and its passengers virtually invisible.

"Should be about two-thirds of the way up on the left side. Got the camera with you?" Warren whispered.

"Got it right here around my neck so I won't lose it," George whispered back, while shifting his focus to a point mid-way up the line of trees.

He inched his head around laterally, while holding the binoculars steady, and examined each branch carefully. When he reached the perimeter of his search pattern, he focused on the next six feet above that and worked his way back. His digital camera with a small telephoto lens moved across his chest with the rhythm of his movements, its long looping strap around his neck so he wouldn't drop it overboard if the small boat suddenly shifted under him. Although a sure-footed experienced boater, he knew that he likelihood of hanging onto both the binoculars and the camera in a rocking flat-bottomed skiff would be slim, especially with the four scotches swirling around in his head. He kept one hand on the binoculars but the other one he wanted free in case he needed it for stability. An old hand at this, he had no expectation of accidentally falling out of the boat but knew that losing the camera could be a real possibility. It was his favorite for this kind of shoot: finding something unexpected. He brought it with him when he transferred to his friend's skiff from his own boat, which would have been too large to maneuver to this precise spot.

Finally, he thought he saw something. Focusing his eyes on an area near the top of one of the tall, skinny, pine trees, he took hold of the camera with his free hand but kept looking intensely at the tree. With extreme care, he switched from the binoculars to the camera—the left hand moving down and the right grabbing hold of the camera and bringing it into position. The small but efficient telephoto lens confirmed his find.

He started to whisper quietly, "Yeah, I—" He then gave out a yell, "Whooooooo—" as the skiff suddenly rocked violently. He dropped the camera as he spread his arms out to keep his balance. The binoculars headed for the water. "What the—" he started to say as he realized Warren seemed to be purposely rocking the boat even harder.

The camera, on its elongated strap, bounced wildly against his chest, leapt up, and hit him in the mouth, and then went over his shoulder to his back. He lost his footing and, as he went over the side, his friend reached out and made a grab for the camera strap.

"I've got it." Grabbing it tight, Warren wanted to get it off George's neck and into the water, where it would be destroyed. The plan wasn't working. It had gone terribly wrong. There wasn't supposed to be that long strap. This was supposed to be an accident, with the camera the only casualty.

George went over the side but the strap around his neck held by Warren pulled his head back. Warren, now panicking and fearing he would be pulled into the water, tightened his grip on the strap. George's head snapped back hard and slammed against the edge of the boat with a terrible cracking sound. His body went limp immediately and the camera strap broke sending the camera flying into Warren, who took a glancing blow to the top of his head. The force of George going over the side pushed the skiff in the opposite direction away from where he went into the water. The paddle went into the water. The pole went into the water. Warren fell backward in the boat— dazed. Frightened birds took flight all around, wings flapping anxiously. The water boiled and rolled pushing the skiff away from the drowning man.

Warren pulled and clawed his way back into his seat. The boat had been completely turned around, and he realized he faced the wrong way as he looked for his friend. He spun around and could see heavy ripples in the water but no sign of George. The urge to jump in after him flashed across Warren's mind but left just as quickly. The water here was ten feet deep and he was no swimmer. He spotted the paddle about twenty feet opposite the boat drifting toward the marsh grass and began hand paddling toward it.

He kept looking back over his shoulder as his hands hit the water. Still no sign of George.

With the paddle in hand he made his way quickly to where he believed they were when George went over the side. The area was almost completely calm again, still no sign of George.

Panicking again, Warren searched in vain, trying to see through the black water. He didn't even know if he was in the right spot.

"Oh, my God! What have I done?" He sat alone in the middle of the boat with his head in his hands. The camera, the focus of his plan, sat in a pool of water at his feet. "It's been at least five minutes. He must be dead. I've got to get out of here. I've got the camera, and I'm sure the pictures are on it. No one knows I was with him. They'll just think he fell out of his boat, drowned, and drifted in here. It happens all the time. There's nothing I can do."

Warren looked around nervously. The quiet returned, the water still again, the ripples gone. The birds were coming back. He quietly put the paddle into the water and made his way back to the main channel through the marsh grass the way he came.

ɛ৲ɔɛ৲ɔ

Warren sat in front of his computer and proceeded to bring up the on-line edition of *The Island Packet. The Beaufort Gazette* with the front page story about finding George Reed's body sat on the table next to him.

He searched through all the local stories and found one

that mirrored what the *Gazette* printed. *Good,* he thought, *no hint of foul play.*

Chapter 2

Tillie muttered to herself as she dusted around the entrance to Sidney Lake's office. "I know she didn't do it. She's a good woman, a nice lady. She's one of my church ladies. No, she didn't do it. It was an axident. I just know it." She carefully kept one eye on the figure behind the desk as she spoke and, seeing no reaction, increased the volume of the last four words.

"What was that, Tillie?" Sidney didn't look up when he spoke but kept working away at the computer, his back partially to his housekeeper. Hearing Tillie mumble as she did the house work was not unusual but, this time, the tone and volume of her voice caught Mickey's attention and the black lab, lying on the floor at the edge of the desk, raised her head and looked directly at Tillie.

"I said she didn't do it."

Sidney now joined Mickey in looking at her standing in the doorway, the pocket doors to the room being fully opened. "Who didn't do what?"

"She didn't kill him."

Sydney, now fully engaged, changed focus from, *The Egoist* by George Meredith, which he planned to include in the fall semester of USC Beaufort's lifelong learning program, but kept himself ready to continue. Turning his chair to face her and looking over the top of his reading glasses, he responded with a puzzled look on his face. "She didn't…what? Someone killed someone?"

"Professor Lake, didn't you see the paper this morning? It was right there on the front page." Tillie stopped her dabbing at the pocket doors with her dust cloth and stood straight and tall in the doorway. Mickey got up and went over to sit directly in front of her, tail lazily wagging from side to side. Although they were, technically, employer and employee, their relationship had grown over the years since Rose's death five years ago in 2009. She watched over him now as she would an older, bachelor brother, and he looked upon her not only as a friend and part of his household, but also as a loyal companion to whom he felt obliged for a variety of reasons.

"I—yes, I did, but I just gave the front page a quick glance and didn't really spend much time on it."

"Mister George Reed was found dead in the marsh yesterday afternoon an' people are sayin' Miss Becky did it."

"George Reed?" Sidney perked up. He leaned forward in his chair and looked at Tillie in disbelief. "The landscape business? I know him. Know Becky, too."

"That's the one."

"I saw her at church yesterday. Her full name is Rebecca. And she killed him?"

"No, she did not!" Tillie stamped her foot to emphasize her objection to his supposition.

"Well, there must be something to it if the police have charged her with his death."

"But they haven't. That's the whole point. The police haven't said she did it."

"Really?"

Mickey decided that this was going to be a longer-than-anticipated interchange and lay down at Tillie's feet.

"If the police haven't charged her, who claims she killed him?" Sidney asked. "I know the Reeds, and none of this makes any sense."

"Egg-zackley! That's what I been sayin'. She didn't do it!" A good firm shake of the head this time. "She's one of my church ladies, and they're all good people. Miss Becky didn't do it!"

He looked at his housekeeper intently. "Let's step back for just a moment. You say that George Reed was found dead in the marsh, the police have not charged Becky Reed, but someone said she did it. Right?"

"Right."

"Who?"

"Who?"

"Who said she did it?"

At this point Mickey's ears perked up, as it sounded as though they were doing an imitation of the owl in the backyard that had been tormenting her.

"Everybody's sayin' it."

"Now tell me, why would they say that, especially if the police haven't said it?"

"It's the way people are. Always lookin' for the bad in things." She took a defensive stance, folding her arms across her ample chest, and tilting her head so that her good right eye could stare firmly at him.

Sidney shifted his bulk and moved the chair slightly away from his corner-positioned desk. Tillie then took a small step into the room so that she now stood at the edge of the carpet and positioned herself just to the right of the leather love-seat on the wall opposite the entrance.

"Tillie, please, there has to be more to it than that."

Tillie thought for a few seconds. Mickey, hearing the break in the conversation, turned her head toward Tillie, waiting patiently for her to speak, and then moved onto the carpet.

"Well, it is kinda funny. I don't actually mean *funny*, I mean strange, like unusual."

"I'm afraid you still have me in the dark." He leaned back in his chair again and this time folded his arms defensively, resting them on his large midsection.

"Well, Professor Lake, if you'd read the paper you'd know what I mean." He could hear the frustration in her voice. "Here, let me get it for you and then you tell me what you think." Tillie immediately turned and left the room heading for the kitchen at the rear of the house, followed by Mickey in search of a snack.

Sidney, on the other hand, shifted his five-foot-eight, 230-pound frame in his chair, turned to his desk, shook his head, muttered to himself, and reached over to bookmark the page he was reviewing.

She came back just as he moved the book to the side. "Okay, you take a look," she said, as two of the three main females in his life made their way back to his office. She handed him the paper, and he spotted the article headline immediately: *Man dies in boating accident.*

"Well, yes, now I see it." He leaned back again.

"Professor Lake, read the story!" Tillie raised her voice as she spoke and put serious emphasis into it. The power in her seventy-year-old vocal cords elicited another one of Sidney's over-the-glasses looks.

He read the story while Tillie and Mickey waited, both impatiently. The look on the housekeeper's face remained intent and focused on her employer. Mickey sensed the anxiety, so the two of them just stood there, waiting, a foot shuffling and a tail wagging.

"Okay," Lake said as he skimmed the story. "It looks like Becky and George went out boating on Sunday afternoon and stopped at a sandbar to do a little sunbathing and swimming. According to Becky, she fell asleep and George took the boat out for a ride. George didn't come back and Becky ended up being rescued from the rising tide by some passing boaters." Sidney paused, looked over his glasses at Tillie, and then read on. "Let's see here. The empty boat is later found stuck in the marsh grass in one of those channels that appears when the tide goes out, apparently out of sight of Becky's sandbar. George's body is later found floating in some tall reeds a good distance away from both the boat and the sandbar, although the story doesn't really give specific locations. There's a mention here of a problem that George had that is believed to be a contributing factor in his having fallen out of the boat and apparently he hit his head on some driftwood. That last part was a comment by the coroner." He again looked at Tillie. "There must be something personal about George that the family would just as well not have printed. That, I guess, is also not unusual for the *Times*, especially if the family is pretty well known locally. Sidney finished reading and dropped the paper into his lap. "It seems like a pretty straight forward accident, Tillie."

"But don't you see?"

"See what, Tillie? What am I missing?" The questions clearly demonstrated his own growing frustration. He wanted to get back to Meredith. He didn't need this.

"Professor Lake, everybody still thinks she did it. Mr. Wilcox didn't prove she didn't!"

"Tillie, I don't understand. You seem to feel that, even though George Reed's death has been declared an accident, the issue is still not settled? Consider two points: one, coroner Wilcox clearly said he believed it was an accident and, two, I don't see any indication of anyone saying it wasn't." His voice rose slightly.

"That's because you don't hear them. Everyone I

know thinks that one of my people killed her husband, and I know she didn't. I wouldn't work for someone as would kill her husband, not that he maybe didn't deserve killin', but I'm a good judge of people. In my business I have to be—goin' in an' out of people's houses an' all—an' I know she didn't do it!" Tillie's voice contained a little heat as well.

Sidney sat silent for a moment, trying to digest the logic of all Tillie said. She was a proud woman and particularly proud of her ability to choose good people as her employers. With a spotless reputation, she could pick and choose for whom she would like to work and not just anyone who offered her a job. Money was not an inducement. Tillie and her friends had, on occasion, turned down job offers that would have given them more pay, but if a good housekeeper didn't like you, your money wasn't going to make a difference. Tillie especially liked her *church ladies*, as she called them, a group of five women who belonged to the same church, were close friends, and frequently made referrals on Tillie's behalf. She liked them and they liked her. She also made a point of letting her friends and family know that the people she worked for were the best people in town. Sidney, who prided himself on understanding what motivated people to take or not take certain actions began to see Tillie's problem, in that she viewed her own reputation as being challenged.

With a softer tone, he finally said, "Okay, Tillie, what are people saying?"

"They're sayin' she did it."

"Yes, I know, but how? What have you *specifically* heard? You know, motive, reason, how it was done, that sort of thing." After having read the story in *The Times*, he still didn't have a good idea of what happened to George Reed.

"Well, the story I hear most often is they had a fight and Miss Becky pushed him overboard and left him. Mr. Reed, he liked to drink a lot, as most people seemed to know, an' sometimes he kinda embarrassed her with the drinkin'. Anyway, they figure he was drunk, they had a fight, she pushed him overboard, and then left him to swim home. She then went to the sandbar, didn't tie the boat up right an' it drifted off with the tide. That Mr. Wilcox, he likes Miss Becky and Mr. Reed, so he just decided to let it go as an axident, which it was. Some other people think Mr. Wilcox and Miss Becky had somthin' goin', you know, an' they planned out the whole thing. That's just wrong! There just ain't no truth to it."

"Well, you're probably right about the last theory but what about the first one?"

A very indignant Tillie jumped on his response. "Professor Lake, she wouldn't do that! If Mr. Reed fell overboard she would get him a line an' pull him back in. If she couldn't, she'd go get help. No way would she leave him to float off an' drown. Even if she was havin' a fight with him, she'd still help him. Miss Becky's a good lady, a church-goin' lady, an' she wouldn't do that."

Sidney sat for a moment with one arm folded across his chest and the other resting on it while he rubbed his chin and gently patted his face. He carefully contemplated his next statement before speaking. "Tillie, there are some things about human nature you're not going to change. Jealousy and envy are two very big ones, which when added to gossip, make for a rather large hurdle." Sidney knew that, even if Becky Reed had been accused and then completely exonerated by the authorities of all possible blame, a significant portion of the population would always think she did it.

"I understand that, Professor Lake, but maybe if someone was just to prove she couldn't of done it, that would make a difference. If someone could just show how the axident could happen like it did, an' it was all logical and everythin', then maybe people would stop talkin'."

Sidney ran his hand through what small amount of hair he had left on the top of his head and then prompted her to make the request. "You have something specifically on your mind, I take it?"

"Well, I was kinda hopin' that you could maybe axe some questions. You know everybody there is to know in town, lots of important people."

"Okay, Tillie, what is it you're actually looking for me to do?" As Sidney measured his words carefully, Mickey sat up from her position at Tillie's feet and leaned against her leg, clearly showing whose side she was on.

In an uncharacteristically sheepish way, Tillie threw the challenge to him. "If you could maybe axe some of your police friends and maybe some of your friends in city hall as to what they really think happened? If I went and did it, they'd just ignore me, brush me off like they always do us island people. An' you know that's true. You, on the other hand, they know you. You're white. They pay attention to you an' you know it. Besides, after talking to them, maybe you could put some ideas together and some arguments I could use when people say some bad things about Miss Becky? I know she didn't do nothin' wrong, I mean she just lost her husband and it's not fair what they're sayin' an' I know there's a logical way to say she didn't have anythin' to do with it, an' if I could say the police truly believe she didn't do no wrong an' that it was all Mr. Reed's own doin', well, then I'd have a good argument to use."

Sidney took a deep breath and Tillie obviously needed one. "This is just a supposition now but what if the opposite turns out to be true? I mean, what if the police really think she was in some way responsible for George Reed's death but realize they will never be able to prove it so they just let it go as an accident? There is that possibility."

"Then they'd be wrong an' I don't want to know about it."

Another pause, longer this time, as Sidney weighed his options to become involved or not and what level of involvement would be appropriate. "All right, suppose I have a chat with Ray Morton. He may be retired now but he still knows everything there is to know about what goes on around here, and if he can give me some good reasons as to why there wasn't more of an investigation of the accident, I'll pass them on to you. However, if I never mention this to you again, it's because you don't want to hear what Mr. Morton said. How's that sound?"

"It's a deal." A look of relief. "I'll stop in tomorrow an' you can tell me what he said. I'll be at the Hamdon's and that's just down the street." Tillie, having achieved her objective, immediately turned and walked toward the back of the house to finish her cleaning.

Sidney looked at Mickey and Mickey at Sidney. "Okay, now what do I do?" He leaned back in his chair, took a deep breath, and continued to talk quietly to Mickey, who, as usual, listened attentively. "What was Wilcox thinking? I understand his consideration for the family in not wanting to add to their grief, but it looks like he didn't ask the state law enforcement department people to have a look at things. An extra day or so wouldn't have made a big difference. But then, maybe old George was so drunk and the evidence on the boat was so obvious that confirming the cause and manner of death was indisputable, routine, academic, 101 stuff. We can hope, can't we, Mickey? Besides, we both know we can never say 'no' to Tillie, can we? We owe her too much, so let's get it over with so I can get this outline I'm working on wrapped up."

⋘⋙

Warren put down *The Morgan City Times. Good,* he thought, *they've got it down as an accident as I thought they would. There's no way they could think anything else as long as they don't get hold of the pictures. Now if I can only get the damn camera to work so I can make sure they're there, then I'll destroy it. But I've got to confirm I've got them.*

Chapter 3

Shortly after lunch, Sidney wrapped up his work on Meredith for the day and decided to take Mickey for a walk. Besides, something nagged at him about George Reed's death and if he didn't figure out what it was he'd find himself thinking about it in the middle of trying to concentrate on Meredith. Steele Wilcox already looked at it as an accident so he must have some evidence to prove it. The trick would be to get Steele or someone else to let him know why. What evidence did he have that clearly showed there was no foul play?

He knew the Reeds from church but not well, only casually from simple chats after a service on Sunday morning. He'd been to their landscape business but only to buy odds and ends for his rose garden. Meetings were casual, time of day, how are the roses doing conversations. Sidney really didn't know anything about them other than being able to recognize them on sight. However, he did know where to go to get a personal, intimate perspective: Alice Ringfoot, the secretary to the pastor of the Bay View Presbyterian Church, who was also a big fan of Mickey's. Having served as the pastor's secretary since 1960, Alice Ringfoot was as much a symbol of the church as the pastor. She knew everything of interest about every member. Miss Alice kept an index card file filled with an invaluable compilation of information, where she made notations about births and deaths of family members, job changes, address changes and personal notes about likes and dislikes, so as not to offend anyone. She never removed or erased a notation. Even if someone moved away, their card was merely placed in the inactive section. Pastors had come and gone and all of them found her knowledge of the congregation to be invaluable. When visiting a member of the congregation in the hospital, the pastor would be armed with information on the person's last major illness, as well as the health of the rest of the family. The name of the dog, cat, bird, or hamster would also be in Alice's private record. The pastor showed up with an enormous knowledge base to please those he visited. Yes, Alice Ringwood would be able to give him some of the background he lacked.

"Hello, Miss Alice." Sidney greeted her as he and Mickey came into the church office.

He huffed and puffed as though the office stood on the top of a hill instead of being only a four block level walk. The secretary's desk served the dual function of guard post and greeter station, as you had to pass right in front of it as you entered. The office itself occupied an interior hallway between the two rectangles of the Church Sanctuary and the Education Building. In addition to secretary to the pastor, she also served as de facto administrator making sure the sanctuary door was always open when she occupied the office. Although an open, unprotected church was a contentious issue with some of the elders, as they were concerned about someone wandering in unannounced and unobserved. The current pastor continued to remind them that such openness was the whole idea of a church in the first place. A compromise involved placing a sign on the front door directing visitors to the side door entrance and inviting them to stop by the office, an entrance to which could be found to the left as one entered the church from the side. The interior door to the church would always be left in the open position, so Alice would be able to monitor the visitors. Besides, nothing and no one ever got past Alice.

"Sidney. And Mickey" She did not lift her head but continued to write on a note card. Not only did she recognize his voice but also, peripherally, the jacket he wore, the latter a definite mid-July give away. Sidney seemed to make a formal occasion out of the most mundane events, regardless of the weather. "Cal isn't in at the moment. He's over with the Reeds going over the memorial service." She finally looked up. "Hi, Mickey. Yes, I'll get you a treat. They're right over here."

Sidney let go of the lead and Mickey went right around the desk to say hello and sniff at Alice's middle drawer where the dog treats were kept. "Isn't it just terrible about Mr. Reed? He was such a nice man. It's so terrible when young people die, just doesn't seem right. Not that George was that young but when you're my age, fifty-three is young, don't you think?" One treat gone, then another. "But then you're young, too. Lately, it seems everyone is young, keep getting' younger all the time. Their daughter just got into town. She lives up in Charlotte and drove down this morning. Such a nice girl. Cal is sitting down with them both. Becky is in a terrible state."

So far Sidney had made out pretty much as well on the information front, as Mickey did on the treat side, without ever asking a question. Being a true local, Alice's great grandfather served on the original organizing committee for the founding of the church, there were very few bits of information about town or church activities that she was not plugged in to in some way. "Actually I wasn't really looking for Cal, I expected him to be busy today. I just wanted to find out about the memorial service. I don't know the Reeds that well, except for church. It certainly was a surprise. You must have known them quite well."

"Oh, yes. Well, certainly Becky. She's in and out of here all the time. She's actually the church historian. So good with a camera. Takes wonderful pictures. That's the main job of the historian: record church events. George was the real photographer, though. His pictures of marsh birds and wildlife are just wonderful. Cal's got one in his office. Let me show it to you."

Alice got up, moved to her left through the open door to the pastor's office, and stopped just inside the doorway. Mickey, by this time, had curled up on the floor behind Alice's desk to keep an eye on the snack drawer. Sidney and Alice were almost the same height with her being five feet six inches to his five foot eight, but she was a tall stick of bones and angles compared to his rotundness and seemed the taller of the two. "See, there it is." She pointed to an expertly framed picture of a snowy egret above the bookcase.

Sidney peeked around the door. "I've seen that picture there for years and had no idea who the photographer was."

"That was his favorite thing to do. He just loved roaming around the marsh in his boat and takin' pictures. He often said that if he had discovered photography when he was young, he would never have taken up with landscaping. That's why he wasn't in church yesterday. Out all night takin pictures of birds and such."

"He must have been a very experienced boater."

"Oh, yes, he was always in that boat of his. Day and night he would be out there with his camera. Actually, he had two boats: one to roam around the marsh in and the other for just general things. You can't get close to wildlife in the big boat, that's just for use in the channels. Y'all don't have a boat do you?"

"No, I don't." Sidney envisioned a new entry being added to his file card.

She led them both back to her desk. "Well, anyone from around here knows the best boat to have is a small, flat bottomed one that only draws about two or three inches. You can go just about any place with that. Get right up close to the shore. Best way to go fishin' and crabbin' in the lowcountry. Did it myself when I was younger."

"George must have certainly known his way around the marsh *and* boats."

"Oh, he certainly did. Knew places I never even heard of and I was born and raised here."

"With that kind of knowledge and experience, how in the world did he ever fall from a boat?"

Alice did not answer for a moment, as though wrestling with what to say. She looked down at her desk as she spoke. "I don't like to say things about people who are gone, after all they don't have a chance to correct flaws like we still do but let's just say it was possible."

"I understand. I believe he did have a reputation as a social drinker."

"And for George there seemed to be an awful lot of social occasions." She stopped and covered her mouth with her hand, as though to stop anything else from popping out. "I guess I shouldn't have said that?"

"The truth is the truth, Alice."

Just then the outer door to the office opened and the Reverend Doctor J. Calvin Prentice, pastor of the Bay View Presbyterian Church came in. Cal, a tall, gangly sort who could easily play the part of Ichabod Crane, seeing Sidney immediately offered a cheerful greeting and extended his hand. "Hello, Sidney, how've you been? And, Mickey, figured you'd be nearby."

"Just fine. Stopped in to find out about George Reed's service."

"Isn't it terrible? I just came from the Reeds. Becky's daughter is in. What a shame about George. My goodness."

"Yes, I really didn't know George very well, just knew him in passing from church but I did want to pay my respects. Alice tells me he was quite a photographer and boater. I had no idea."

"Oh, yes. George was quite a photographer. Did you see this?" He moved toward his office and pointed to the picture above the small bookcase.

"Alice just showed me that." Sidney followed him to the doorway. "I've seen that picture for years and until today I never knew it was George's."

"He did wonderful work with wildlife. He took me out with him one evening in that little boat of his and it was amazing how he could sneak up on just about anything. He used a pole to maneuver in the marsh grass. There was a metal ring at each end of the boat and he would just jam that pole through one of them into the muddy bottom and hold us just perfect against the tide." Cal gestured with his arms imitating the action of pushing the pole into the soft bottom of the marsh. "That's the other thing he knew so well: the tides. If you ran into him at any time of the day he could tell you exactly where the tide level was at that moment."

"I guess his love of the water makes the accident all that more bizarre."

Cal studied Sidney for a moment. "You have a minute to stop in? I've been meaning to bounce a few things off you." He motioned for Sidney to come all the way inside and pointed his hand toward the desk surrounded on two sides by chairs, bypassing the conference table that was just inside to the left.

"Of course."

"Alice, do I have any calls?"

"Just Howard Northridge about this year's scholarship candidates. He said he'd call back."

"Good. Sidney, come on in." Cal held the door as Sidney moved in front of him and then closed it. Mickey stayed outside with Alice to guard the treat drawer. The pastor removed his jacket and placed it over the hanger affixed to the back of the door, revealing the short sleeves of his blue check shirt, an item that Sidney would never purchase much less wear. There was something about short sleeve, dress shirts that just didn't fit into his dress code. They seemed to be an attempt to be formal and informal at the same time. Sidney's preference would be to choose one or the other and not try to blend the two, although he was only too aware that the current trend was to blend everything from clothing styles to ethics. "Just grab a seat." Cal quickly checked his desk for messages to see if someone might have slipped past Alice and left him a note, a feat most unlikely to be sure, but he always checked anyway. "You know you mentioned the word bizarre and that's the same word that Becky used," he said slipping into his chair. "She just doesn't see how it could have happened. She said George was the most sure footed person in a boat she knew."

"She doesn't think it was anything other than an accident, does she?" Sidney took the right one of the two chairs positioned in front of Cal's desk, ignoring the one on the side. He sat back, crossed his legs as best he could, and made himself comfortable for a chat with one of his closest friends.

"No, no, I don't think so, but she's having difficulty

believing it could have happened. She's in shock, of course." Cal leaned forward as he talked. "I suppose it's a natural reaction when someone in the best of health dies unexpectedly. When such things happen, it's not unusual to have denial step in. This is probably the toughest part of my job." As Mickey quite often served as Sidney's sounding board, especially when Hattie Ryan was away, Sidney had, at times, become Cal's. Ministers did not usually have many really close friends in their congregations, as there is always a consultant-client relationship with just about everyone. With Sidney, the relationship developed around Cal's interest in Victorian literature, quotes, and references which often punctuated his sermons. Sidney's vast and practical knowledge served as a resource for Cal in his effort to be accurate with his quotes and historical time-lines. Sidney, on the other hand, enjoyed the philosophical discussions and the interesting interpretations that Cal would often present. The two had become good friends on a social and intellectual level: one teacher to another. "I must admit it is strange though."

"What?"

"His falling out of the boat."

"But isn't that the definition of an accident? An occurrence that is unusual, unexpected, out of the ordinary. I mean there isn't anything to suspect otherwise, is there?"

"Oh, no. I certainly don't think so." Cal paused. "Although, people do talk."

"In what way?"

"It's so ridiculous but I do wish that Steele Wilcox hadn't been so quick in the handling of everything. I'm sure he thought he was doing Becky a favor. They were good friends—the Wilcox's and the Reeds, I mean—and not just Becky and Steele, although they were good friends, too, but not as individuals, as couples. Do you

understand?" Cal fumbled and Sidney assumed the gossip reported by Tillie that tried to tie Becky Reed and Steele Wilcox together made its way to Alice and hence to Cal.

"Yes, I think I do, and I do agree with you on the quickness of everything but then it must have been very clear to Steele exactly what happened and certainly no evidence of foul play."

"Oh, I'm sure that's the case." The pastor leaned back and started to play with a pencil. "It's just that people can be so, how shall I say it, cruel, maybe. Gossip is such a terrible thing. I really have to do something on that topic soon." Cal, not known for his preachy sermons, felt more comfortable with the intellectual/literary model for his Sunday lessons. The congregation was made up of people who were not particularly interested in being preached at; told how to live their lives or scolded about an aspect of community life.

They were more inclined to pat the minister on the head and say, "Very interesting this morning, Cal. Good job. I enjoyed it." And then go on about their lives secure in the knowledge that they were well aware of right from wrong and could make the correct decisions without out-side influence.

"I must admit I've heard some things as well. Wil-cox's desire to avoid embarrassment for the Reeds may be doing just the opposite. My understanding is that George probably couldn't have passed a breathalyzer test that afternoon and Wilcox saw no reason why that needed to be public information, after all George was dead and no one else was impacted in the accident—except his own family." Sidney leaned forward in his chair. "Why make public something that doesn't need to be?"

"I agree, but the fact that George tended to over in-dulge from time to time was not exactly unknown. Con-firming that his condition was a contributing factor in the accident might have been a better thing to do."

"Yes and no. Given the nature of a small town like this, I think the gossip would still be there. You're convinced he had a few too many and then just slipped overboard?"

"That's obviously what Steele believes. Becky, on the other hand, hasn't said it outright but I don't think she is entirely willing to admit to it yet. She was used to the fact that once twelve noon hit, the bar was open for George, and the liquor cabinet on the boat was always full."

"She still thinks it was an accident, though?"

"Oh, yes. She just doesn't seem to agree on how it happened."

"Does she have any ideas of her own?"

"I don't think so. When someone dies unexpectedly from an accident, especially a meaningless one, it's very difficult to come to grips with it. There's nothing heroic about falling off a boat and hitting your head. There's an anger, a disbelief that develops. A life is ended and it's hard to believe it could happen so easily."

"Yes, I can see that. Well, I think I've taken up enough of your time," Sidney said, firmly grabbing the arms of his chair and pushing himself to his feet. One of his prime requirements was to always find chairs with arm rests. "What are the arrangements for George?"

"Everything on Thursday. There will be a private service for him in the chapel at McLaughlin's. Just for the family. That will be at ten a.m. Burial will be in Marsh Glenn Cemetery at eleven, with a short grave side ceremony and then a memorial service here in the sanctuary at twelve-thirty. Becky's circle, I think it's the 'Ruth' one, will put on a luncheon in the community room afterward." Cal, with his tall but light frame, practically leapt out of his chair. "In fact, I've got to get all this to Alice so she can make the arrangements."

"I'll let you get to it then. I'll see you on Thursday if not before. Oh, by the way, didn't you say you had a *couple* of things you wanted to talk about?"

Cal thought for a moment. "Yes, yes. Well, I thought about doing something a little controversial with regard to the bible reading on next Sunday but I've talked myself out of it for the time being. My mistake at the Fourth of July service last week is a little too recent for me to do anything experimental."

"Ah, the Jenkins family, I presume?"

"Right as usual. Having put all that effort he put into the Fourth of July service only to have no one remember any of it other than the Jenkins family, all eight of them, marching out of the church from the second row up front when the choir began to sing the "Battle Hymn of the Republic." No, I think I'll lie low for now."

"Well, if you're planning to go off the beaten path again just let me know. Sounds like it might be a great discussion topic for after dinner with a good sherry or brandy."

"Is that an invitation?" Cal said with a smile.

Always."

Cal, knowing that Sidney spent more time in church observing the people around him and their reactions than following the service itself, knew his friend always had a good feel for how a topic would play with the congregation.

An effective preacher knew that Sunday church service was theater and while not supposed to be entertainment, contrary to the proliferation of popular music and commercial choirs playing for applause, it was important to keep the audience awake and involved.

Not that Cal would intentionally avoid a topic he believed would raise the blood pressure of those sitting in front of him, but he wanted to make sure the approach he took did not detract from the lesson. The trick was to teach and not to offend in the process.

Sidney positioned himself to get out of the chair. "And now I think I've taken up enough of your time this afternoon."

As Sidney stepped out of Cal's office, he saw a tall, lean, Southerner dressed in a light blue golf shirt and dark blue slacks step up to the secretary's desk. His cap was in his hand showing his blond hair and his goatee was clearly visible in profile, "Mornin', Miss Alice. How're you this fine day?"

"I'm doin' well, Caldwell. What brings you here today?"

Mickey never moved but just kept to her curled-up position almost under Alice's desk.

"Oh, the Wednesday night supper. Miss Lilly talked me into givin' the presentation this week. Need the key to the Education Building door."

"Of course, I know that. I made up the schedule." She picked up the key that was on her desk just in front of her and handed it to him.

"So I have you to thank for this," he said with a bright smile taking the key with its blue, plastic identification disk clearly marking it as the correct one for the education building.

"Caldwell, good to see you," greeted Sidney from the door of Cal's office. Mickey's head now came up.

The startled visitor turned. "Sidney, didn't realize there was anyone here. Parking lot was empty except for Cal's and Miss Alice's cars. And Mickey being so quiet I didn't ever see her there."

"Living in town has its advantages."

"That's right, you're just down the street, aren't you? Afternoon, Cal," he added, seeing the reverend follow Sidney from the office.

"A mere five minutes away," Sidney responded. "I'm looking forward to your presentation on Wednesday. A view of the Civil War from the perspective of a Southerner who is a student of the subject is always enlightening."

A suddenly serious Caldwell Talbot replied, "Ah, prefer the War of Northern Aggression, since the states that formed the Confederacy had every legal right to do so."

Sidney, taking note of the change in Caldwell's mood and manner answered: "I have a feeling that Wednesday will prove to be time well spent." Mickey also got to her feet.

"Ah hope so. A good many of your colleagues at the college would do well to focus on the real facts of the war and not just what the Yankees wrote about it." This was vintage Caldwell Talbot. "What brings you here on a Monday?" He made the question more in the form of a challenge than a simple inquiry.

"Just checking on the memorial service for George Reed."

"Shipping the body back north, I guess, like most of the Yankees." There was a sudden hardness to the tone.

"I don't believe so." Turning to Alice, the definitive source for everything, Sidney looked for confirmation. "Isn't George Reed being buried at Marsh Glenn?"

"Yes, he is. George and Becky bought a plot over there about five years ago."

"Most surprisin'," Caldwell continued. "A Yankee wantin' to be buried in Southern soil. Especially one whose family fought against the South. Mostly, they don't want to be caught dead down here, literally. They just use us like they always do." The comment seemed almost matter of fact in a reflective mode, almost as though he was talking to himself.

"I don't think George was that way, Caldwell," said

Alice. "They've been members of the church for almost twenty years and built that landscape business of theirs up from scratch."

Talbot developed a scowl. "Takin jobs and business away from Morgan people. Reed and I have had some words about that from time to time. Plenty of good folks around here from Clemson. We don't need Pennsylvania people tellin' us how to grow plants in Southern soil."

"Goodness, Caldwell, the man just died a terrible death. This is no time to re-fight the war," Alice scolded.

"Makes no difference." Now a sense of frustration and futility entered his voice. "Too many people coming from other places telling us how to do things. We know how to do things just fine. We don't need people telling us we're doin' things wrong. It's only them it's wrong for. They don't like it, they're welcome to leave, go on back where they come from. Hell, if it was so great where they came from and everything was done right there, what're they doin' down here? George wasn't all that different, just here longer."

"Caldwell," said Cal, "I don't know what to say but I do know this is not the appropriate time for this subject matter. I understand how you feel. We've discussed this often enough but this is not the time or the place."

Sidney and Alice remained silent once Cal stepped into the exchange. Caldwell's views about the influx of retirees from the north were well known and he always made it a point to speak his mind whenever the opportunity presented itself. The trick was to determine how much of what he said represented intentional Yankee baiting and how much was hardcore belief. Caldwell often gave presentations about the War of Northern Aggression and he loved to work over a transplanted Northerner whose relatives passed through Ellis Island and had only a limited history-book knowledge of the Civil War.

At them he would throw out names and dates and quote from both pre and post war legislation.

"Okay, a Yankee died so I shouldn't talk bad about Yankees. Did I like George Reed? Actually, I did. We got along pretty good. George and I had some lively discussions. He knew where I was comin' from. Anyway, okay, that's enough for now. I didn't come to talk, I came to check out the audio equipment and projector down the hall stairs and, if it's all right with everyone, that's what I'll do. Good day to you." With that, he headed for the door to the interior hallway and the entrance to the education building, opened it, and left.

A consensus of those in the room would have sworn that each of them muttered the words "good riddance" but no one spoke, they just watched him leave and heard the door slowly close behind him.

By the time Sidney and Mickey left the office of the Presbyterian Church, the sun stood high and hot, too hot to continue walking. Besides, that bit of nagging at the back of his head had become a full-fledged thump, and he needed to do some thinking and planning before he started asking any more questions. Caldwell's reaction startled him.

ೞೞೞ

George Reed's camera sat on the desk in front of Warren. Periodically during the day, he kept coming back to the office to see if he could get it to turn on. He had some success an hour ago after he took the battery out and dried if off with a hair drier but couldn't bring up any pictures. So he just left it with the back open and the hair drier blowing warm air on it. This time it worked and he found twenty-eight pictures taken during the last week of a wide variety of birds in the marsh and around the dock where Reed kept his boat. But they were all taken during the day. Where were the pictures from Saturday night? Those were the ones he needed to destroy. They were the pictures he knew had him in the background. That's why he needed the camera. Where were the pictures?

Chapter 4

"Hello? Mr. Lake? Anybody home?"

"In the kitchen, Geoffrey. Come in." Long ago, Sidney found the kitchen to be one of his thinking places. The routine of cutting, chopping, mixing cleared his head and left it open for solutions to break through. The size of his girth gave evidence of many intellectual searches.

"I didn't think you would be working today?" Sidney moved from the kitchen counter to the small center island. Living in the downtown historic district had its disadvantages. The updating of the kitchen with new appliances and cabinets and some other renovations, such as the addition of the island and a pass through to the combination dining room living room proved to be real challenges, as the original outside footprint of the building had to be retained. The original small size of the room, a design of 125 years ago, remained but minus the small eating area.

"Officially, we're closed. You heard about Mr. Reed? Hi, Mickey."

"Yes. Terrible business that." Sidney looked up from the carrots he was about to slice.

"That's why I came by. Mrs. Reed shut everything down for the week so I have plenty of time to help you with your roses like I promised. Don't really have anything else to do so, here I am." Geoffrey took up a position against the counter and Mickey came over to say hello. Working outside during the summer gave him a wiry look and hardened his six foot frame. He leaned over to scratch behind Mickey's ears.

"Never mind the roses, you could help me with Reed."

"With Reed?"

"I'm afraid I've done it again. I've agreed to look into something I probably shouldn't and, given where you work, you may be able to help." Sidney's involvement in the seemingly innocent death of a New York banker over on Hilton Head made him the center of attention in Beaufort County for a while, publicity he never felt comfortable with.

Geoff looked puzzled, almost as much as Mickey, who tried to decide whether she should stay with Geoff or go back to her standard position at Sidney's feet as he worked with food.

"You are aware of the circumstances surrounding Mr. Reed's death?"

"The boat, the sandbar, all that kind of stuff? Yeah, I read about it this morning. Also got a call from Bev, she usually opens up. Mrs. Reed asked her to call everyone and let them know the shop would be closed for the week." Geoff had already dressed for work when he received the call and wore a green tee-shirt sporting the company's logo: tiny crossed rakes over a potted plant emblazoned on the left breast.

"Did this Bev person say exactly what Mrs. Reed said to her?"

"Not really. Just said Mr. Reed died in a boating accident and the store and shop would be closed for the week, said she would keep in touch to let us know what was going on. She was kind of in a hurry trying to call everyone. Bev knows I usually come in early so she called me first."

Sidney continued cutting. "Well, I understand there have been some comments made relating to Mrs. Reed's possible involvement in her husband's death. A good friend has asked me to help her prove the comments wrong and chalk them up to malicious gossip."

"You're kidding," Geoff gasped, surprise evident in his voice. "Have the police arrested her?"

"No, and I don't think they will. My concern is with rumor and innuendo."

Geoff left the counter and positioned himself on one of the two stools at the front of the island where the professor continued chopping as he spoke. "Interesting. Umm, I guess some of those arguments they had at the shop could give someone the impression they didn't get along too well. Yeah, it wouldn't surprise me to hear a comment or two."

"And do you think there might be some truth to them?" Sidney stopped his chopping and looked over his glasses straight at Geoffrey.

"Oh, I don't know. Really haven't paid much attention. I mean, I'm a summer employee. I'm heading back to USCB in mid-August. Mrs. Reed seems like a nice lady. Do I think she had something to do with her husband's death? I don't know but I'd bet if she did, it was probably unintentional. How did you get involved in all of this and what are you making?" seeing the potatoes and fresh peas on the counter.

Sidney recounted the conversation with Tillie.

"So you're working for Tillie." Geoff made the comment with a wry smile. Needling Lake was not something Geoffrey would normally do with someone—there being a more than forty-year difference in ages—but their relationship had become more and more comfortable as they worked together on his roses, and Geoff's majoring in English literature and philosophy didn't hurt either.

"I hadn't really thought of it that way, but, yes, I suppose you could say that. Shepherd's pie."

"And your job is to prove Mrs. Reed didn't do something she hasn't been accused of. I don't think I've ever had Shepherd's pie." He snared a loose piece of carrot as it popped off the cutting board and came his way.

"You, as usual, have gotten to the heart of things. Yes, I suppose that's precisely what I've been asked to do." Sidney recognized a trait in Geoffrey he admired: the ability to quickly cut through data and get to the heart of a subject without being distracted by non-essential information.

"Okay, cool! How can I help, and does it include dinner?" He popped the carrot into his mouth.

"I'm not quite sure yet, at least of the help part. You're always welcome to dinner. Because of the lack of information, the newspaper article was just bare bones, I'm having difficulty fully understanding not just *what* happened but especially *where* it happened. For some reason, I have a feeling that will be critical. And yes, I know it was on the Morgan River but if I could actually visualize the location, it would be a big help. I think it may have an important bearing on everything. You read the newspaper account this morning?"

"Yes."

"Did you get a sense of exactly where everything occurred?"

"Actually, I didn't pay that much attention to it, other than it confirming what Bev said."

"The paper's on the counter over there, read it through again." Sidney pointed with his knife toward the end of the counter on the other side of the room, away from the food preparation area.

As Geoff began reading, Sidney moved the thoroughly diced carrots into a waiting pot and then covered them with liquid from a bottle of spring water. Mickey then changed allegiances and decided to sit next to Sidney again. Although Sidney didn't get to be 230 pounds by dropping food on the floor, Mickey knew there was always the possibility something could come her way. Sidney often thought of dieting but never actively pursued it. He knew only too well that real weight loss required life style change and exercise, neither of which he had any intention of doing. The words stubborn and unreasonable passed Hattie Ryan's lips more than once before leaving on her summer research vacation to the Lake District in England.

"The problem as I see it," Sidney observed, "is they never say where the sandbar's located, where Becky Reed took her nap, and they don't say where the boat and the body were found, other than to say they were both someplace in the marsh. If we just knew where that sandbar was"

"Yeah, I can see where the paper isn't much help," Geoff said, after quickly scanning the article, "but the sandbar thing may be easy, if it's the same one they use all the time. Mrs. Reed showed it to me, said it was a great spot and I should sneak out there once and a while. She showed it to me on a map in the office. Never did get a chance to try it, though."

"You have a boat?" Sidney said, stopping what he was doing and looking straight at Geoffrey. "Do you still have that map?"

"No, but Susan does—the boat that is. Susan Abbott. Actually, it's her father's boat but we've used it to roam around a bit. I think I know where that map is."

"Excellent! That'll give us a frame of reference for everything. Very good, Geoffrey." Clearly buoyed by the information Geoff provided, Sidney continued in an enthusiastic and eager manner. "Our other problem is one of time—time of day. There is no indication when all of this happened on Sunday. However, since the tide was coming in and most sandbars, undoubtedly, don't appear until the tide is halfway out and disappear the same way on the way in, and if the tide change occurred about one p.m. yesterday—already verified that—we're probably looking at a three to four hour window—maximum. Say, no earlier than twelve noon, given that Mrs. Reed was in church that morning, and no later than three p.m. Also, apparently she was asleep when he left and no idea when he left or how long he was gone, or even the direction he went. When she did wake up, the boat and George Reed were obviously out of sight." Sidney's habit of enthusiastically working out problems while he cooked sometimes resulted in missing or unusual ingredients which could make attending a dinner at Lake's an adventurous undertaking at times.

"Do you think the newspaper knows the answers to most of these questions and just didn't print them?" Said Geoff, who in the process of shifting his weight on the stool, the belt of Geoff's jeans caught against the edge of the counter and made a scraping noise, not unnoticed by Sidney.

"It would not surprise me. The story was particularly vague, although, I suppose some might say that is not unusual for a local newspaper."

"Another thought. I happen to know a couple of students from the college who are working as interns over there this summer. I could do some checking."

"Do that. Geoffrey, you're full of help today. I also have some ideas on how to obtain more detailed information on where everything happened. Between the two of us I may be able to get this off my plate sooner than I thought." Sidney stopped all his preparation work and looked directly at Geoff. "We'll compare notes later. Keep in mind, Geoff, that what we are trying to do is to prove she had nothing to do with her husband's death. If she had pushed him overboard, she obviously would have had to be on the boat to do it. If she was, then she would have had to jump over the side herself and swim back to the sandbar." Picking up the pencil next to his cookbook, he took a sheet of paper from the back of it and began to draw as he spoke. "However, as the boat was far enough away from the sandbar so it was not visible to her rescuers, that means it was drifting inward on the tide and Mrs. Reed would have had to swim against the tide to get back to the sandbar."

The paper was now full of lines outlining a waterway and a bunch of arrows pointing in a variety of different directions. "So, distances here are critical. My suspicion is that even if Mrs. Reed were a tri-athlete or a masters swimmer, neither of which she is, I don't believe she could swim against the incoming tide, as it appears to be almost ten feet at this time of year. The same is true if she drove the boat back to the sandbar and didn't secure it properly. It probably would have been visible in the marsh and certainly in sight of the sandbar." Sidney's animation gave evidence that he believed he had managed to sort everything out.

Geoff got up from the stool. "I can see why the position of the sandbar in relation to everything else is so important and especially the boat. Looks like a slam dunk to me."

"Possibly. Certainly, when one thinks it through, one can easily understand why the coroner didn't see the need to press for an elaborate investigation."

"So my job would be to work out the location, as accurately as possible, of the sandbar to prove she wasn't on the boat when George fell in."

"Well put. I need to talk with Ray Morton to get the official side of things but if it all comes together, as I believe it will, I'll have the arguments Tillie needs to logically refute the accusations she's been hearing."

"Sounds good to me. What about the roses?"

"Let's forget the roses for a few days."

ɞᴄᴔ

As Geoff maneuvered his pickup truck down Howard Street and headed for the drawbridge across the Morgan River, he wondered why Sidney Lake would want to get involved with trying to clear Becky Reed's name. He'd known Sidney now for two years. Mowing his lawn picking up leaves and, lately, helping with the rose garden. They grew comfortable with one another. And then the English literature connection blossomed. The long porch conversations over iced tea and lemonade analyzing *Bleak House* to *Jude the Obscure*. Through it all, Tillie was always there. Even though she worked for Sidney only once a week she would stop by and pass the time of day. Those last four months when Sidney's wife Cynthia was so ill, Tillie came every day. She washed, she cleaned, she cooked, she ran errands. She kept Cynthia company. They talked, they prayed, had a laugh or two and shared family stories. Yeah, Geoff could understand why Sidney would get involved in almost anything for Tillie. It was a form of pay-back. The kind that could never be completed and never should be but also one where you had to try whenever you could.

So Geoff would help his friend pay back a debt that could never be paid and switched his thoughts over to the task at hand: figuring out what happened to the map Becky Reed gave him, the one where she drew some marks showing the location of the sandbar. He didn't remember taking it home so he assumed it has to be at Roots and Rakes. When she drew the location for him they were in the outside shed where the yard manager had a desk and work area. The shed had a light and he often spent time there reading during breaks in his schedule. In fact, he had some of the research material for a paper he did last semester in the bottom drawer of one of the file cabinets.

The drive took him past areas that looked across the lowcountry of South Carolina. The vast expanses of water and tidal marsh were everywhere and made him feel comfortable and at home. So much of the region reminded him of parts of southern New Jersey where he was born and raised. On the drive over he kept visualizing his conversation with Mrs. Reed and the exact location where he thought he left the map.

The distance to the Reeds' garden and landscape center was just five minutes across the bridge on Deer Island. Becky Reed actually sat down at the desk in the shed and marked up one of the local Chamber of Commerce street maps that he often used to locate customers. The maps covered Morgan, Deer Island and the surrounding area and contained all the major streets and landmarks. He remembered her saying that while it was not as accurate a map as one would use when boating, the shore points were in the right places and, with quick triangulation, the location of the sandbar would be easy to find.

The sun dipped in the west as he pulled up to the fence at the rear of Roots and Rakes. There were no cars in the parking lot out front, as expected, since Becky had closed down everything for the next few days. Around back it was the same. He opened the rear gate, drove in, stopped, and then closed the gate behind him, although he did not lock it. No point in going through the lock and unlock process for such a short stay. He parked behind the shed and made his way to its front entrance. As he came around the side of the building, he spotted a car pull up to the back gate and watched the driver get out. He seemed to be carrying something in his hand. Something long and narrow like a piece of pipe. The driver reached out with his left hand and grabbed the padlock. Seeing it unlocked his head came up quickly as he scanned the yard between the fence and the main building. Geoff stepped away from the shed to get a better view and the driver of the car spotted him, hesitated then immediately turned and made a dash back to the car, jumped in, backed up and took off in a cloud of dust. "What was that all about?" Geoff said out loud.

From where he stood he could not identify the person. The car appeared to be green, sort of, and he thought it might be a GM type with four doors. "Nothing to steal here, fella," he said "unless you're into wood chips and manure." But then he realized that the business would be a good target for someone trying to break in since Becky Reed shut it down for the week, and no one was likely to notice anything missing until they reopened on Saturday. It wouldn't be the material stored in the yard that would be the target but the computers, irrigation equipment, and expensive plants and pots in the store. He gave the spot where the car stood another hard look, visualizing everything so he could describe it later if necessary.

Finally dismissing the intruder, Geoff headed back toward the shed, opened the never-locked door, and turned on the light. The desk sat just inside to the left, with a long work table next to it. Some file cabinets and a few folding chairs could be seen on the opposite wall. The shed was used to record bulk purchases of gardening material and to serve as a scheduling center for the irrigation work and plant deliveries that R and R made. His search went quickly with the map being found in the desk's top right hand drawer. He took a quick look at it to make sure it had the markings on it and then tucked it into the back pocket of his jeans.

Mission accomplished.

Geoff then set about closing everything back up the way he had found it. He also made a mental note to give Bev a call and tell her about the green car and suggest she might want to do a quick inventory check.

ᘓᘍᘓᘍ

Warren pulled over to the side of the road. "Damn! The place is supposed to be closed." His hands pounded the steering wheel. "The pictures weren't in the camera so they have to be in the landscape office." He took a couple of deep breaths. "Damn you, George Reed." Finally he began to calm down and analyze the problem. *Okay, the pictures are not in the camera,* he began to reason, *which means either they were never there or were erased when he moved them to his computer for editing.* He paused, trying to gather his thoughts, looked at the road ahead. Staring but not seeing. *What if, after all this, it's the wrong camera? He's a photographer. They all have more than one, even serious amateurs do. They're probably all together in that spare room he pointed out to me. The one that's in the equipment area of the loading bay. He said that he used it for a dark room. If it's anywhere, it has to be there. He wouldn't use the company office computer to play with pictures. There has to be one in the old dark room. But how do I get in and when?*

Chapter 5

S o you're a detective again," said Ray as he handed Sidney a sweet iced tea. Alcoholic beverages before the dinner hour were not permitted in the Morton household.

"No, I am not a detective. The only detective work that really interests me is the literary type. I'm just trying to help a friend solve a problem based on an unusual event."

"People falling out of boats around here is not exactly unusual."

"You know what I mean."

"Still sounds like detective work to me." Ray eased himself into the oversized porch chair across from Sidney and placed his own iced tea on the small table next to him. He did his best to suppress a smile as he made himself comfortable and contemplated the best way to continue needling his friend.

They made a fine pair as neither of them looked as though they ever missed a meal. Although two inches taller than Sidney, at five foot ten, the marine trained body had begun to slip since retirement and his 210 pounds began to be more visible. "Tryin' to know what

the police know about an official investigation is a
mighty suspicious thing to do."

"Yes, yes, I expected that. However, you're not the
police anymore so I'm not being suspicious and I'm not
trying to be."

"Well, what makes you think I know anything more
than what y'all read in the paper?" Ray did not have a
Southern accent, being born and raised in California, but,
after being in Morgan for twenty years, he could drop
into one if he had to and he learned over the years that
Southern speak often contained a natural playfulness.

"Ray, please. Even the newspaper knows more than
they print and you know more about what goes on in the
county and city than just about anyone else I know. Most
people have real hobbies when they retire. You spend
your time sitting around city and county council meetings
absorbing everything that goes on and, when you're not
doing that, you're curled up in a booth at the diner with
all your old police buddies." Sidney tried unsuccessfully
to suppress a smile. "Actually, you just need to get out of
the house and out from under Marie's feet, as that's the
only way she'll keep you in food and give you a place to
sleep."

Ray laughed and shook his head. "You know when I
retired Marie told me she married me for better or worse
but not for lunch. Been retired three years now and it was
the smartest thing she ever said. We don't get under foot,
have our own space, it works. Know some people from
the job that when they both retired found out they really
didn't like one another, split up within a year—after almost thirty years of being married. Well, anyway, yeah, I
do know a thing or two about how things work."

The give and take between the two built up over the
years. They genuinely liked one another. The retired cop
and the English professor, an interesting association

brought together by Mickey. Sidney believed that all domesticated creatures needed to be useful and his Labrador retriever needed to hone her breed's skills. He immediately put her into training and continued with it even after the classes ended, being a firm believer in lifelong learning. The job of retrieving the morning newspaper became Mickey's.

The training went well—bring in the newspaper and get a treat—and Mickey took to it right away. Then one day Ray, who lived two doors down from Sidney, showed up at Sidney's door looking for his newspaper. It seems that Mickey had decided to not only bring in Sidney's paper and get a treat but also went searching for other papers as well. Ray simply followed her home. Sidney apologized, offered Ray a cup of coffee, and they'd been sitting around talking ever since.

"But why do you need to know any more than what's already been reported?" Ray continued.

"All right, let me explain," which he did, putting a good deal of emphasis on the exasperation that Tillie expressed.

"So the idea is that you're supposed to prove that Becky Reed didn't kill her husband even though no one said she did, officially?"

"Look Ray, I'm not trying to be intrusive. You know how I feel about Tillie. Besides, she takes a lot of pride in working for good people in the best parts of town. All I want to do is tell her there's no way that Becky could have killed George because, well, because it just wasn't possible. Which is true, isn't it? I mean the police really don't think she's involved, do they?" Ray sat in his chair and thought for a long moment. "Ray?"

"All right, look. The truth of the matter is that whenever a husband or wife dies unexpectedly the prime suspect is always the spouse. You know that. Even the cop shows on TV got that right, especially when there are no witnesses and the death is either from 'natural causes' or a weird accident. So, yeah, they certainly have to consider Becky as a possibility."

"But ruled it out." Sidney showed some concern with the line of Ray's comments and almost cut him off before he finished.

"Not so fast. You want to know what the story is or not?"

"Okay." Lake, duly chastened, sat back in his chair, and raised his hands, palms facing Morton as a sign of submission.

"Good. My understanding is that whatever investigation they did didn't go anywhere because there's nothing to go on. George had a bump on his head consistent with being hit by a piece of wood. They figure it was a piece of driftwood by the boat where he fell in. The marsh is full of old trees, logs, whatever. Yes, he had been drinking. Yes, he was known to have a drinking problem. Yes, he did drown. Nothing on his boat led anyone to assume there was any form of foul play. Steele and the chief's people took a basic good look at everything. They have no idea how he fell overboard and are assuming it was just a freak accident. His fly was zipped."

"His what?"

"Look, a good many of the male bodies that are found floating around the marsh usually have their fly's unzipped. It's how George fell in once before, only he had people with him that time. He had a few too many beers, stepped over the side of the boat onto the ledge to take a leak, boat hit a swell, and he was gone. The three guys on the boat with him picked him up. Try that alone at night with the tide moving and no one will ever find you in time. Anyway, there's absolutely nothing to go on, which is probably why Steele didn't take his investigation any further. Why waste taxpayer's money when you don't have to and upset the family and a friend, in the process."

"So that's it?"

Ray hesitated. "Yeah."

"Why do I have the feeling that something's missing. It seems pretty cut and dried to me. Do you see a problem that I'm missing? Is there something bothering you about all of this?"

"In all honesty, if I was still around, I probably would have had some words with Pete about signing off so quick. It's not that I see anything really wrong, it's just that there wasn't any reason it couldn't have waited a few days. You know, just tie up any possible loose ends."

"Okay, but that didn't happen so what about my problem?"

"Which one?"

"You're a big help. I need to *prove* that Becky Reed could not have been involved with George's death. I'm not looking for court of law evidence, just something reasonable. Any ideas?"

"Well, let me think." Ray folded his hands on the back of his head and pushed back in his chair.

Sidney sat watching him while Ray looked into space directly over Sidney's head, a spot where the sun would be setting in a couple of hours.

The Sidney Lake, Ray Morton friendship was certainly an interesting one: the Easterner and the Westerner, one being born Virginia and the other California, the English professor and the retired marine sergeant/policemen both now inhabiting a sometimes foreign world. They both moved to South Carolina from those other now alien places. Ray's introduction to the Palmetto State came as a drill instructor at Parris Island, in the heart of the bucolic lowcountry, just outside of Beaufort. During his career, he was posted to the Recruit

Depot a number of times and he and Marie decided to make the nearby lowcountry town of Morgan their new home. When retirement time came, Master Sergeant Raymond Morton and Marie knew they wanted to spend the rest of their lives along coastal South Carolina.

"I suppose the tide would do it. That would be my first cut, given I haven't had a good chance to study anything," Ray continued after some serious thought. "Given the particulars of the situation, you could probably work out that if she pushed him over and left him, returned to the sandbar, where the boat eventually came loose in the rising tide and drifted to where it was found, which, if I remember right, is one of the theories Tillie mentioned, you could verify that the boat could not have made it to the location where it was found by being pushed inland by the movement of the tide around the sandbar, especially since it was out of sight from there."

"That sounds relatively simple and straight forward."

"Yeah. In fact, I wouldn't be surprised if that's what Pete and the boys saw right off when they found the body and the boat, which is why it never went any further."

"So why didn't someone say so?"

"Why? An accident is an accident. Besides a cop's job is to pursue the presumed guilty not prove someone innocent. That's for someone else to do—like you, for instance."

"I needed that."

"You asked."

"Okay, let's say your theory is true, how do I put all this together?"

"An experienced detective like you should have no trouble," Ray said, tongue in cheek as usual. Sidney gave him the over the glasses look in return. "All right, I'll get serious but I still think this is a no brainer for you. Look," he then said in a matter of fact, sing, song way, "obviously you need to know where this all happened. Three locations: the body, the boat, the sandbar. Next you need to know what time of day the drifting occurred and the position of the tides at that time. Pretty straight forward stuff."

Sidney, as Ray had obviously surmised, already worked out most of this on his own. With Geoff already gathering some of the missing information, if he could just get Ray to pitch in he assumed he could have all his arguments together for Tillie by tomorrow and be done with the whole matter. "So how about giving me a hand?"

"What give you a hand?"

"Help me develop my argument. Have an informal chat with your City Hall Café buddies and find out the actual reason Steele Wilcox and Pete Hornig pasted the accident label on George Reed's death so quickly. Based on that, I can put together my arguments to pass on to Tillie. You're the cop."

"Retired cop."

"Sounds good to me. What else have you got to do? Besides, it'll get you out of Marie's hair and give you another excuse to roam around the county building." Ray sat silent again, scratched his head a bit, looked to one side then the other. "Come on, Ray," Sidney prompted.

"Maybe," he finally said.

"Look, you said we needed to know the three locations and the time of day. If you could convince some of your old comrades—especially those who were at the scene—to give you an idea of how Steele and the Chief approached everything, then we could pour over the information and come up with a way to solve my problem with Tillie. I'll buy lunch."

"Oh, well, with that kind of an offer, how can I refuse?"

"Somehow I knew food would do the trick."

"I get to pick the place."

"Deal."

"Okay, but I need you to do something, as well." *Oh boy*, Ray thought, *I can't believe I said that*. It had been with those same words that he enlisted Sidney's help once before and ended by almost getting them both killed over on Hilton Head. Coincidentally, that also started with a body in the water.

"Sure," Sidney immediately responded.

"If you're going to work out marsh and tidal locations to convince Tillie you'll need a chart of the Morgan River. You may not know much about the tidal marsh but, trust me, Tillie and her friends do and you better be dead accurate or they'll never believe you."

"So where do I get one? Boating, as you know, is not one of my strong points."

Ray thought a moment. "Not mine either but I don't think we need anything super special. Why don't you just go down to The Previous Page and pick up something basic or even a recently used one? Tell Jarvis what you're looking for and I'm sure he can come up with something that will do the trick. We don't need anything new and fancy. Besides, I want you to save your money for lunch."

છએછ

Arriving back at his office, Warren knew he had to do something, but what? Or was he overreacting? No one knew about the forgeries. There'd been no public mention anywhere. It'd been five years now but he hadn't been too greedy, at least until last Saturday night. No, the pictures George Reed inadvertently took that night would undo everything, raise too many questions. Him and his damn nature photography, and at night, yet. No, it would ruin him, his family, everything. He had to find them. It had to be the old dark room, and it had to be this week before the landscaping business opened up again.

Chapter 6

After leaving Morton and then briefly stopping by his own place, Sidney made the three-block trip over to The Previous Page on Market Street, one of the few remaining old, local businesses still left on the street. With the influx of retirees from the North, the old downtown shopping district just didn't work anymore. The local shrimp and oyster canneries were all gone and the jobs as well. The transformation to a tourist mecca complete with gift shops, art galleries, jewelry stores, and small cafes and restaurants, as well as the mandatory acquisition of the local bank by a national chain, completely revitalized and up scaled Market Street. While the old facades remained, the stores and shops—now mostly owned by transplants from New York, New Jersey, Ohio, Pennsylvania, and other alien locations—no longer catered to the resident townspeople.

The locally owned pharmacy, driven out by CVS and Walgreens; the stationery store, now a Staples; local markets, now a sprawling Food Lion and Kroger; and all of them now located in strip malls at the edge of town. And while the wealthy locals—who ran the real estate companies and controlled the political environment—

were happy to sell land to the outsiders, they also bemoaned the changes that occurred. Morgan was primarily a one street town, although now with the much-hated-but-gladly-accepted federal funding assistance from Washington, efforts were being made to expand the commercial district along the side streets.

The three bells that rang over the door added to the charm of the used bookstore as Sidney entered the shop. It sat on the edge of the commercial area where rents were a little cheaper, as opposed to being down a block where the main tourist traffic congregated. The bells had a comforting and welcoming sound about them unlike the modern electronic buzzer or chime used by so many new places. The Previous Page had a local reputation of being a cut above the average used bookstore in a small, out-of-the-way town, in that there were no hidden treasures here. Admittedly, it looked disheveled and unorganized with books everywhere—a definite tourist draw—but Jarvis Oliphant, the owner, knew the value of every volume on every shelf in every aisle and if he did come across anything of true value he quickly moved it to a separate section, put it into his own personal collection at home or earmarked it for sale on the internet.

He also carried new material, mainly signed copies of books written by local authors, as well as tourist guides, maps, books and brochures of the lowcountry and anything else in written form that he thought he could sell to a tourist. He could spot serious collectors looking for bargains the moment they came in and sort them out from someone simply looking for an out of print book to read. Sidney frequently visited the shop and had passed the time of day with Oliphant from time to time but couldn't warm up to him.

A member of an old-line family, Jarvis played the combined role of bumbling good ole boy and Southern gentleman with the mixture of chatter and an over the top politeness facade he presented to customers. He never seemed to be out of character.

Sidney looked about the room trying to get his bearings. His plan to enlist the help of Jarvis in finding the appropriate Morgan River charts hit a snag as the *L* shaped sales counter next to the entrance stood empty, so it looked as though he would have to go exploring on his own. He had no idea where to find nautical subject matter.

Locating fiction, history, biography, classics, and some other sections would not be a problem, as they were in an area he often browsed. Sidney drifted toward the back of the book-shelved, crammed part of the store, where he knew the office and store room were located, in the hope of still finding the owner and enlisting his help. A quick look inside the even more crammed and seemingly disorganized space of the office did not uncover the elusive Jarvis. However, seeing the computer on the desk just inside the doorway still showing the Brontë Society website, Sidney presumed Jarvis was not far away or the screen saver would be on. As he leaned over and began to take a closer look at the computer screen, Jarvis came up from behind.

"May ah help you?"

"Yes, Jarvis, I definitely think you can," Sidney said before turning to face the owner, who at six foot three had come closer and looked over Sidney's shoulder.

"Sidney, ah didn't recognize you."

"Not surprised. You usually find me on my hands and knees looking at titles. I wouldn't be surprised if that wasn't a more familiar position for you to recognize most of your regular customers. How have you been, Jarvis?" Sidney extended his hand with a smile and Jarvis took it eagerly with a bit of a chuckle in return.

"Oh just fine. You may be right about seein' folks from a different view. Lot of bendin' an' reachin' goes on in here. Picked up some new books over the weekend an' was just sortin' em out in the back here—" He pointed to the desk behind Sidney that was piled with books and papers. "—am doin' a little research when ah got a strong urge for a Coke," he said with another chuckle. "Lookin' for somthin' special? Seein' as ya seem to know the place almost as well as ah do. Ya usually have the literature section corralled and know where to find everything."

"Definitely out of my element this time. I was just looking at your computer here." The screen display pictured the page related to the Brontë Parsonage Museum and Library.

"Yeah, ah tap into all the major literary web sites, as well as the on-line used book sellers." Jarvis reached in front of Sidney, clicked on Favorites, which displayed web sites for not only the Brontës but Dickens, Austin, Hardy, Williams, Joyce, and every major author imaginable, then clicked on Book Dealers and brought up Alibris, Amazon, Barnes and Nobel, Oak Knoll and a series of others.

"You do some serious competitive pricing, it would seem."

"Internet sure has changed things. Ah can find out just about anything ah need to about any book or author anywhere. Always nice to know what you have. Sure is different than it used to be. So how can ah help ya today?"

"Trying to find some charts of the Morgan River."

"My, that's a little bit out of your usual interest. You need new ones or old ones?"

"Fairly new one, I think. One that shows the Morgan River and marsh areas around it. I don't own a boat so it's not as though I'll be out there using it all the time."

Jarvis began to walk toward the front of the store and

the sales desk. "A little nautical education for the professor then?"

Sidney followed along. "Yes, that's probably what you'd call it. Ray Morton and I were just sitting around talking about the George Reed accident that was in the paper this morning, and I realized I was lost in the conversation not knowing where everything was, you know, the sandbar and everything. Did you know George?"

"Eh, yes ah did, a bit."

"Did you know him well? I knew George and Becky from church but not socially."

"Oh, no. Just came in from time to time, also met at some local chamber of commerce type things and such."

"Being a landscaper, I guess he spent his time roaming about the old gardening books. I know you have a very extensive section on old Southern gardens and even some on gardens in Morgan. I have a rose garden that I fiddle with and I'm always looking for ideas myself." Sidney eyed the gardening section as they headed up one of the aisles. "Yeah, I suppose that would be a big interest for a landscaper. Although, I understand he had a big interest in photography too. It certainly was strange the way it all happened but then I guess boating accidents are a way of life in the lowcountry. I have enough trouble negotiating the roadways around here without trying to maneuver a boat in that river, with the way the tide moves." They reached the front of the store.

"Yeah, if ya don't know what your doin' out there, ya end up stuck in the mud pretty quick. Ah got some maps an' charts over here," he said, pointing to an area to the right of the sales desk, "an' ahm sure you can fine what your lookin' for. Prices are marked on 'em. Let me know when you're done. Need to sort some things out at the desk here."

"Thank you, Jarvis. I'll see what I can find." While

most Southerners looked for opportunities for pleasant conversation and would rather pass the time of day chatting about local events than almost anything else they could think of, Jarvis, although pleasant enough, didn't quite seem his usual chatty self this afternoon.

Sidney began to rummage through the maps looking for one that showed the Morgan River. Ray told him to make sure he found one that had depth markings on it but Sidney didn't really know what to look for. After about five minutes, he had chosen two of them that he thought would do the job and headed over to the desk. Jarvis's local, Southern accent was a treat for the tourists, who when they heard it assumed he wouldn't know one book from another and figured they could find a bargain. Jarvis also knew it and played his part to the hilt. Sidney had learned a long time ago that strong, Southern accents were not unlike strong, New York accents, in that they were not an indicator of intellect just as glibness in speaking was not an indicator of intelligence any more than inarticulateness was a sign of stupidity.

"Well, I think I have what I need unless you have some suggestions for me," Sidney said, returning to the front desk.

"Let's see whatcha got." Jarvis picked up the two maps Sidney had chosen and knocked some papers off the counter in doing so. In picking them up he then knocked over the pad and pen he used to make notes about which books were selling. "Gotta get this place better organized." The bumbling and clumsiness continued. Jarvis just didn't seem to be able to turn off his tourist act. He then began to look at the maps. "These should probably do. Ya got the whole river covered with both of im. If ya knew exactly the spot ya wanted ya could get somethin' just for it but I think these will probably do the job."

"That's the problem. I don't know where anything happened, although Ray does and, when he talks, I'd just like to put something visual to it. Terrible habit of mine, I'm afraid. I always have to fully understand the topics of discussion. I just hate being in the dark."

"Well, like you ahm not much of a boater. Lived ma whole life round here and had lots of fun roaming around when I was kid but those days are gone, just never took to the water. Have a couple of boats o'course. Mainly for the grandkids to go fishin' with. They know where everythin' is out there. Paper didn't say where George Reed fell in did it?"

"No, it didn't. Actually, the paper didn't say too much about anything but then that's pretty much how things are done here: protect the family first. Don't say anything negative if you don't have to"

"Nothin' wrong with that. Nice part bout livin' in a small town like Morgan. Even with the college over in Beaufort getting' bigger an' all those tourists folks from the North thinkin' about settlin' here, we's still a small town. That'll be $25.28 for the two of em." All the time Jarvis was talking, he was also writing and working up the sales tax with a desk top calculator and pad and pen and never really looked at Sidney.

Sidney thumbed through his wallet for the cash. "That's probably true. Someplace larger would have had a more extensive investigation of the accident too. Maps certainly are expensive."

"One of those you have there is waterproof. Won't get ruined if it blows overboard. Accidents do happen. 'Specially on the water, which is why ah try not ta go there." Jarvis took two twenty-dollar bills from Sidney and started to make change.

"I suppose there's good and bad to that but then when you've got something that was obviously an accident, and everyone agrees that it was, why stir everything up? Of course, there's the other side too in that someone could take advantage of the situation."

"Maybe yes, maybe no." Jarvis gave Sidney his change. "Don't need a bag, do ya?" The comment was dismissive.

"No, no. I'll just take them with me."

❧❦❧

The map that Geoff retrieved from the landscaping shed now had three locations clearly marked *S* for sandbar—put there by Becky Reed—*B* for body and *WC* for watercraft—put there by the two interns at the *Morgan Times*. He realized that, while showing the points of interest on both sides of the river and providing a grid of the downtown shopping area, there was no real way to accurately pin point the true location of anything in the river, especially where the boat and George Reed were found. Geoff came to the same conclusion as Ray Morton in that a marine chart of the river would be needed and now headed for Susan Abbott's figuring she might have something he could use. The Abbott's lived on the Morgan River, were an old Morgan family, and owned at least two boats that he and Susan often used to roam around the marsh, in addition to the larger two-masted sailboat the Abbotts used for deeper water excursions. Just before arriving at Susan's, Geoff called Sidney and left a message on his machine explaining that he had the information they discussed but would not be able to make dinner. He would stop by to see him around nine in the morning, if that was okay, as he had another errand to run that evening. Not knowing of Sidney's excursion to The Previous Page, Geoffrey planned to obtain a chart from the Abbott's and have Susan accurately plot the points on it, as she was the experienced boater, and then present it all to Sidney with everything clearly and accurately marked and identified. The plan fell apart when they found the power boat slip empty. It being such a nice evening, Susan's parents took the boat for a ride and the local charts along with it.

"Why do you need the charts, anyway? You've never really been interested in the river before," Susan said, staring right at him, blue eyes suddenly intense. They were standing on the end of the Abbott's dock looking at the empty boat slip.

"Actually, I'm doing a little something for Sidney Lake."

"I didn't know he was interested in the river."

"Well, I suppose you could say he's not really interested in the river."

"Then why does he want a river chart?" Susan placed her hand on his arm and looked at him intently.

Geoff called her a touchy-feely person who always had to make physical contact with a person when talking with them, a habit that sent the wrong signals to many a date.

"It's for research he's doing."

"I thought he was an English Professor?"

"He is but this is different."

"Is it some sort of secret?"

Geoff thought for a moment and looked at Susan standing in front of him. The habit of sharing everything with her came easy to him but now he wondered if he should tell her about the conversation with Lake and wondered if Lake expected Geoff to keep the matter to himself even though he didn't specifically say so. On the other hand, Geoff and Susan had no secrets between them and, given the look on her face, could he afford not to tell her?

"You know Mr. Lake didn't specifically swear me to secrecy but, on the other hand, I don't think he wants it generally known what he's doing."

"Geoff, now you've really got me interested! You know I can keep a secret. I promise I'll not tell another soul." Her grip on his arm tightened.

He almost made a comment but managed to let the moment pass. Challenging her on her secret keeping record would not be a good way to enhance a relationship. Not that she would reveal something intentionally to hurt someone.

She just answered questions honestly without thinking and then became embarrassed and apologetic if it turned out wrong.

"Oh, well, what the hell." He made his decision. Good or bad he would go with it and accept the consequences. "Professor Lake is looking into the death of George Reed and he asked me to get some information for him."

"He's what!" Susan grabbed his arm with both hands this time.

"Look, there are a lot of rumors going around that Becky Reed killed George and—'"

"Yeah, I know. Do you think she did it? Is he trying to prove it?"

"No, just the opposite. He's been asked to show that she didn't do it. It's just an informal thing. Someone who's a friend of Mrs. Reed heard all these stories going around and asked Lake to prove them wrong."

"Isn't that the police's job?"

"Actually, no. As Professor Lake put it the police are supposed to catch the person that did it and not prove that someone didn't." Geoff started to walk off the dock with the idea of heading for his truck but Susan was still holding on.

"I guess that makes sense. Okay, what do we do

next?" She continued to hold him tight and stopped him from going any further.

"We?" He stared into those blue eyes framed by the shoulder length blond hair and Atlanta Braves baseball cap.

"Of course. Even if the charts were here neither you nor Lake would know what to do with them. You wouldn't know one marine marking from the next."

Geoff looked at her and knew she was right. Nautical charts were a world unto themselves. The local Coast Guard representatives seemed to spend almost all their time trying to convince the local boating community, especially transplanted retirees new to the tidal marsh, to take the Auxiliary courses. "Point taken. Well, if we're going to do this, we'd better get going," taking a look at the darkening sky.

"Go where?"

"Back to town."

"No. If you want a chart we go to the marina." They stopped again.

"But the marina's the other way. Why couldn't we just pick something up at one of the bookstores downtown?"

"Because the Old Fort Marina has old, new, used and everything in between. They don't just have new stuff, they buy and sell used stuff. They have everything from clothing to equipment to books and, yes, maps and charts. Besides they'll be a lot cheaper than downtown and if I know you, you won't have more than five cents to your name and you're buying, unless Mr. Lake has provided you with an advance and you're working with unlimited funds."

"Yeah, sure but I don't even know if you're supposed to know anything about any of this, I mean about checking up on Reed."

"But I do know and we're a team. Besides, you'll find

a way to tell him." Leading the way, she headed for his truck.

Geoff shook his head as he looked at her and rolled his eyes. "Okay, we're a team." But he still didn't look forward to the challenge of explaining Susan's involvement to Lake.

∽∾∽

The ride from where the Abbott's lived and the Old Fort Marina, with three stop lights and two stop signs, gave Geoff ample opportunity to fill Susan in on everything he knew. He couldn't leave anything out with Susan's rapid fire questioning technique. A fourth grade teacher in her first year at Bay Front Elementary School, she learned the art and skill of questioning nine year olds as a survival tool as well as a technical one. The questions needed to be simple but straight forward and to the point.

When Susan got going she knew, instinctively, how to hone in on the information she needed. By the time they were halfway to the marina, she knew everything about Lake's involvement and what Geoff had learned from the chamber of commerce map and the interns.

"This is not going to be easy to pinpoint," she said looking at Geoff's map with the three marks on it, as they drove into the parking lot of the marina. "These tourist maps are nowhere near scale. Yeah, we definitely need a pretty good chart. We're going to need a chart that gives us minor channel readings. The depth markings are real important. They'll tell us not only what kind of boat can go where, but also how fast the tide will empty an area. The general commercial ones usually keep to the main channels. Most boaters are looking for the Inter-coastal Waterway charts. We need something better than that."

Once inside the Old Fort Marina Store, it proved fairly easy to get around provided you knew exactly what you wanted. In addition to the store, the marina complex had a restaurant, showers, lockers, a repair and maintenance facility, and just about everything boaters going up or down the inter-coastal waterway could want. Geoff and Susan just stood inside the door and surveyed the main sales room. To Susan's surprise, everything seemed to have changed. Nothing was where she remembered it. The front sales counter being unoccupied they decided to split up with Geoff searching on one side of the room and Susan the other. They had been there no more than a minute when a short, skinny, young, sort of blond haired woman came in the door and immediately stepped behind the counter, her smoke break over. Geoff and Susan, having made no progress whatsoever descended on the front desk almost immediately.

"Excuse me," said Susan, "Where would we find charts of the Morgan River? I haven't been in lately and nothing seems to be where it used to be."

"Charts? Y'all mean like maps and things?"

"Yeah, you know for boating, finding one's way around the marsh." Susan couldn't believe that someone working in a marina would have to confirm that a chart and a map were the same.

"Ah just take care of the register. Just started today. Mr. Carson, the boss, hasn't had a chance to show me everythin' yet. He's in the back checking over some new stuff that came in, if you can wait just a minute I'll ask 'im?"

"That would be great. He would certainly know."

As the clerk headed for the back room, Susan and Geoff explored the check-out counter. They also looked about the room and digested the disorder. There were boxes everywhere: on the floor, on the counter, stacked against the counter, on the window sill. There were pamphlets on the counter offering tourist information, guides to shopping on Market Street, a map of the river like the one Geoff had in his pocket with the marks on it, information about bed and breakfasts and brochures about coming events. The vintage cash register took up most of the room on the counter and, being somewhat of an antique in the computer age, did not perform the now common inventory and accounting functions. Where and how one would write up a sale appeared to be a mystery unto itself.

"He said you'll find what you're looking for over with the books and magazines over there on the left," the clerk said returning from the back room.

"I guess that makes sense," said Geoff.

"Actually they're facin' the window on the other side of that first shelf"

"Thanks."

As Susan and Geoff made their way to the magazine racks, a man dressed in Bermuda shorts and a golf shirt came through the door to the back room and headed for the front desk. He gave them a look as he walked by and seemed to focus on Susan. A good five minutes later, with two charts spread out before Geoff and Susan, the man drifted in their direction. "Find what you're looking for?"

"Yes, I think we finally have," Susan answered. "I'm Susan Abbott."

"Of course you are. I thought I recognized you. I'm Dennis Carson. See your Father over at Rotary all the time. Had lunch together last Wednesday, in fact."

"That's right, I forgot the store changed hands. You sure have a lot more stuff than Bubba Charles did. Weren't you retired or something?"

"Or something sounds about right. Can only play so

much golf. Seemed like a good idea at the time though, just playin' golf an' hangin' around the club. After about a year and a half it was pretty obvious I wasn't gonna make the senior tour. So here I am, workin' harder than ever but lovin' it. Still sorting a lot of things out. Sorry for the mess. Decided to carry more used and exchange items."

"This is Geoff van Horst, a friend from the college."

"Pleased ta meet ya," Carson said, extending his hand but instead of looking directly at Geoff, his eyes focused on the Roots and Rakes logo on his shirt. "Sorry about Tammy, soon as I can find a replacement up there, she's gone. I wasn't the one who hired her. Sometimes it's just not safe to go away for any reason. Lost my regular girl while I was away and one of the fellas I left running things hired her in a pinch. How that girl thought she could work at a marina and know absolutely nothing about boats and water and sailing just amazes me? Got a feeling I've seen you around as well," he said, turning to Geoff.

"Not in here. But you sure have a large collection of used books. I may just come back soon. Used book shops are like candy stores to me, I guess that goes with being an English major."

"Swapping books for people goin' up and down the inter-coastal has turned out to be pretty good business. Lot a book people on boats but not a lot of spare room so I let them swap them out. Charge a small fee but they always buy something else anyway. Developing serious quality as well volume an' it's taken up more space than I thought. Gonna turn the storeroom into a new book area. May even do some book events. So you found what you're looking for? I guess it's not literature you're after today."

"No, Susan and I are planning to do a little exploring

of the marsh up and down the Morgan River and wanted to find some maps, er charts, Susan's the boater, that had the minor channels on them."

"It's pretty easy to get stuck. See people sittin' out there all the time waitin' for the tide to come in. You're father's quite a sailor, Susan."

"Oh, yes, Daddy has been all over with that sailboat of his. Took us on a trip to the Bahamas one summer and has been all up and down the coast and into the Gulf of Mexico." Susan suddenly felt uncomfortable but she couldn't put her finger on why.

"You handle sail as well?"

"I can but not like him. Actually, I tend to prefer motors."

"An' you, Geoff?"

"I'm strictly a land lubber. No salt in my veins. I'm kind of a straight line person, prefer to go from A to D without visiting B and C." Geoff made a zig sagging motion with his hand imitating the tacking of a sailboat and, as he did, the tourist map with the marks on it dropped to the floor.

Carson saw it drop and reached over to retrieve it. "I can see where this map wouldn't be of much help." The marks Geoff made were clearly visible from the way he had folded it. "They're great for walking around downtown but won't be of much help on the water." He continued to look at the map as he spoke. "Wouldn't your daddy have lots of charts you could use?" he said to Susan.

She fumbled in her reply. "Oh, yes, well, but he stays in the main channels and we were going to do some exploring. I don't think he has anything we could use."

Carson handed the map to Geoff. "He probably has the whole place committed to memory, anyway. There probably isn't a nook or cranny in the river he doesn't know."

"Kinda like my old boss," Geoff blurted out. Carson looked at him questioningly. "George Reed."

"George Reed? Oh, the landscaper. That's what the shirt is," pointing to the logo. "I just couldn't believe it when I saw that piece in the paper this morning. Family must be in shock. Terrible shame. Terrible shame. Just goes to show how dangerous it can be out there. Yeah, Reed, Reed, terrible shame. He was quite a man on the water, you know. You can be sure if you sat down at a Rotary lunch with George at the table, the conversation would sooner or later be about the marsh and its wildlife. So you work for Reed?"

"Just the summer. Lawn care, installing and repairing irrigation systems, that sort of thing. Going to USCB. English Lit. Looking forward to graduate school. Actually, I kind of have two summer jobs: one for the Reeds and the other for myself. Help people out with their flower gardens on the side. Sidney Lake in town has me working on his new rose garden. I didn't know Mr. Reed that well. Mrs. Reed did most of the work around the store. She's closed everything down for the week."

"Not surprised. Sure was a terrible thing to happen. But that's the water—a great temptress as well as master and servant. We think we have it under control and then...what do you do for Sidney Lake again?"

"You know Mr. Lake?"

"Taken some of those adult continuing Ed courses from him. Now that I have this place probably won't be able to do much of that any more. Betcha that's where else I've seen ya. Used to have book store down in Jacksonville before I sold it and came up here. Bein' on the water's my first love but books are my second—thought golf was. Decided to finally put my priorities in order. You were about to say what you're doing for Professor Lake."

"He's trying to build a special area for hybrid teas. They're awful tough to grow in the lowcountry."

"Tell me about it. Sidney and I are in the same garden club in Morgan. Gets a bit competitive sometimes. Might just have another chat with Sidney. Y'all pretty much have what you want?"

"Susan's the expert."

"Oh, I think these'll do just fine," Susan said, nervous-ly. She guessed that not telling Carson why they really wanted the chart set her on edge. Lying made her uncom-fortable especially knowing she didn't do it very well. Blurting things out was more her style. Not because she would intentionally give away a secret but she just didn't know how not to tell the truth when asked. Thinking on her feet, as they say, was not one of her strong points. She also found that she didn't like Carson. Something about his manner, the way he looked when he asked questions, he seemed to be looking beyond the just get-ting an answer to the usual chitchat. She felt more as though they were being interrogated but then she rational-ized it could just be her defensiveness about not being truthful.

"Good. Tammy will take care of ya when you're ready. Just be patient. Nice to meet you both. And Geoff, you come on back and browse whenever you like."

"Thanks. I may just do that."

Geoff and Susan, with charts and map in hand, headed for Geoff's pick-up as quickly as they could. The Morgan Diner was their next step. They had a lot they wanted to talk over. In front of them was an evening of plotting and analyzing, in addition to a few other recreational activi-ties on which Geoff had originally thought he and Susan would spend a good deal of his unexpected free time.

⌘⌘⌘

The local television stations in Savannah, Georgia finally caught up with the death of George Reed and carried a couple of different stories. Of course they didn't last more than two minutes so there wasn't much depth to them. They gave the standard report from the local authorities about the nature of the accident and then filled in with some boating safety advisories. Then they showed some stock videos of the coastal marsh and that was it. Another bullet dodged. Warren relaxed a bit and gave some thought to how to get into Roots and Rakes late at night.

Chapter 7

The service yard at Roots and Rakes came to life in the headlights of Geoff's truck, the almost completely dark area creating shadows that danced everywhere. He unlocked the gate of the chain linked fence in almost a trance like state, lots of things rolling around in his head that had nothing to do with fixing an irrigation system: his time with Susan on Monday when they visited the Old Fort Marina, the poring over the charts, the argument later in the evening and on Tuesday making up after the meeting with Sidney. Then tonight the Wednesday night supper followed by Caldwell Talbot's presentation that he had to leave just before it finished. He didn't even remember the ride from the church until he found himself outside the gate.

Getting back into his truck he drove into the dark service yard and left the gate open behind him. When performing an irrigation installation, he usually tried to be at the job site as early in the morning as possible during the summer in an effort to avoid the main heat of the day. But this time the sun would not be coming up as it just disappeared from the western horizon. He also decided to drive head first toward the back of the main building, keeping his headlights focused on the area in front of him rather than try to back up to the doors of the loading bay. His normal routine would have him entering his upcoming task into the work book in the shed's ledger before taking the material he would need but with the headlights facing in the opposite direction, he couldn't even see the shed.

Being here at this time of night was unusual for him but he wanted to hear the rest of Caldwell Talbot's take on the Civil War and held off leaving as long as he could. Besides, interrupting Caldwell in the middle of his presentation, well, that was not an option. Bev called him on his cell phone more than an hour earlier to ask if he would fix an irrigation system gone awry. She cleared it with Becky, since R and R was officially closed for the week, and said it would be okay to ask Geoff if he could do it first thing in the morning. The callers were an elderly couple living in one of the old cottages on the far side of town and were most apologetic, it being the day before George's funeral, but they had to turn off the water to their house as there was no separate turn off for the water to the irrigation system.

They were okay for this evening as a neighbor asked them for dinner and let them use their bathroom but they really needed it fixed first thing in the morning if possible.

The call came in about half way through Caldwell Talbot's lecture. He turned his phone to silent during the presentation and only checked it—surreptitiously—once, hoping to hear from Susan. Normally he would leave it on vibrate but Caldwell made it clear he would personally evict anyone from the room whose cell phone rang or interrupted him during the presentation. He even asked everyone in the audience who carried a phone to take it out and look at it to make sure it was turned off. Once Caldwell announced a ten minute break in his presentation, he noticed the message from Bev and called her back.

Sherman and the Lowcountry, as advertised, proved to be educational, revealing, informative and entertaining. Geoff did obtain a better understanding of the emotional factor of the Civil War South as Caldwell outlined the truly vindictive nature of Sherman's campaign and how he directed it not at the Confederate Army but the citizens of Georgia and South Carolina for demoralization purposes. The march achieved its of goal of cutting the heart out of the general population by destroying family farms and small town businesses and then burning libraries, both public and private, schools, churches, family as well as courthouse records.

Caldwell managed to go over the top as usual by comparing the Union Army to the brutality of the Taliban in Afghanistan and the disciples of many of the Ayatollah's followers in Iran, and he made it all believable with example after example. There were objections and raised voices but Caldwell cut them all down to size, again with specific fact built upon specific fact. Geoff never even considered getting up to answer Bev's call until the break came. He had no intention of becoming part of the evening's entertainment.

When initially driving through the gate he thought he saw a light coming from the main building but he knew he had to be mistaken. No one had been there all day, at least he presumed that to be the case, and the emergency night light in the office couldn't be seen from the angle he took toward the building. The only light in the yard was attached to the shed and that blew out over the weekend—something he should have fixed on Monday if they had been open—although it barely gave enough light to see much of anything anyway. Only Bev paid any attention to work issues today and she limited herself to checking the answering system. *No*, Geoff thought, *it couldn't be a light, not coming from this angle.* The building's three sections stood as a great, dark shadow in front of him with the office section in the middle separating the display area from the storage and supply area. In the dark everything seemed larger and certainly spooky.

The gentle wind rattling the palm trees didn't help either. Darkness and dramatic shadows had that effect. Geoff got out of his truck and walked slowly to the door of the storage area where the tools and spare parts he needed were located.

The darkness and the shadows made him nervous as he approached and just wanted to load up the supplies into his pickup, park it outside his apartment this evening, and then leave directly from there to the cottage first thing in the morning.

Guided by the lights of his truck shining on the large, metal, garage doors, he made his way to the back of the building. The intensity of the light and its glare further increased the depth of the darkness. The doors were designed to allow him to drive the truck directly into the loading bay. He took out his key as he approached the rear entry door, which was off to the left of the garage doors and provided individual access to the storage area.

The door was slightly ajar. Could it be the reason he thought he saw a light? With all the confusion of the past few days, could Bev simply have forgotten to check the service area door when she last locked up and left, which she usually did from the front office door?

The door being left unlocked was not particularly unusual. He had been guilty of it a number of times. Because of its location, it was often forgotten when the last person left for the day and exited from the front of the building. In fact, Becky Reed had found it open so often that she considered posting a sign in the office to remind whomever was leaving last to make sure they closed and locked the rear door.

As Geoffrey pushed the door open and gingerly stepped over the threshold, his shirt caught on something, and he heard a tearing sound.

"Shit," was his instinctive answer. He then reached for the light switch to his right as he moved inside and flipped it on.

With the quick change from dark to light, it took him a few moments to see clearly and his primary focus was his shirt. These were not his work clothes but a pale blue dress shirt, the one he had worn to the Wednesday night supper and Caldwell Talbot's presentation earlier, and now it was torn.

"Damn," he said exasperated and then he caught sight of why his shirt had become ensnared. The door jamb was splintered. Someone had broken into R and R.

Are they still here? When did this happen? He froze and looked around the cavernous space, scanning the floor to ceiling shelves and bins lining both sides of the room. He saw nothing out of the ordinary. He heard nothing. Scanning the room back and forth, he moved inside. *Should I call out?* His mind raced in a hundred different directions. He then realized that the act of turning on the light was a call in itself. He still heard nothing. The far end of the room had windows that looked from the office into the storage area.

Everything was dark except for the usual night lights. *Should I leave? Out into the darkness? Maybe not. What a time to leave my cell phone on the seat of the truck. Why not just stay put? If there is anyone here, they're obviously not in the service area, which means they're in the office or in the attached greenhouse.* Both locations had numerous doors and windows for escape. *So stay here and let them get away and you don't get hurt and you don't see anyone. Why not just act normal? Make like you didn't see the damaged door and lock and go about getting what you came for and leave. Call Bev from the safety of the truck away from the building. Shouldn't I call nine-one-one and report the break-in? What if it's already been reported by Bev and the cops already know about it? Okay, let's just get what we need and get out of here.*

Moving at what he thought would be his normal pace, he began assembling equipment on the floor in the center of the room: a tool box, some irrigation line hose, connectors, all the time trying to keep in view the window that looked in from the office, just in case someone was still around. Although, since no one made a move or sound, he started to feel more comfortable and began to rationalize that the break-in must have been on Monday, the day he noticed the green car by the back fence, or even yesterday.

He never did remember to tell Bev about the car so no one had any reason to check on anything in the storage area. Someone was probably in on Tuesday to water plants and make sure the irrigation systems were working, again, no reason to check the storage area.

He worked his way up to where the controllers were stored, right near the door to the office, where the switch to operate the garage door was located on the wall. He peered through the large window next to it.

Suddenly, hearing a noise; he turned, saw a shadow, lifted his arm to defend himself, and ducked at the same time, but—

తుతుతు

Warren picked up the phone at R and R's sales desk and dialed nine-one-one. "Looks like there's been a break-in at the Roots and Rakes Landscape business. Better check it out."

"Sir—"

He quickly hung up. His hand shook and he replaced the receiver. *God, I hope I haven't killed him too. No one is supposed to be here. It's all getting out of hand but I've got to find those pictures. Where the hell is the camera he used on Saturday night? There's nothing here but the old developing equipment. Damn, I've got to get out of here.*

Chapter 8

With Caldwell Talbot's presentation over, the crowd began to mill about, gathering in small groups to comment on what they heard as well as renew acquaintances and pass the time of day with friends. The meeting, as well as the dinner, was open to anyone who had an interest and there were about 150 people in all for the talk. Sidney chatted politely with Helen Oliphant, the used bookstore's owner's wife, when General Lawrence Brewster broke in. Although having a reputation of being a bit gruff and tending to be direct and to the point he could also be surprisingly engaging when he wanted to be. Retired army, six foot four and 250 pounds he moved to Morgan four years ago and usually had no difficulty making his presence known.

"Sidney, have you seen Caldwell? Hello Helen, excuse me for interrupting but I have to find Caldwell before he leaves."

Helen acknowledged his greeting with a nod to him.

"He was over there in the corner a few minutes ago. Edith's right behind you. I'm sure she knows."

"Just wanted to needle him a bit about a couple of points he inaccurately presented."

"Oh, I'm sure he'll just love to hear that."

"Only, fair, Sidney, he had two hours to push his views. I only need five minutes to rebut him."

Helen looked at him and said, "Well, good luck."

Sidney added, "You'll need it."

Then Brewster turned to Helen, "Where's Jarvis?"

"Atlanta. One of his book conferences. Always likes to keep up with the industry trends. You know how intense he can be on the subject of antiquarian books."

"Yeah, tell him I need to speak with him. When will he be back?"

"Tomorrow but very late in the evening."

"Helen, General, Sidney," said Steele Wilcox, joining the group. "Quite a presentation, wasn't it?"

"Hey, Steele," the general said, "good to see you." They shook hands. "Can I catch y'all later? I just can't let Caldwell get away without my getting my two cents in. Excuse me for just a minute." He then turned and looked for Edith Talbot.

"Good luck," Steele said. "Glutton for punishment that man."

"Given their history, I'm not sure I want to be a party to that conversation. Caldwell may be one of the most uncompromising people I've ever met. I can still remember the argument he had with my husband about his carrying more books about the Civil War that were written by Northern historians than Southern ones." Helen just rolled her eyes and shook her head from side to side as she spoke.

"You're probably right about that. I seem to remember General Brewster having a run in with Caldwell Talbot, not that that's difficult to do. Brewster had been asked to give a guest lecture at the college on the Civil War from a military strategy point of view and Caldwell didn't like the idea of a Yankee presenting, what he perceived to be, a Union view of the war to Southern students. Caldwell, as you may have figured out by now, is not particularly shy about taking on just about anyone when it comes to the Confederacy. However, to give him his due, Caldwell is, actually, a superb historian, even if he doesn't have the academic credentials. Brewster and he had a battle of letters to the editor a few months ago and almost an altercation at the college."

"Did I hear the name of a certain member of the Southern Heritage Society mentioned?" interrupted Cal Prentice, coming up from behind Sidney. The pastor placed his hand on Sidney's shoulder as he came alongside, not a difficult feat to accomplish, given their difference in height.

"You most certainly did. I was just mentioning his letter writing contest of a few months back, the one with General Brewster.

Just then Susan Abbott joined the group. Sidney spoke first. "Hello Susan, where's Geoff? You know everyone here?"

She exchanged hellos with Wilcox and Helen Oliphant.

"He got a call from Bev at R and R and had to leave. Something about an emergency irrigation fix or something. Said he would try to get back before we all left."

"Terrible thing about George Reed, wasn't it?" said Wilcox.

"Sure was," came a voice from behind. It was Lawrence Brewster back again.

Sidney started and turned. "I'm sorry, General, I must have been in a bit of a daze. Thought you went after Caldwell."

"Gone. Edith said he had to rush out to another commitment. I'll catch him tomorrow. So you were in a daze, eh, Sidney? You don't look old enough for senior moments."

"One never knows these days. The trick is to live long enough to have them. Seeing what happened to George. I didn't really know him that well, but when someone around your same age accidentally dies, it does make you think. You knew him pretty well, didn't you?"

"Yeah, I must admit we'd become good friends," replied the general.

"Mind if I ask what brings a retired army general and a landscaper together?" Sidney had become acquainted with General Brewster over the last year through the Morgan Garden Association, where they were both members. Brewster, president of the group, took the position after his wife, an avid gardener, died a little over a year ago.

"Birds."

"Birds?"

"Birds. I feed them, he photographs them. I don't know if you've ever noticed but I've got a pretty elaborate bird feeding set up in my yard backing up to the marsh. George used to come and set up his cameras out there from time to time. I've got a picture of a painted bunting you wouldn't believe. We'd just sit around with a bottle of wine and watch nature at feeding time. Hey, Steele, tell Sidney here what a great bird photographer George was."

"Oh, that he most certainly was." The coroner stepped into the middle of the two of them. "Yes, George knew his birds all right. Knew where to find um, knew how to sneak up on um, not a place in the marsh he didn't know how to get to." Wilcox was the picture of the perfect undertaker: the black suit, white shirt, black tie, white handkerchief in his breast pocket. He also had the marvelous ability to go instantly from smile to frown, to sincere

concern, to a bright smile again. It was generally believed
that a run for mayor was not far off. Although a close
friend of the Reeds, he refused to handle the funeral,
pushing it to McLaughlin's to avoid any hint of conflict
of interest with his coroner position.

"You know I heard that. Something about his being
able to maneuver a flat bottomed boat with a pole."

Steele and the general both chuckled. Steele continued, "Oh, yes, he could dance around that boat better than
some folks that were born here."

"Interesting." Sidney paused and Steele caught it.

"Truth is, no matter how sure footed you think you
are, slips on a boat are very, very common." The jolly
manner was suddenly serious.

"I suppose you're right—"

Brewster cut in. "In a way, I suppose you could say
it's a bit like the fellow who runs marathons and trains
doing ten miles a day and then falls down of a heart attack. You tend to forget you're vulnerable; you have limi-
tations; if you're not careful you can get burned."

"A fair analogy," said Wilcox. "So you didn't really
didn't know George?" The question was addressed to
Sidney, the cheerfulness beginning to return again.

"More acquaintance than anything. Met at church,
have a mutual housekeeper—that sort of thing."

"Ahh, George, Becky, and I go back a long way," he
said almost wistfully. "Was one of their first commercial
customers twenty odd years ago, when they first started
Roots and Rakes. Been good friends ever since. Brewster
here I met because he's just a big troublemaker," the general laughed while Wilcox gave him a playful punch in
the arm. "Didn't like the way ah was flying the flag outside my place and came over to complain. Told me to get
a light on it or take it down. Funny how friendships form.
If y'all hadda told me that George, me, and this big, ole,

rough, Yankee bear would end up being friends, ah wouldn't have believed it."

"Are you also a bird watcher?" Sidney continued to register everything he heard and saw.

"In a way. Tend to absorb what George and the general would throw at me. Four of us would play cards every few weeks. They'd all get talking about birds sooner or later. George sure did love to take pictures. Mid-day or mid night it made no difference. He'd figure out what was migratin', where they were and off he'd go. Drove Becky nuts now and then. She never knew where he was. Becky's the only reason the business did okay. Denny always said she was the brains behind R and R's success."

"Denny?" The introduction of the name didn't register with Sidney.

"Sorry. Dennis Carson. You must know him from the college. He's always takin' those adult courses of yours over there. He subs as our fourth now and again. Came up here from Jacksonville. Bought Bubba's marina a little ways back. Takes care of my boat. Think he did George's too. Thought you would know im."

"I may have, I just never put it all together. Now that you mention it, I think we were all together for dinner at the general's here a couple of months ago. It all just went right by me."

"Well, don't feel bad," said Brewster, putting his hand on Sidney's shoulder and giving a chuckle, "you academic types all seem like you're in a fog anyway."

"Speaking of fogs," said Wilcox, "what's this I hear about someone breaking into your place?"

"What's that got to do with fogs?"

"Assume you must have been in one not to turn your alarm on."

"I thought this was supposed to be Mayberry, no bad

people here. Everybody leaves the door open."

"You must be starting to believe what the chamber of commerce has been puttin' out. You don't see us folks that were born here leaving our doors open."

"Yeah, I guess so. Anyway, I can never remember how the damn thing works. Pushing buttons and codes— lot easier to just shoot the bastard."

Wilcox laughed. "You gotta be home, though."

"I guess so."

"So what happened?"

"I don't know, I wasn't there."

"You must be a big help to the police," Sidney said.

"They know more than I do. Said the window pane on the kitchen door was broken and they found one of my paintings over by the marsh. No idea why he would leave it there."

"Probably realized you had no taste in art," Wilcox needled, "an' just threw it away. Nothin' else worth taking?"

"Have lots of good stuff," the general said, feigning indignation, "even if that painting was only worth $500. In fact, I just inherited a bunch of old, valuable, books from an uncle of mine. Have a lot of them still in boxes in the den."

"If they're still in boxes, how do you know they have some value?" Sidney said. It seemed as though everyone was ganging up on the general, but he just smiled as if he liked to be kidded and loved a good joke as well as the next person. The trick was to not cross the line. You did not want General Lawrence Brewster angry with you for any reason.

"I asked Jarvis over to have a look," the general said, giving a nod to Helen. "He said there was some pretty good stuff in there."

"So how do you know something wasn't taken?"

"Don't, yet. Jarvis is supposed to come over tomorrow and work on it. He started making an inventory list for me and will double check what's there against what he's gone through so far. If something is missing, we'll tell the sheriff."

"You mean the chief," Wilcox said. "You live in Morgan so Pete Hornig's got jurisdiction."

"Chief, sheriff, whatever. I'm sure they'll all figure it out."

Sidney couldn't resist. "Just like they figured everything with regard to George's accident. You're still positive it's just a simple accident? No strange circumstances that would point to anyone helping him over the side?"

"No, no, Sidney. Come on, it was no secret that George was a bit heavy on the Southern Comfort side. I checked everything out and, believe me, he had enough alcohol in him so that he'd have trouble keeping to his feet on a cruise ship much less that forty footer of his. In fact, I even warned him about it once and Becky and he went round and round about it on a number of occasions. No, I don't see any other way it could have happened. There's a big log out there someplace with part of George still on it. Sorry, Helen. Don't mean to be so graphic."

"Oh, I understand. I'm just glad it was an accident and nobody to blame but himself."

"Everything completely tied up?" Sidney said.

Susan watched Wilcox intently for his answer, knowing why Sidney asked it.

"Actually, I'd be a lot happier if they could find that log he hit and there's a mark on his neck I need to ask Becky about, but those are miscellaneous loose ends that won't affect anything. No, I'm happy to stand behind my accident report."

"But without that log, you really don't know for sure if he actually fell or was pushed. Right?"

"Sidney, he was all alone. There was no one with him." From the irritation in the response it was evident that someone had been challenging his opinion.

Susan couldn't resist this time. "But if no one saw anything, how can you be so sure?"

"Honestly, now, there's no evidence of any one being out there with him. It's an accident, pure and simple. Everyone seems to be coming up with conspiracy theories. There's nothing to it."

"Only natural. So tell me about the robbery," Sidney said.

"Best I can tell, the painting was the only thing of value taken. And they did find it, just at the edge of the property, in the marsh grass. Kind of a mystery in itself, that."

"No one reported anything? No one saw anything?"

"Apparently not."

"But why leave the painting behind?"

"Maybe the thief *thought* someone saw him," Susan offered.

"Very good," said Sidney. "Very good. The thief was very likely spooked by something or someone and the 'spook-or' probably had no idea he frightened the 'spook-ee' and interrupted a robbery."

"Geoff had a similar experience the other day at R and R." Susan mentioned Geoff telling her of his spooking what could have been an intruder at the Reed's landscape business but left out his going there to get the map. "Someone showed up when the place was closed and when they saw someone still there they took off."

"Could have been anyone," Steele said. "Don't want to read too much into it. Hey, look, I have to be on my way. Probably see everyone at the memorial service tomorrow."

Everyone in the circle agreed and the coroner took his leave.

Susan spotted Alice Ringfoot waving to the group and assumed she was trying to get the pastor's attention. "Reverend Prentice, I think Alice is calling you."

Cal took a look toward the back of the room. "Excuse me for just a minute."

Right after he left, Helen Oliphant decided it was time to leave and she also made her way to the door.

"You know, Susan, I hope you didn't mind our giving you the lesson on downtown protocol," Brewster said. "It's one of those unwritten things about the town that ya kinda just get to know."

"Oh, that's all right. I've lived here all my life, as I said, but since I'm out of school now and teaching, I've constantly being amazed at all the things I had no idea went on right in front of me."

Cal rejoined them. "Alice was waving at you Sidney. Tillie left a note with Alice for you. Didn't want to interrupt us. Made Alice promise to get this to you. Tillie said it was important. "

"Tell you what, folks, time for me to be headin' out as well," Brewster said. "Susan, give my regards to your father. Cal, Sidney, catch up with y'all tomorrow."

Sidney took the envelope, opened it, and stared at the paper. "Well, I'll be."

"Something the matter?"

"No, well. I guess I'm just a little mystified." He looked at the note again.

"Can I help in some way?"

"No." Sidney kept looking at the note. "It's just that Tillie asked me to check into something for her and now she says I don't have to because she already has the answer. I've been working on it for three days and I certainly don't have the answer."

"I have no idea what you're talking about."

"Cal, keep this to yourself."

"Sure, you know me."

"Susan, I know Geoff told you all about it. Tillie was concerned about the gossip going around with regard to Becky. I know you've heard some of it. You know, the idea that she may have had something to do with George's accident."

"I've heard some of those, yes."

"She asked me if I'd look around a bit and prove that she could not have had anything to do with it. So I have. In fact, I've been doing a lot of looking around and have bothered a lot of different people and done all sorts of research and, while I actually believe it was an accident just as Steele does, I couldn't prove Becky wasn't out there when George went over the side. In all honestly, I can't figure if there *is* any way to prove it."

"You're not saying that she did it?"

"No, no. The point is, I don't believe you can *prove* she didn't do it any more than Chief Hornig can *prove* she did. No one was there—no one saw anything."

"But Tillie says she can prove Becky didn't do it?"

"Not exactly. She just says she has the answer. Meaning, I guess, that somehow she has proven Becky innocent to her satisfaction."

"Then she may have come to the same conclusion that you did. Maybe she sees that since there is no way to prove her guilty then she is definitely innocent."

"Possibly, but I have to believe there's more to it. She was convinced she didn't do it from the start but what could she have found out that we didn't? I found the exact location of where that sandbar was, the exact location of where the boat was found, the exact location of where George's body was found, and mapped it out on nautical charts of the Morgan River, and we still couldn't prove anything. Even the police came to the conclusion that there's no way to prove it either way."

"You mean they actually suspected her?"

"It's their job to suspect everyone. No, they don't really think she did it."

"Shouldn't that be enough? I mean, that the police don't think she did it."

"No, that's where we started. The police and the coroner have ruled it an accident. They didn't say she was innocent, they don't do that. The police just have no evidence to warrant an investigation of anyone."

"I'm beginning to see the problem. Given the nature of gossip in Morgan, yeah, I can see where total and complete proof of innocence would be a necessity."

'Right, I agree, and so does Tillie. So I have to believe that what she's discovered is not something that just proves Becky not guilty but complete proof of innocence, which is something I haven't been able to do. Reverend, Tillie, and I have to talk."

ೞ

As Sidney walked home from the church, Tillie's message about no longer needing his help continued to gnaw at him. Admittedly, there were mixed emotions involved. The good news was that Becky seemed to be finally off the hook and Tillie seemed to have her desired, irrefutable argument in Becky's defense. The problem that bothered him was that she found her answer not only without his help but also that he continued to have no clue as to what she came up with and who gave it to her. Sidney liked things neat. He liked solutions that made sense, were logical, and conformed with the available facts. No, there was definitely something missing. Did Ray Morton know something that he didn't tell him?

Since he had to go right past Ray's on the way home, he decided to stop and pump the retired policeman a bit more. Making his way up the front steps, he checked his watch and, making out that it was still before nine-thirty, gave the lighted button for the Morton's bell a ring. Dinner at the Morton's would have finished about an hour and a half ago and unless they had an appointment somewhere he expected they would be home. Of course he could have called ahead using his cell phone—if he had it with him, which he didn't

Knowing Caldwell's passionate dislike of being interrupted when speaking, he just decided to leave it on a table in his bedroom. Ninety-nine percent of the time nothing was so urgent that a message on his land line filled the bill just fine. He also knew it was not too late to be interrupting them, especially as the welcoming front porch light clearly identified the bell he just pushed. There were also lights on in the house, giving Sidney reasonable assurance he would find someone at home. He felt embarrassed for having involved so many people in his investigation, thinking of Ray and Geoff and subsequently Susan Abbott and Cal Prentice. Sidney, not the most outgoing of people, kept mostly to himself. If it had not been for his late wife, Cynthia, he would have had little social life at all. Mickey was his only confidant, although he had to admit Hattie Ryan was gaining some ground.

The challenge presented by Tillie intrigued him on a number of levels and the intellectual exercise of trying to prove Becky didn't kill George perked him up by providing an opportunity to interact with people. It also irritated him because he had not properly completed his task.

The door opened to reveal a rushed and hurried-looking Ray. "Good, it's you. I don't have to call you then."

"Excuse me?"

"Your boy, Geoffrey. He's just been taken to the emergency room."

"Geoffrey? What happened?"

"Don't know. Heard the report on the radio." Meaning the police and emergency call band he often listened to.

"I'd better get myself over there. He doesn't really have anyone in town."

"I'll drive. Come on. I'll have you there in a flash." Ray took Sidney by the elbow and directed him toward the steps he just came up. Ray's car was in the driveway next to the house. Marie's car was in the one car garage.

"Okay."

They both headed down the stairs when Ray suddenly stopped. "Marie," he called back over his shoulder. "Taking Sidney to Central Memorial, I'll be back in a while."

"*What*?" came the response? Footsteps could be heard running from the kitchen. "Is he all right?"

"Not him," Ray called back as the screen door to the house opened and Marie stood on the threshold. "Geoff."

"Oh, my."

෧෨෧

During the ten minute drive to the hospital, Ray relayed what he had heard. A nine-one-one call resulted in the dispatch of paramedics, an ambulance and a Morgan patrol car to Roots and Rakes, where they found Geoff unconscious and lying in a pool of blood. There was no indication of the cause or the extent of his injury. Ray learned that much since the patrol car, which had been nearby, arrived first and notified the paramedics what to expect.

"I have no idea or information about anything else. The report was pretty cryptic, as it should have been."

"I suppose he could have tripped on something. I saw him earlier this evening and Susan said he'd got a call from the R and R office manager about something and he left just as Caldwell was finishing up. I didn't get a chance to talk with him, though." Sidney suddenly realized that Geoff was important to him. He truly liked Geoffrey. Yes, he was a bit brash and undisciplined in the way he approached life but that was a sign of the times. Everyone seemed to be that way, except Sidney, of course, and some of his associates at the College's lifelong learning program. He liked having Geoff around. He was young, he was intelligent, and he had a mind that was filled with far more knowledge about the world than Sidney ever had at the same age.

"He's a hardheaded kid. He'll be all right. If they're alive when the paramedics get to them, they tend to stay that way. Tell you what, I'll drop you off at the emergency room and then take a run over to R and R. It's only a couple of minutes in the other direction. Hornig's guys will be there for some time yet, and I'll see what I can find out. I'll catch up with you on my way back."

�����

The emergency waiting room was a simple affair: about forty metal and plastic seats spread out in small groupings, a check-in window and a room on the side where walk-in's could be screened by a nurse to determine what action would be required. Sidney rushed through the two sets of double glass doors and headed immediately for the check-in window, which was directly in front of him about thirty yards away. He looked neither left nor right but made directly for the glass partition and the male clerk seated behind it.

"You have a Geoffrey Van Horst in emergency?" he

said, avoiding any of the niceties he might normally have used.

"Geoffrey Van Horst," the clerk repeated, not surprised at the anxiety Sidney expressed. The man picked up a file folder just to his left, opened it and looked over a list contained within. He acted calmly and efficiently, not responding to the tension that Sidney radiated, as if he knew it was his job to be calm and Sidney's to be anxious.

"He would have just come in by ambulance." Sidney's both hands were on the small counter area which also contained a pass through area between where the glass partition ended and the counter began so that forms could be signed and passed back and forth.

"I don't see anything here. If he just came, in I probably don't have the information as yet. Are you a relative?" He looked up at Sidney.

"No, he's just a good friend, a college student. I just heard he was here."

"Sidney?" came a voice from behind him. "Is something the matter?"

"Cal," he said, turning and surprised to see the preacher. "It's Geoff. There's been some sort of accident. I think they just brought him in. What are you doing here?"

Sidney, in his interest in getting to Geoff, had paid no attention to the other people in the waiting room and breezed right past Cal. There were at least ten other people. Some were alone and others in small groups. Most were waiting to hear news from inside the double doors that were on the wall just down from the admitting clerk's office. Others were walk-ins waiting to see the nurse that was in the other office area on the opposite side of the room.

"Mark Halley suffered a heart attack a few hours ago. Betty called me. They still have him inside. Betty's in the restroom. He seems to have stabilized. They'll probably move him to the intensive care unit in a little while. I told her I would stay with her. What's this about Geoff?"

"Don't know. Ray Morton heard it on his radio and drove me over. They don't seem to have any information on him yet," Sidney said, referring to the check-in clerk, who just looked back at Sidney and shrugged.

"An accident of some kind?" Cal said.

"Cal, I just don't know. All I do know is they found him over at Roots and Rakes."

"Let me see what I can find out. Do me a favor and watch for Betty Halley. Do you know Betty?"

"Yes, I've met Betty."

"Good, just tell her I'll be back in a minute." With that, Cal gave a wave to the man behind the check-in window, who acknowledged him and reached for the door release buzzer. Once through the large double doors he headed directly for the central monitoring station, directly down the corridor. To the left of the station were another set of double doors that led to the ambulance bays.

"Excuse me, Nancy, I'm looking for someone else this time." The semicircle where she was sitting was a flurry of activity. There were three other nurses with her, two of which were standing and speaking with other nurses and doctors, all holding clip boards filled with papers and charts. Another nurse was leading a woman toward an open room. She had dried blood all down the front of her, her left eye was closed and her face all puffy and bruised.

"Busy night, Reverend?"

"Not as busy as your night, I'm sure," the reverend said, taking note of the activity.

She managed a smile. "Yes, but my nights are always like this. Who this time?"

"Geoffrey Van Horst. Should have just come in."

She took a quick look at a batch of papers in front of her. "Boy, you're quick. They just rolled him in. They're working on him now."

"Does it say what's wrong?" he said trying to get a look at the paper she was reading from.

"No, but it looks like a lot of bleeding. Those are the paramedics that brought him in coming out of room seven. Maybe they could help." There were four double rooms behind where Cal was standing and across from the central station. The far one on the right was number seven.

"Thanks, Nancy." He quickly moved across the hall and headed for the two young men that had just come out of the room. "Excuse me," he began." I'm Cal Prentice from the Presbyterian Church in town."

"Oh, sure," said the six foot plus, sandy haired, twenty something paramedic. "I recognize you. See you almost every Sunday. I sing in the choir at First Baptist across the street. Corry Matthews, and this is John Harris," They shook hands. "He's a Catholic but we don't hold it against him." They all smiled. The second paramedic was almost a mirror image of the first but a bit older. "What can we do for you?"

"Was that Geoffrey Van Horst you just brought in?"

"Eh, yeah," paramedic two responded. "I'm pretty sure that's the name. I'm not sure about the Geoffrey part but Van Horst sounds right. Kind of an unusual name for around here so it stuck. Larry, that's our third, usually does the paperwork."

"How is he?"

"Tough to tell. They're working on him now," answered number two.

Number one stepped in. "We managed to control the bleeding—head wound." He shook his head. "Very messy. One of your flock?"

"A good friend. Actually, he's one of yours," referring to paramedic number two. "I know him from the college. He has no family here. Another close friend is outside," motioning toward the waiting room as he spoke. "Was anyone else hurt?"

"No," said number one as all three walked back across the room to the monitoring station. "He was in a building. R and R landscaping, you know, the one over on eighty-seven. Guess he worked there. Not sure what he was doing there tonight though."

"He does work there, yes. I thought it might have been an accident. A car or something."

"No, it looks like he took a pretty good whack on the head. At least that's what I think it was."

"Oh."

"I can't be sure. Someone else will have to decide what happened."

"But he seems okay?"

"We got him stabilized pretty well. He started to come around on the way in but went out again. They'll take good care of him."

"Yes, I'm sure they will. Well, thank you for your help." Cal knew he couldn't press for too much information. He didn't want to get the paramedics into trouble and he didn't want to put them into the position of having to refuse to answer his questions.

"No problem. Hey," he said in parting, "I think he'll be okay."

As the two paramedics moved away and headed for the monitoring station to complete filling out their paper work, Cal tried to peek into the room where he now knew Geoffrey was located. He stood outside the three quarter closed door and did his best to peer in. It looked like the curtain was drawn completely around the bed, but he could see a good deal of activity.

"Another one of yours, Reverend Prentice?"

Cal turned to see a male nurse standing behind him. "Oh, George, yes." George had earlier been working on Betty Halley's husband. "Geoffrey Van Horst is his name, came in while I was out front with Mrs. Halley. Thought I'd try to see what was happening."

"Took a nasty hit on the head but seems okay. He's awake and alert. We've still got a lot of tests to run on him to get a fix on the extent of the damage, if there is any. You can wait outside and I'll let you know what's going on and when you can see him."

"Thanks George. I appreciate it."

As Cal returned to the waiting room area he spotted Sidney sitting and chatting with Mrs. Halley. As he made his way across the room the automatic doors to the outside opened and Ray Morton and two Morgan police officers came in.

"How's Geoff?" Ray immediately asked Sidney after saying a few words and then leaving the two policemen, who were buzzed into the patient area.

"Don't know. Cal, here, was just inside checking."

"Do you know Mrs. Halley?" said Cal to Ray.

"I...errr..." Ray stammered.

"We met at one of the Wednesday night suppers at church," she helped out. "You were giving a presentation on relations between the sheriff's department and the Morgan police department."

"Yes, I remember that."

"Mrs. Halley's husband, Mark, is in emergency. Heart attack," said Cal.

"Oh, I'm sorry to hear that," Ray said while taking her hand. "How is he?"

"He seems to be doing fine now. They're going to move him upstairs in a little while."

"Oh, that's a good sign."

"Yes, but how is the young man?" she said addressing Cal and all heads turned in his direction.

"Best I can tell he's doing okay. He's awake but hit his head very badly. They said they still have some tests to run."

"They think it was a break in," said Ray. "Probably walked in on them."

"Why would someone break into a landscape business? What does one steal from such a place? Plants?" said Sidney incredulously.

"Good question but it makes a good target, under the circumstances: place closed for the week due to the death of the owner, no one expected to be around. If you need money for drugs, you sometimes go after some very strange places."

"But what would they take?" continued Sidney? "Plants are too bulky and still have to be converted into cash. There wouldn't be any cash since the place has already been closed for three days and I don't imagine irrigation equipment comes under the heading of high priced items. The valves and so on can't be worth more than a couple of dollars each. Even computer equipment doesn't have a lot of value anymore."

"Sidney, you're being logical, as you always are. Most petty thefts, break-ins, are not really done by people who think straight or even really think. Like the bank robber who writes the hold-up note on the back of one of his own deposit slips. Thefts and violent acts don't have to be logical."

"Okay, point taken," conceded Sidney. From his association with Ray over the years he had developed a great appreciation for the modern policeman, who spent most of his time dealing with the mundane and seemingly irrational nature of the crimes they came in contact with. Sidney found the concept of training someone to think in an illogical manner in order to catch a thief a fascinating idea. Also, the idea that there can be a rational pattern to irrational behavior had become of great interest to him.

"Are they're sure it wasn't an accident?" offered Cal. "Could he have tripped and hit his head?"

"Nothing cast in stone yet. Although the guys at the scene are pretty sure he was hit. They've seen enough to know. They'll get a better idea once they've had a chance to talk with Geoff."

"Well, it's still possible we're over dramatizing. Everyone is always looking for conspiracies these days. I think the benefit of the doubt is the best approach," said Cal, ever the optimist.

"I agree," chimed in Mrs. Halley. "Always best to look for the good in people."

"Good idea for clergyman—bad idea for cops," was Ray's reply as they all looked at him.

"I'm not going to get in the middle of this one," Sidney said Then he turned to Ray. "Was there any indication of a break-in?"

"Could be. The rear door had some damage but no immediate way to tell if it happened tonight. Hornig's people will work that out. Geoffrey might help with that too. They've put a call out to Becky Reed as well."

"Just what she needs. Wouldn't the alarm system have gone off?"

"Only if it was turned on. Or maybe some one knew how to turn it off. Not unusual. As you said, the most valuable items they have are the plants and they're all pretty much outside surrounded by a chain link fence that may or may not be locked and just about anyone could get over it. No, my first instinct is that Geoffrey walked in on a couple of addicts who saw the closed for the week sign and decided to see if there was anything of value around for them to steal."

The door to the patient's area opened and all heads turned in that direction to see George coming toward them. "Mrs. Halley, we're going to move Mr. Halley up to the ICU in a few minutes. It's on the second floor."

"How is he?"

"I think he's doing all right. The cardiologist upstairs is Dr. Clark. Just ask for him and he'll give you a good overview."

"I'll go with you Betty," said Cal.

"Oh, thanks," she said getting ready to move. "I do hope your young man will be all right," she said to Sidney as she gathered up her purse. Cal then walked with her to the elevator that was down the hall way on the other side of the room.

Before disappearing, Cal gave Sidney a hand signal indicating that he would give him a call.

"How is Van Horst, by the way?" said Sidney to George.

"He's doin' okay. They're taking some tests now. Be a while before you can see him.

Police have first crack. You're the professor friend?"

"Yes, Sidney Lake and this is Ray Morton." They all shook hands.

"George Carter. Give it about a half hour or so."

"Thanks."

As Ray watched George disappear back through the doors from where he came, he then asked, "Say, Sidney? What were you coming to see me about tonight?"

"Oh, yes," Sidney had completely forgotten how everything started. "Tillie left me a note saying she proved Becky Reed couldn't have had anything to do with George's death and didn't need my help any longer, so I was going to tell you I didn't need yours but I still have some questions."

Ray gave Sidney a questioning look. "Did she say how

she knows, because I couldn't say that definitively and I'm sure the Morgan police can't either?"

"No, and it has me puzzled as well. I was going to see her tomorrow and get her to tell me what she's learned. I can't imagine what she's found out."

∽∽∽

Warren slowed the car to stay just above the speed limit. The back road to Savannah was a speeder's paradise and every sheriff's deputy in the two counties it crossed knew it. Although he also knew they preferred to set up their traps along I 95 and the US 278 connector to Hilton Head, which were more lucrative, he didn't want to chance it. Beaufort and Jasper counties were not supposed to be on his agenda tonight. He had some serious thinking and planning to do over the next couple of days. Where in the world is the camera or computer with the pictures on it?

Chapter 9

O kay, Tillie," Sidney said, walking to the left side
of the Charleston stairway entry to the Gregory's,
where Tillie interrupted her sweeping and waived
a greeting to him and Mickey.

This part of the street was one of Morgan's prime locations, as it rose up to a height of twenty-five feet above
the mean high tide level. The road followed the river and
had old home after old home lined up on one and two
acre lots filled with a multiple variety of ancient oaks,
twisted and turned from the tropical storms that visited
each summer. Most of the houses were restored but a
few, at either end of the prime residential area, were waiting for the next influx of non-Morganites to buy them up.
Money was coming in from Atlanta and Charlotte of late.
Northern money seemed to be more interested in the up-
scale gated communities and new housing rather than
renovation and restoration in the historic district. Track-
ing down his housekeeper gave Sidney an opportunity to
accomplish multiple tasks at once: a morning walk for
Mickey, and a conversation with Tillie. River Street sat
on the down slope of the rise that gave The Ridge its
name. "You have to tell me what you found out."

"She didn't do it an' I know it for sure." The arms were folded, the jaw was set, the issue settled, and she had no interest in hearing any rebuttals to her arguments. "Watch the mud there by your feet, Professor Lake. The sprinkler system is overshootin' again." Tillie knew of Sidney's emphasis on clean, shined shoes. Most people would be wearing shorts, sneakers and a tee shirt to walk the dog but not Sidney, for him it was kakis with a crease, a long sleeve shirt worn loosely to smooth the bulge of his frame and neatly polished walking shoes. Sidney shifted position slightly and Mickey sat down.

"But how, Tillie? How do you know she didn't do it? Just saying so doesn't mean you have a better argument then you did before."

"Oh yes it does. Because Mr. Daniel said it was impossible." Tillie was standing above him as she was on the second step of the stairway.

"Mr. Daniel?"

"Mr. Daniel Doyle. He was born and raised on the island and knows every inch of water around it. More than eighty years he's been on the water an' if he says there's no way Mr. Reed could end up where he did and the boat where it did and Miss Becky on that sandbar—Can't happen, he said. Impossible!"

"Why?" Sidney couldn't believe this Mr. Daniel's word was enough.

"The tides."

"Wait. Indulge me for just a minute." He was determined to get a better explanation. "First of all how does he know where the boat and Mr. Reed were found? It wasn't mentioned in the paper, so how does he know the location?"

"Saw them both."

"Saw them?" Sidney envisioned Mr. Daniel watching George Reed fall overboard.

"Yes, sir. Mr. Daniel spends more time on the water than he does on land. He was just checkin' his traps as usual. He saw Mr. Reed's boat out there hung up in the marsh grass with nobody in it an later he saw the place where the police pulled Mr. Reed's body out of the water."

"And the sandbar?"

"Oh, everybody with a boat knows where that sandbar is."

Sidney just shook his head. Here he's been running around for four days developing and analyzing information, getting all sorts of people involved and unable to come up with a definitive answer to Tillie's plea. "They do eh? And he claims that because of the tides, Mrs. Reed could not have gotten back to the sandbar from the boat, given where it ended up?"

"That's right. He said she'd have to walk on water to get there or the boat get to where it was by driftin' from the sandbar. Im-possible."

"Interesting." Sidney, knowing he and Ray, as well as Susan and Geoff, had pored over the charts for the Morgan River, needed more. "You think I could talk with Mr. Doyle. I mean, would he talk to me about this?"

"Don't see why not. Just tell him who you are and that Tillie sent you. He already knows you, though. I tole him I axed you to help. How's Mr. Geoffrey doin' this mornin'?"

"Eh, doing much better. How did you know about Geoffrey?" Looking surprised that Tillie knew of the attack on Geoff.

"Ain't too many white people scrubbin' floors in hospitals, especially at night. They saw you at the hospital worrin' about Mr. Geoffrey, knew I worked for you so they let me know. Somebody sure banged him in the head."

Sidney just shook his head again and smiled. Life in a small town. No secrets. "Good thing his head is as hard as it is. Nothing broken. They should let him out this afternoon. He's going to stay in the guest room for a few days. I told him I didn't want him staying alone in that room of his.

"That's good."

"Something wrong?"

Tillie looked right past Sidney and focused on something in the neighboring yard. With only one eye that worked right, she had to actually move her head in the direction she was looking. "No, I just realized that's where they found the painting that come from General Brewster's place. Funny place to leave a painting."

"Where?" Sidney turned his head.

"Over there," she pointed. "The marsh curves around back there so that from the front steps here you can look right past the rear corner of the Bennett's. You see that big angel oak there? Well, to the right you can see some myrtle. It was right there against the myrtle."

"The Bennett's would easily see it from the back of their house."

"They're up in Maine. Been a way a few weeks now. No, Mr. Gregory spotted it and went over to take a look, then called the police. Whoever took it musta been spooked pretty good to leave it behind. Heck, Mr. Gregory said it wasn't very big."

"Tillie, is there anything you don't know?"

"Ha," she laughed, "in my business they ain't too many secrets. Ain't a awful lotta truth sometimes either. That's why I wanted to make sure the Miss Becky story was set to right."

"Just shows you have a good heart."

"It's the Christian thing to do. No point bein' just a Sunday Christian. You've got to do the right thing all seven days. My grandmother always told me that for six days you're supposed to practice bein' a Christian and on the seventh you give thanks for having made it and axe for help for the next six."

"You're all right, Tillie. Say, do you think anyone would mind if Mickey and I took a walk over there?" indicating the area of the marsh where the painting was found. "In fact, why don't you come with us?. You could help me think through a few ideas I have."

"Sure, nobody's around. Everybody knows you and Mickey anyway." With the mention of her name, Mickey got up in anticipation of moving on.

As they started for the neighboring property, Sidney said, "So where do I find your Mr. Daniel?"

"Every day about four he'll be at Coffin Landing. That's where he keeps his boat. Just axe for him. He'll be either commin' or goin' but he'll be there. That's his mendin' and fixin' time."

"Okay, thank you Tillie. I'm glad you're satisfied with Mrs. Reed. Sorry I couldn't have been of more help." Sidney paused for a moment trying to collect his thoughts on how best to proceed and then decided to just jump in. "Tillie, I know you're satisfied with what your friend said and I know for you the whole Reed affair is over but I would really appreciate it if you would come with me when I visit with Mr. Doyle. We both know how the low-country is and I don't think your friend will be as open with me when I ask him a question as he is with you."

She thought for a moment. "Yeah, you're right and I know it. He really don't know you even if I say you're ok. I was kinda thinkin' that. Yeah, I'll go with you besides if he decides to talk in Gullah, you ain't gonna know what he said. Yeah, we'll go together but Mickey'll have to stay behind. Makes black folks nervous when white men come askin' questions an bring a big dog along."

As the three of them moved across the lawn and over toward the Bennett's Sidney thought, *Yes, the Reed matter is all settled for you but not for me.* As he continued walking, he began envisioning the marsh and George Reed falling overboard with the boat drifting away. Suddenly, a vision also came into his head of someone coming up behind George, hitting him on the head and pushing him over the side. *Where did that come from? Must be combining Geoffrey and Reed.*

They walked slowly and easily across the grass to the marsh edge and the target myrtle, with Mickey exploring every odor she could find along the way. They both stopped at their target—Mickey sniffing about the myrtle and Sidney giving the area a general look.

"This is one of the best views on the whole of The Ridge. Wow. Look at the view you get from here." The Ridge name was an obvious one as the area sat on a gentle slope that ran from the rear of most of the houses down to the marsh and the Morgan River. Sidney estimated that the rise on average would be about twenty feet with the high point being just slightly above that, which protected the homes from the storms and hurricanes that have come across the area since time began. The original residents were a branch of the Yemassie Indians who, having learned from experience, put their village on the ridge seven or eight hundred years earlier.

"Tillie, I know you're happy with what Mr. Daniel said but for some reason I've got a feeling there's more to this than a simple falling out of a boat."

They stopped and Sidney released Mickey from her lead so she could wander a bit.

"I know. I mainly didn't like that Miss Becky was bein' talked about but it's got me to wonderin' too. Mr.

Reed, he was a boat man. More alive on the water than he was on land. A lot like Mr. Daniel. I don't see either one of them ever fallin' out of a boat sittin' quietly in one of those marsh channels. No matter how much they was drinkin'." The view from where Sidney now stood was one you could watch all day and never become bored, a bit like watching the fire in a fireplace. The gentle breeze through the marsh grass not only provided movement but also color variations, as the sun caught different angles on the vegetation as well as the water. Even here at the shore he could see the movement of the tide pushing the water in the channels, a continual lapping and movement against the grass and reeds.

"And what went on here doesn't make sense. Why would a thief leave the painting here. This house is empty, which everyone seems to know, so no one can see you. In fact, with all these trees and shrubs around, I doubt if anyone from the Gregory's could see either. The down slope makes for a good screen too." The area contained a wide variety of vegetation and a fifty foot natural barrier between where the marsh and the formal landscaping began. Looking toward the marsh, Sidney could see a view lane to the left of where he stood that provided a panorama of the river and the marsh, while to the right there were a variety of tall pines and some white and red oaks and tall crape myrtle. The opening in the tree line provided a view that the Brewster's and the Bennett's shared. Birds kept swooping down out of the trees and over to the variety of bird feeders in Brewster's back yard where there were also three birdbaths automatically fed by the irrigation system.

"I kinda agree with you. So why leave the painting? Maybe to come back for it later? No, doesn't sound right. Any self respectin' thief would o' tried to hide it in some way. Why come back a second time and risk being seen out in the open?" Mickey, not listening, began sniffing to the left of the myrtle and led Sidney out to the more open area where the marsh began.

"Unless he wanted it to be found."

"Or maybe he was spooked."

At that point two egrets took to the air in front of Mickey, where they had been wading in the grass looking for a late breakfast. Sidney jumped. "Ah, like that, Mickey, yes, just like that. Maybe he spooked some roosting water birds or better yet maybe an alligator." Mickey, unperturbed, continued into the marsh and stood in the water. "No swimming today. We're just walking. Water comes in pretty close here doesn't it?" Mickey just stood there looking out at the river watching two sailboats gently tacking back and forth as they headed in a Southern direction. "Yes, probably just that simple. He thought he saw or heard something, panicked, dropped the painting and took off. Interesting thought isn't it Tillie?

ᗯᗯᗯ

Sitting on the small balcony of his hotel overlooking Bull Street, Warren felt comfortable. The Savannah newspapers were on the chair next to him. No mention of George Reed. He watched all the news reports on the local channels this morning and again—nothing. George Reed's death was old news. An accident no one would hardy remember in a few weeks. But Warren didn't have a few weeks to find the pictures. Now that the heat was off, it was time to get aggressive. And there was only one place left to look.

Chapter 10

So it was definitely a break in?" Sidney said, sitting on the conversation side of his front porch with Ray Morton. The area backed up to the windows of the living room and contained an outdoor furniture grouping of three chairs and a sofa around a rectangular coffee table. Sidney sat in the chair on the end looking down the porch while Ray had taken one of the chairs that had its back to Howard Street with the sofa across from him. They were both sipping iced tea and occasionally watching the local traffic and the tourists being ferried around by horse drawn tour carriages, although Sidney showed more interest in them.

Periodically he would give a wave of the hand or a salute with his iced tea glass, actions strongly recommended by the chamber of commerce. The actions delighted the tourists who immediately returned the wave and took pictures. Some of them, imagining the bucolic retirement lifestyle of a small, Southern, coastal town, would actually decide to move to Morgan, or a similar place, but once arriving they would be talked into an adult community, living behind a gate and never really experiencing the lifestyle that convinced them to move to the region.

"Yeah. No doubt. Have you had a chance to talk with Geoff?"

"Not really. Brought him home early this morning and put him right to bed upstairs. He's out cold with all that medication he's taking. They told him he was very lucky. Apparently he took quite a hit. Geoff attributes his survival to having his head filled to capacity with an overabundance of English literature and George Meredith and thereby producing a glancing blow."

"George who?"

"Nothing. An ongoing discussion we're having. Any idea who hit him and why?"

"Difficult to say. Whoever was there came in through the back door just the way Geoff did. Can't tell how many there were. He was hit from behind. Said he made some noise in the hope that if anyone was still there they would take off out the front. Obviously didn't work. The lights were on."

"Wanted to make sure no one was there before I went in," said a bath-robed and head bandaged Geoff from the doorway to their left.

"Well, look who's up and around: ole rock head? How you feelin' Geoff?" Ray said in greeting.

"Are you all right to be moving around," cautioned Sidney, being protective—a new role for him.

"Yeah, I'm just tired of sleeping. If that makes any sense. Mind if I sit for a while?"

"Take a spot on the sofa and put your feet up there," instructed Sidney, indicating the chair off to the side slightly and in the corner of the porch. "We were just talking about you."

"So I heard." He made his way to the sofa and sat himself down on the right side of it where he would be facing in the direction of Sidney and Ray when he put his feet up on the chair.

"Was it you who turned the lights on last night?" Inquired Ray.

"Oh, yeah. I had no idea someone was in there. I went to use my key the same way I always do. The door was unlocked but I thought someone just forgot. It's happened before. Only suspicion I had was when my shirt caught on a splinter in the door jam. Even then I wasn't sure. Never saw anything. Never heard anything." Geoff shifted the rear pillow to the side and braced it against the arm and put his feet up.

"What about the burglar alarm" said Sidney? "I thought all business had them. In fact, everyone seems to have them anymore. I think everyone in that gated community down the road from Roots and Rakes has them and they even have armed guards at the gate."

"We never use it. Mrs. Reed had it put in for insurance purposes. Keep the rates down. There's nothing there to steal besides it's impractical. We have a lot of people going in and out before and after hours. That's why I was there. I was supposed to fix a system first thing this morning. Some of the other crews get back late. Mr. Reed used to be in and out at all sorts of hours. Nobody would ever remember the code, so why bother."

"How do you figure they got behind you?" said Ray. "From what I could see, everything in that room is wide open except for that door that looked like it went to a closet. Think they were in there?"

"Possible. Again, I really don't know. I'm not really sure how far into the building I was when I got hit."

Ray nodded: "The guys who found you said you were just past that doorway. They also said it looked like you deflected part of the blow. Any recollection of that?"

"Not really, except for a sore arm." Geoff moved his left arm. "I seem to remember hearing something, starting to turn and that was it."

"I think they'll take a hard look at that closet room in the hopes of finding something but in a commercial space like that it won't be easy."

"Do they know if anything was taken?" Sidney said to Ray.

"Not that they could tell right off. Becky Reed and her office manager, I think that what they called her."

"That's Bev," Geoff said.

"Yeah, they're over there now trying to see if anything's missing."

"I can't imagine what someone would take. Unless..." Geoff hesitated.

"Unless what?" Ray leaned forward slightly, his instincts sensing something.

"Well, that closet you refer to wasn't really a closet, it was George Reed's dark room."

"Dark room?" said a now very alert and focused Ray Morton.

"He was a photographer as well as a landscaper," interrupted Sidney.

"Sometimes he left cameras in there," continued Geoff. "He had lots of them also other types of stuff for editing pictures."

"I thought everyone had gone digital and printed pictures off their computer?" questioned Ray.

"Not Mr. Reed. Oh, he did have digital cameras but he started taking pictures and doing his own developing a long time before cameras went digital, claimed they weren't always good enough for what he was trying to do. He had a complete set up in there: chemicals, enlargers, you name it. He said he was more comfortable with film and he really liked the idea of having a negative, although, he said a lot depended on what he was shooting. He always had a camera with him. Those small digital ones were great for on the spot pictures but when he was really looking to capture a specific bird or a nest it was always a thirty-five millimeter with a telephoto lens. Oh, he had special lights, tripods, a whole knapsack full of stuff he used to go off with."

"And everyone pretty much knew about what was in that room?"

"It was pretty common knowledge, I guess. Everyone who worked at R and R knew about the dark room. He'd always be dancing about the front office with one of his cameras. Lots of times when he was really happy with something he shot, he'd bring the just developed prints up front for everyone to see."

"Well, we may have found a motive for the break in," said Ray now leaning back once again and reaching for his iced tea next to him on a small table.

"By the way," Sidney said, directing his question to Ray, "do you know who made the nine-one-one call, the one about the break in, since Geoff obviously didn't?"

"Came in anonymous. Just said there was something funny going on over at R and R and someone should look into it."

"Male or female?"

"Male. Southern accent."

"Any ideas?"

"Have to believe it was one of the people who hit Geoff. Got scared, with all the blood. Didn't want to face a murder rap. It's not unusual with this kind of thing. They weren't really trying to hurt anyone but they had no plans of getting caught either."

Sidney frowned. "You keep referring to *them*. Why, are you sure it was more than one?"

"General profile around here. Break ins like this are not usually done by loners. Usually drugs behind it some place, and they're always in a group. Two, maybe three people. Safety in numbers. Serious thieves usually go after something of real value and they tend to be loaners."

Sidney thought for a moment. "Like paintings?"

"Yeah, paintings, jewelry, large blocks of cash. Real money." Ray stopped for a moment and then added, "Hey, want real money, start a company, take it public, and then milk it dry." This was a hot topic for Ray of late. When he retired he took some of his *free* funds and, at the suggestion of a local broker, invested them in two companies that went bankrupt.

"That does seem to be the trend," Sidney mused. "As you know there can be a lot of creativity when it comes to theft."

"Didn't I hear that someone ripped off the Morgan First Bank last week?" Geoff inquired.

"Oh, that was pretty good, yeah." Ray was about to continue on his tirade against the vultures of Wall Street but the switch in topics seemed to cheer him up. "Stupid on the part of the bank but pretty gutsy on the crook's part. They haven't caught her yet but they're pretty sure she worked for that fast food place in Founders Square Plaza." Ray had a grudging respect for non-violent thieves with a sense of flair or creativity.

Sidney looked puzzled so Ray continued. "You didn't hear about that one? You ought to read more than that Martin guy."

"It's Meredith."

"Meredith, Martin, you need to get out more."

Geoff sat slightly wide eyed, not used to hearing Sidney Lake needled. "So what happened?" he said.

Ray leaned forward again, really getting into his story. Although not a Southerner, he had absorbed the art and culture of *the story*. "It was so simple, it was brilliant. You see, most of these fast food places don't like to keep cash on the premises, so they keep weeding out their registers all day and move the cash to the local bank branch.

At the end of the day whatever is left goes to the night depository, which is all fine and good policy, since you don't want to keep anything of substance in a local safe. Not good to tempt people and even more so, not good for insurance premiums. However, opening up is a problem since the fast food place has no real cash on hand except for some minor leftovers from the day before. All the registers are empty. Where to get the cash? The bank. So before the bank opens up for general business, they have people doling out cash and coin to the fast food places so they can set up their registers. Somebody from the restaurant shows up at the door, they buzz him in, he provides a list of what they need: rolls of quarters, dimes, nickels, pennies, and a bunch of one's, five's, and ten's nicely bundled. They put everything into a sack. He signs the slip and back to the shop he goes."

Sidney smiled. "I think I know where this is going."

"Hang on," Ray said. "So the other morning a nice little girl shows up at the door to the bank wearing a hat and shirt featuring the logo of the restaurant. She flashes a nice smile and gives the clerk inside a wave. The clerk, well, he sees the uniform and that nice smile and gives her a wave back, comes over to the door, unlocks it, and in she comes. She flashes that smile again and they chat on about having to be to work so early in the morning and what a great day it would be to head out to Hunting Island and the beach. She then hands him a list of what she says she was instructed to get by the morning manager. One of the tellers asks about Joe or Bill who is the one they usually see in the morning. She says he's out sick or quit so Leo, her manager, sent her over. The teller fills the order. She signs the receipt and gathers up all the coin and currency into the night depository bag the restaurant dropped off the night before, flashes the smile, chats on with the guy who opened the door for her, who then unlocks it again, and off she goes. Fifteen minutes later, Joe or Bill shows up and a second teller fills the same order. Two hours later the bank suddenly discovers they duplicated the restaurant's daily cash request and our little lady is long gone. Pretty slick."

"Do you think they'll get her?" Geoff said.

"Probably. She's definitely local. Didn't get more than a grand between the rolled and banded cash from the bank and the leftovers from the deposit bag. It's probably spent by now. But I have to give her credit. She didn't use a gun, didn't threaten anyone, no one got hit on the head," Ray said, looking at Geoff. "If you could channel that little lady in the right direction, she'd probably do okay—"

"Hi, everybody," interrupted Susan, who'd managed to come up the front steps undetected, as everyone was so focused on Ray's story. "Shouldn't you be in bed?" she asked, directing her comments at the bath-robed Geoff spread out on the sofa.

"Oh, hi, Susan. Needed fresh air. Good for the healing process," was his reply.

"Hi, Mr. Lake, Mr. Morton. It's awfully nice of you to watch over Geoff this way." Mickey came out from her position in the back corner. Susan gave her a pat. "You too, Mickey. I've heard about you."

"We'll find some way for him to make up for it," Sidney said.

"Shouldn't you be in school now?" Geoff said.

"Cut my after school work short so I could come over."

"What time is it?" Sidney asked.

"Just about three-thirty."

"Oops, I've got to be at Coffin Landing at four." Sidney rose from his chair. "You all stay here and chat."

"Tillie's tide guy?" Ray said

"Yes. Want to come along?"

"You don't want me there if you expect him to tell you anything. The islanders will never give you an opinion on anything if they think there's a badge around, especially one they don't know, even a retired one. No, you go on your own. I'll stay here with the love birds and maybe Mickey and I will find something better to drink than sweet iced tea."

☙℘℘

Coffin Landing sat on the Morgan River across from the downtown area and about a half mile to the south. With waterfront property being so valuable and, increasingly, gobbled up for development, it represented a surprising remnant of an earlier time. There were no coffins there now, as there were during the Civil War, when the Landing served as the place where the local hospitals—most of the large houses were converted to temporary hospitals during the war—would send their dead while all the paperwork was finished and burial arrangements were made. Some bodies were buried locally, while others were shipped down to Beaufort for burial in the large cemetery there.

A bait, tackle, and seafood store now stood on the spot of the coffin storehouse. The water around Coffin Landing had enough natural depth to it so that it supported a good size dock, the current home to five commercial shrimp boats and quite a few smaller ones. It was here that Daniel Doyle spent more than seventy years on one or another of the shrimp boats and the rest of his time shrimping and crabbing in the local waters on his own. He knew every inch of the marshland.

Not a shoal or a channel escaped his net. There was not a fish, shrimp or crab he couldn't find and, if they weren't where they were supposed to be, he could tell you why.

"Mr. Daniel," Tillie said, addressing the smallest of the four black men of seemingly indeterminate age who were sitting in the shade of a tall live oak tree at the back of the store. Two of the men were sitting at a table made of a couple of boards on sawhorses and playing dominos while the other two were working on a crab cage.

"Dis mus' be de man frm de college," said one of the men doing the repair work and spotting Sidney just behind her.

"Yes, sir, I am," Sidney volunteered.

"Tillie say you might cum by. Glad to meet you." Doyle started to get up.

"No, no, stay there." Sidney reached out his hand and took Doyle's in his. It was an experience he would long remember—like shaking hands with the bark of a tree: strong, hard and rough. Sidney's paper-trained hand never felt calluses like it. He thought his hand would be a bloody pulp when he got it back.

"Dis here's Deacon Mackie and they's Robert Brown an Aaron Smalls. Tillie, you knows um all"

"Sure do."

They shook hands all around and Sidney noticed a small smile on Doyle's face that indicated a knowledge of what kind of an experience Sidney's hand was undergoing. "Cum on in here an' sit youself down otta da sun." He motioned them toward two folding chairs nearby. "You ebber be out here befo'?"

"No, I haven't," Sidney said.

Everyone went back to what they were doing, except for Daniel.

"Do much fishin'?"

"Actually, I don't think I've been fishing around here. Around anywhere, actually." Sidney took the empty chair, which was in the shade just across from Doyle, while Tillie started a conversation with Deacon Mackie in Gullah.

The chair moaned a bit as he sat down, not used to a customer of such weight. A welcome cool breeze came up off the water to greet him as he shifted in the chair to make sure it was sturdy.

"Spend you time fishin' in books, eh."

Sidney thought he saw one of the domino players stifle a laugh. They were obviously planning to follow every word of the conversation while continuing to talk and play the game. "I suppose you could say that the only shrimps and crabs I run across are characters in novels." He was not unfamiliar with the sound of Gullah, although he realized Doyle seemed to be staying away from the strong aspects of the language. Sidney had heard Gullah often and the college even put on plays where Gullah story tellers gave the history of the islands.

He had heard conversations between local residents before and knew, if they decided to really start speaking among themselves, there would be no way he could follow them. Doyle, having been around as long as he had, knew how to communicate and be understood by just about anyone he wanted to speak with.

Doyle chuckled. "You otta try fisin' some time. Jus' put youself out dere an' drift long in da marsh. Good for ya. Folks need some sloe time. Not good ta be rushin' so much. Miss da good life. Rushin' so much you go rite by it an' doan' know it." He kept working on the cage as he talked, inspecting the ties and the lines.

"I can't disagree with you there. Tough to change habits though. It is peaceful here." Sidney looked past Doyle out to the tall, marsh grass and the easy lapping of the water against the shore line and the tide easing the water past the nearby dock, where only one of the shrimp boats was now moored, the rest of them were out off the Edisto coast.

"Yeah, dis a good spot." Doyle looked straight at him. "So tell me Mr. College man, what can ole Daniel do for you?"

"Well, you know about George Reed's accident last week out on the water, and Tillie here worried that some people might think his wife had something to do with it, even though the police didn't think so. I was helping her show it was really an accident but there didn't seem to be any way it could positively be proved the lady couldn't have been involved. Tillie then told me this morning that you said it was impossible for Mrs. Reed to be involved, but I don't think I fully understood how you could be so sure."

"Yes, sir. Impossible," he said with a shake of his head. Deacon Mackie sat there and shook his head as well and Tillie followed suit.

"She said something about the tides."

Doyle rubbed his chin and gave Sidney a long once over look.

Tillie bristled. "If Mr. Daniel says it couldn't be done, then it couldn't of been done. You go on an' tell Professor Lake what you said about the tides. You can tell him, Mr. Daniel"

Another long pause. Then with a slight nod of his head, he began. "Is real simple. Ya see frm where dat Mr. Reed wuz found, da water don't go very far. They's a hole right dere, a good, deep fishin' hole. You drop somphin' in dat hole an' it pretty much stay dere, which is why da fish like it. Mr. Reed, he woudda gone in da water right where day foun' 'im. Now Miss Becky, she wuz on dat bar an' dat big boat of her wuz up da channel where Mr. Reed wuz found. But if she take da boat to da sand bar an' den let it go, it won't go up da channel where dey foun' it cause the tide, it go the odder way from dere, an' da boat woudda end up in da channel to da north of where dey foun' it." Doyle was careful and precise as he spoke.

Sidney figured he would play devil's advocate as much as possible. "But what if she swam from where the boat was found back to the sand bar?"

"Deacon, why doan you tell 'im about dat swim you had. Deacon here's got da mos' swimmin' practice as he falls otta boats more en da res of us."

More chuckles from the domino players.

"Now, that's not true. You give the man here the wrong impression."

"Da hell, it ain't," Doyle said with a smile. "Fact is, you got some swimmin' done in dat very channel, I recall."

"Now that wus a *real* accident. Tripped over the line marker."

Doyle waved his hand at Deacon. "Tell the man."

"All right." Deacon addressed Sidney directly. "The way it works in that spot is that it's pretty straight an' the water moves real fast at risin' tide. Besides, as Mr. Daniel says, you can't get to the sand bar from there. You got to go about a quarter mile out the channel an' then catch the tide in the river to bring you over where the sand bar is. It just ain't logical to go from one place to the next. If that boat drifted in there by itself, nobody left it going against the tide. They woudda found it further inland."

"Okay, based on what you've said, I can see why Tillie feels confident that it was an accident, and Mrs. Reed didn't have anything to do with it. Just a thought, though, why did you say that when you fell in it was a *real* accident?"

Deacon looked over at Doyle who sat there and rubbed his chin, quietly thinking for a moment. Then he cleared his throat. "'Cause that Mr. Reed, he didn't have no accident."

❧❧❧

"Well, at least he's not dead. Just a bump on the head," Warren said after reading the brief story on the local news website.

He got up from his chair and walked over to the window, bringing his bourbon and water with him. *Accidental death.* The story bothered him because it mentioned George Reed's accidental death. It didn't tie the two events together other than to say it could have been an opportunity burglary since the business was closed due to Reed's death and they were taking advantage of no one being around for a week. The problem, as he saw it, involved the death and the burglary being in the same sentence. Even though the article did not suggest a connection, maybe someone seeing them mentioned together just might think they belong that way.

"Gonna have to do somethin' soon. One and one don't add up at the moment for anyone but for how long? I know where those cameras got to be. Can't wait any longer." He took a sip of the bourbon. *How did this all go so wrong? All I did was make a few adjustments to some signatures. It didn't amount to much. A few bucks maybe. No big deal. Yeah, but I had to go and certify it so it would be worth more. Can't undo it. Got to go forward.*

Chapter 11

Ray nursed a scotch and water while Sidney swirled his white wine and looked at the nautical chart laid out in front of him on his dining room table. Geoff stood in the doorway to the kitchen with Susan next to him.

Ray waved his drink at the chart. "So he said you couldn't get a boat in there?"

"No, he said you couldn't get Reed's big boat in there," Sidney responded while he looked at the spot on the chart where the body of George Reed was found. "It's too big or weighs too much or whatever."

"So the boat doesn't go there. The body floats in on the rising tide."

"Mr. Doyle says, no. He said you could drop a body off Reed's boat at ten rising tides in a row, out in the channel where the boat would have to be, and it would never make it back to where the hole is."

Ray scratched his head. "So you can't get his boat in there and the body won't drift in. So how does it get there?"

Geoff shrugged. "You drop it over the side."

"From a boat that draws about six inches or less," Susan added.

Mickey barked.

"Looks like everybody's got it all figured out," Ray concluded.

"Everyone," Sidney agreed, leaning back from the table and the chart, "except the local police, the coast guard, and the coroner. All the people who are supposed to figure it out. What I think we're looking at is a group of people who should know better, seeing what they expected to see, seeing what someone wanted them to see."

"Yeah," Ray agreed, also leaning back in his chair and away from the table, "but you can't really blame them. It's a perfect set up. A guy who drinks too much is found in the water. He's got a bang on the head and too much alcohol in his veins. His boat is floating away in the tide. He's a local everybody likes and has no enemies. Only one who might have had a reason to bang him on the head is his wife, as all wives now and again would like to kill their husbands—remember that, Geoff—but there's no physical way Becky Reed could have done it and ended up on that sandbar." Geoff was about to make a comeback remark but Ray kept going. "Everything is consistent with an accident. An accident that is not exactly uncommon around the lowcountry. People fall off their boats all the time." His chair came forward. "In fact, George Reed was known to have done it more than once."

"Okay, you made your case for the local police missing this one," Geoff finally said, deciding not to make a smart remark.

"Geoff, if you're going to participate—sit." Sidney motioned him to one of the chairs. "You're supposed to be resting."

Susan walked to the table with him and pulled up another chair for herself.

"So we go to the police," Sidney continued.

"Wrong," Ray said, leaning back in his chair again and balancing his glass on the arm.

"Why not?"

"Sidney, let's go easy here. We've got a situation where everybody who's somebody has signed off on this. This is not New York, it's Morgan. Everything that goes on here is personal. The police chief is appointed by the council so he doesn't have to face an election like the coroner, who would like to be mayor, but sayin' bad things about the chief reflects on the council. There's a right way of doing this and a wrong one. The one thing you want to avoid is the suggestion of a missed investigation, so any announcement about the investigation being reopened must look more like a continuation of the original investigation, as though the chief and the coroner knew it all along and just didn't want to make their suspicions public. It's called saving face. These guys have got to show everyone that they're really smart and on top of everything. They have to hold a press conference that basically says they suspected foul play the whole time but didn't want to tip their hand so the perp would think he or she got away with it."

Geoff snorted. "You use 'perp' down here? I thought that was a New York thing."

Ray gave him a look that said *If you were a palmetto bug, you'd be under my heel right now*. He then added, "Yeah."

"Sorry."

"As I was saying, the trick is to make it their idea."

"But won't they just shrug it off if they can't find a motive?" Sidney asked.

"This may be a small town but these guys are not stupid and neither is SLED. They'll figure it out."

Everyone sat quietly thinking for a moment.

Geoffrey rubbed the bandage on his head. "You think there's any possibility that the guys who hit me on the head could have murdered George Reed?"

It was the first time any of them had used the M-word in connection with Reed's death, and they all realized it. George Reed was most likely murdered and this was no longer just a friendly exercise.

Sidney looked at Ray. "What do you think?"

"Interesting idea. Of course, the idea that George Reed was murdered puts everything back on the table. It may be a coincidence, someone breaking into R and R on the day before Reed is buried and then maybe not. Certainly, the day of and before the funeral, one would think, it would be a day when no one would be near the office and be the safest. The same logic you could use for the petty theft."

"Well, what if Geoff here is right and the break in was related to George's death?"

"Wait a minute, Sidney. Just think through what you're suggesting. If you go on the assumption that Geoff walked in on Reed's killer or killers, that means that Reed was involved in something or possibly had something they wanted."

"Maybe he was blackmailing someone," Geoff suggested. "He was a photographer. Maybe he had some pictures that some guy would like to make sure his wife didn't get to see."

"Nice try, Geoff," Ray said, "but this is Morgan not Los Angeles. Think Mayberry. Believe me, there are no secrets here. If somebody was fooling around with somebody else in town, the word would be out real fast. If you want to fool around, find someone down in Hilton Head or Beaufort or Savannah. Hell, you guys got involved in this to begin with because of gossip."

"Geoff may be right to an extent, though," Sidney said. "The key is to determine if anything is missing."

Geoff shook his head. "The problem there is to know if something *is* missing. I mean, the room they were in was a dark room. No one ever really went in there but George Reed. Even Mrs. Reed stayed away."

"Unless…"

Everyone turned to look at Susan.

"Unless Geoff interrupted them and they have to come back again."

They were all silent, then Ray raised both hands, palms forward. "All right, let's think that through for a moment. The reality is there are three possibilities: they didn't know what they were looking for, they found what they were looking for, they didn't find what they were looking for."

"If they had no idea what they were looking for," Sidney said, "then there's probably no reason for them to come back, so we can throw that out right away because they found out it's too risky. If they found what they were looking for, then for sure they're not coming back. There are two more options, not one. First, they didn't find what they were looking for because they didn't have time to complete their search. In this case. they probably still won't come back because a) it's still too risky and, b) if they couldn't find it, they might assume no one else would either. Second, they had ample time to look and realized that the object of their search was not there."

This was typical Sidney Lake: taking what seemed to be the obvious and moving it onto another level, which was why Ray learned to respect his opinions. Police spent most of their time taking insignificant events and tying them to seemingly unrelated activities. Sidney, when analyzing a painting, especially a portrait, spent most of his time on the accent pieces: the pipe on the table, the dog on the chair, the book on the lap, the way the hands were folded, the color, size, name of the flower in the vase or lapel. These spoke volumes to him, as did the items he expected to see but which were not there. Hattie Ryan, his closest friend, often chastised him for not paying attention during a conversation when, in fact, he was paying too much attention—just to the wrong thing. In a restaurant, he spent more time listening to the conversation at the adjoining table than the one in which Hattie tried to get his participation.

He also had a habit of looking right past her to better observe the activities of the waiters and patrons.

"In presenting a case to your friend, Chief Hornig," Sidney said to Ray, "it might be very useful to give him the break-in at Roots and Rakes as the defining event that they could use, as the argument for going public and declaring George Reed's death as suspicious, to say the least."

"That's not bad, Sidney. Even if it turns out not to have anything to do with Reed's death—not be connected at all—it's still the kind of event that gives him the opportunity to show he's on top of everything."

Sidney nodded. "What we need, though, is to make your old chief curious. What would you say to you and me taking a look at that dark room and seeing if there's at least something there that might raise a question, as being a possible connection to Reed's death, no matter how remote?"

Ray thought for a moment. He said nothing as he played with the ice in his now empty glass. He moved back and then forward. "Okay, I'll buy it. I think that would definitely bring Hornig on board. Yeah, I think that would do it."

"Another point to consider. On the assumption that George Reed was alive when he entered the area—" Sidney put his finger on the chart where Reed was found. "—which, for reference purposes, I'll call Doyle's hole, then he went there with someone else, someone he knows, someone with a boat with a shallow draft, someone who knew Reed might have an interest in going to that spot."

"Which means there may be something there that would interest him and the person knew Mr. Reed well enough to know it," Susan concluded.

She had been quietly watching Ray and Sidney work through the manner in which they hoped to get the police back into George Reed's death but she couldn't hold back any longer. Although Geoff had suggested to her—one did not *tell* Susan, as he'd found out early on in their relationship—that the two of them just sit back and stay out of the way. Let Lake and Morton work it out. However, Susan didn't work that way, especially since Geoff had already put in his two cents. Geoff's first reaction to Susan, when being introduced at a reception of the Smalls County Library Association, was that she seemed to fit the perfect description of a Southern brat. Her rapid-fire questioning hit him full force but he managed to recover quickly, which seemed to impress her. At the beginning of their relationship he questioned whether her interest in him was because he was a Yankee, which would give her the opportunity to tweak her father's nose, or whether she really liked him.

Sidney got up from his chair, walked over to his left, and looked out the window. "Okay, it looks like we have a couple of things going here. We still have a few hours of light left and that storm sitting off the coast shouldn't be here till much later tonight, so let me suggest something. In order for Ray to feel comfortable and credible in talking to Chief Hornig and, Ray, you're the one to do it not one of us. One, we need to confirm that there may be something in the Doyle's hole area that would be an inducement for him to go there with his killer and, two, we need to get a better understanding of what is or is not in that dark room. If you would be willing to help out, Susan, I—"

"Oh, yeah. Sure. Definitely," she said practically jumping out of her chair.

"Why am I not surprised? I guess I don't have to twist your arm. Okay, what I believe would really be helpful, since you have access to the kind of boat that we would need, would be for you to go to the Doyle's hole area and see if you can come up with a reason why George Reed would find it interesting, even compelling, to go there." Sidney walked toward them with the empty wine glass in his hand and gestured with it. "Why someone George would know would be able to talk him into going there on a Sunday afternoon. Ray and I, in the meantime, have to get a handle on the dark room, the value of its usual contents, and which of them might be missing or, if still there, would still be of interest to George's killer."

"Okay," Ray said, "one major point. I will go along with all of this, as long as everyone understands that our objective is not to find out who murdered George Reed, if, in fact, that's what happened, but to develop enough credible, circumstantial evidence as arguments that would compel Pete Hornig and Steele Wilcox to reopen the case."

"Agreed," Sidney said.

Geoff looked at the three of them. "What do I do?"

"You're going to call your friend Bev and tell her that Ray and I will be dropping over to pick up some notes and papers you left there, which you said you left in a desk of some sort in the shed on the property, and then you're going to stay glued to your cell phone and provide support for Susan, should she need it."

"Okay," Geoff said, nodding, "but one other thing. If I remember correctly from the original rumor mill as presented by Tillie, one of those rumors linked Mrs. Reed with Wilcox. Again, long-shot time, but what if Wilcox is our 'perp,' and the reason everything was shut down so quickly was because he was protecting himself?"

Ray answered, but only after a pause when everyone was staring at him. "That's why it goes to both of them. Yeah, it's a long shot, but as I said, everything's on the table. And another thing, ready or not, we lay this out tomorrow."

∾∾∾

Warren switched from the local news over to the Weather Channel to get a better idea of the storm that loomed off the coast of Georgia. He had a decision to make: go after the camera's and pictures tonight during the storm or, depending on its severity, hold off an extra day. The maps popped up on the flat screen TV hanging on the wall opposite the bed. The reporter seemed pretty sure it could reach tropical storm size but definitely not hurricane force—he definitely did not want to be out in a small boat in a hurricane—but he felt a storm with some wind, thunder, and lightning could work to his advantage. *Yeah, this could work just fine.*

Chapter 12

As Ray pulled into the parking lot at Roots and Rakes, he eased his car into an open space between two other cars that were parked in front. Then he turned to Sidney. "Who was that on the phone just before we left?"

"Lawrence Brewster. He wanted to know if I could stop by later this evening. Seems as though Jarvis Oliphant has been helping him with all those books he inherited, and Brewster just received an inventory list from his late uncle's lawyers in Charlotte. When I spoke with him the other day, he said he asked for Jarvis's help because there was no list and he had no idea what he had received. Now, with the list, he needs to go through it and compare it against what he has. Jarvis has gone out of town for a few days, and he was hoping I would be able to help him and maybe give him an idea if there was anything of real value missing due to the break in last Saturday. The police and insurance company are after him to come up with a value for the break-in, if there is one. Besides, he wants to get it all out of the way before the Morgan Garden Association cocktail party which he's hosting this weekend. Say, that just reminded me of something else," he continued as they made their way to the front door through a gauntlet of flower pots and hanging baskets. "The other day Geoff came over here and retrieved a map he left and someone pulled up to the parking area by the back fence but, spotting Geoffrey, they took off. I wouldn't be surprised if there's a connection with last night."

"Do you know if he reported it?" Ray asked. "Was it in his formal statement about last night?"

They stopped for just a moment.

"I've no idea."

Ray stopped before opening the door. "Did he get a look at the car?"

"Not really. Could only say it was not an SUV, it was a dark color, and it looked full size."

"How many people did he see?"

"I believe it was only one. But that doesn't mean there couldn't have been someone still in the car."

"Remind me to give Geoff a call as soon as we get out of here. Sometimes what you don't see is as important as what you do." Ray then opened the front door and held it for Sidney. "It's definitely worth pursuing. It's one more tidbit we can turn over to Pete Hornig."

"I'm afraid we're not really open," said the thirty-something woman behind the counter who faced them as they entered. She was wearing jeans and a tee shirt.

"Yes, I know," Sidney said, continuing to walk toward the counter. "Is Becky Reed still here? You're Bev, aren't you?"

"Yes."

"I saw you at George's funeral. Geoff said to say hello."

"You must be Sidney Lake."

"Guilty." He immediately wished he hadn't said that. "And this is my designated driver, Ray Morton."

"Hello, Bev," Ray said while extending his hand. "Don't pay any attention to anything he says. None of his students ever did."

Bev smiled. "And how is Geoff doing? What a terrible thing to happen."

"Much better. His head is a lot harder than even *we* thought."

As Sidney responded, Becky Reed came out of the office. She too wore jeans and a tee shirt but her shirt carried the message: *Gardeners have the best dirt.* "Hello, Sidney, Ray. Glad to hear that Geoff is doing better. I've really grown to like him. I can't believe what happened."

"All very strange. I see the police have gone," Sidney said, gesturing at the lack of a police vehicle in the parking lot and no one visible inside.

"Yes, finally. They were here all night and this morning. Still have the place closed off back there," she said, indicating the large storage and loading bay that could be seen through the windows behind the sales area. "The detective said they were pretty sure whoever attacked Geoff didn't even come in to the office area but they wanted us to verify that nothing seemed to be missing. Apparently, they came in and out the rear door. I guess you're here to pick up the books and notes Geoff said he left. I did find those. They were in the work shed where he said they were. They're over here." She gestured at the end of the counter.

"Thanks, these will keep him busy for a few days. Did you ever figure out if something was missing?"

While Sidney and Becky talked, Ray took in the whole room and its set up in relation to the rear storage area. He carefully looked at the relationship between the office and the sales desk, as well as the door they had just come through and the large display area of indoor plants off to the right, where another doorway led to the attached greenhouse and the outside. Last night it was dark, and he really didn't get a good look at anything. His main focus had been to find out what had happened to Geoff. Now he looked at everything with a different purpose.

"If there is, I don't know what," Becky said with a shrug of her shoulders and a look toward Bev.

Sidney rubbed his chin. "Geoffrey thought that, too, initially, but when he realized that someone may have been hiding in George's dark room, it occurred to him that someone could have been after the cameras and other equipment in there."

"Actually, I thought of that as well, but, no, everything's all there. The only one that I know for sure is missing is the one camera he usually kept in the boat. That was a small digital one. He always kept it with him just in case he came across something interesting. Most of the one's in the back were thirty-five millimeter with various telephoto lenses. Developing the pictures was almost as much fun for him as taking them. Especially the night photos. He loved to sneak up on wildlife at night in the marsh and those old thirty-five millimeters were his favorites for that. I'm sorry if I seem to be rambling on. It's so strange without him."

Bev put her hand gently on Becky's shoulder.

"I keep expecting him to come walking through the door," Becky whimpered.

Sidney could see her eyes begin to fill.

Ray jumped in before she could start to cry. "I was really impressed by his photographs. Marie took me to that exhibit at the arts center last year, knowing that I wouldn't go on my own, George had some pictures on display. Was he working on anything special recently, like when he did those pictures of the wood storks?"

It was clear to Sidney that Ray had done his homework. Sidney doubted that he actually went to that exhibition with Marie. She had probably mentioned it to him afterward or even earlier in the week.

"No, I don't—Yes, yes, he was. He told me he was trying to do raccoons. He said he was fascinated by their swimming from sandbar to sandbar and then through the marsh. In fact, he must have been out until two in the morning on Saturday night roaming around in that little skiff of his with the pole."

"Those little boats will go anywhere, won't they?" Ray said, while still taking in everything around him.

"Oh, yes, and George prided himself on being able to sneak up on just about anything. He would sit in that skiff, hiding in the marsh grass for hours until he got the picture he wanted."

"Have you seen any of the raccoon pictures?" Sidney asked.

"A few. He was still working on them. I know he developed some that he did last week but I'm not even sure he finished all of those. He brought home the ones he finished. He planned to bring them into the office and show everyone. He was really proud of them. In fact, Caldwell asked me about them the other day."

"Caldwell? Talbot?" Ray said, obviously surprised.

"Yes, he apparently knew George was taking pictures of raccoons and asked him for some pictures. He's an active environmentalist."

"Caldwell?" Sidney echoed.

"Yes, he apparently has a thing for raccoons."

Sidney could hear Ray mumble, "I don't think I want to go there."

Becky continued, ignoring Ray, if she heard him, but a definite smile appeared on Bev's face. "He's an unusual person," Becky said. "I don't always know how to take him, although he and George seemed to get along okay. But then that was George. With Caldwell, I could never be sure when he was serious or not. There were times he would make me feel as though I was doing something wrong just by being here. Like he'd be delighted if I left and went back north and then, at other times, he'd be as friendly and gracious as could be. I love this town. This is my home. I often wonder if some of the local anti-Northern people even realize how irritating their 'Yankee' this and 'Yankee' that can be. Anyway, he was looking for some raccoon pictures that George had promised him he could use in a presentation he's supposed to give. I think he said it was next week."

"I guess it never pays to put people in boxes. They'll surprise you every time. Look, we're not going to keep you," Sidney said, pushing back from the counter and reaching for the books on its end.

"Oh, that's all right."

"Say," Ray said, "would you mind if we took a quick look in George's dark room. I don't think I've ever actually been in one."

"I don't think so. The police still have the room blocked off but I'm sure there's no harm in looking in, besides, if anyone should know what they're doing, it would probably be you. I'll take you back"

They walked through the doorway to the storage area. The lights were already on. The dark room entrance came up immediately on the left. As they moved into the cavernous room, strips of yellow tape blocked their access. The door opened out. Becky reached in to turn the light on but Ray stopped her. "I wouldn't want to disturb anything until the line is down, although I'm pretty sure they're finished in here. Besides, there's plenty of light from the ceiling fluorescents out here. There are two light switches?"

"Yes, one is for the regular light and the other for the red light he uses in the dark."

"I don't see any cameras," said Ray.

Sidney was trying to look around them both but wasn't having much luck

"The police took them."

"Of course."

"What is the string running across the room with the clips on it used for?" Sidney inquired, finally seeing into the room.

"That's for drying film and prints. These are developing pans." She pointed out the four trays lined up in a row. "He kept all his chemicals on the shelf above."

"Not much room in here is there."

"No, this was really just a closet that George converted. He expanded it a bit with plywood and then painted everything black and also put that dark cloth over everything," she said, pointing at a felt like material that wrapped around the inside of the entire room.

"Looks like there's really only room for one person in here," said Sidney.

"Two are okay as long as they're not moving around much but it was just right for George and his pictures."

"There's no file cabinet in here is there?" Sidney asked.

Ray just kept scanning the room and its relationship to the rest of the building.

Becky shook her head. "No. As soon as he finished with the pictures, he brought them home. All his files are in the den. Sometimes he might leave an individual file or two here during the week, but he always brought everything home on the weekend. That's where he does his real analysis. He has magnifying equipment there and everything. He would also scan some of the pictures into the computer and manipulate them there."

"I'm impressed," Ray said. "He worked in both worlds."

Sidney nodded. "With all those one hour photo places that used to be everywhere now just about gone this is all very interesting. It'll probably be a lost art, though, in a few years, with digital completely taking over everything," he mused. "The ultimate technology trap. I don't think people realize the danger they're facing in losing valuable documents and photos."

They both looked at Sidney questioningly.

He shrugged. "A pet project of mine. From a research point of view, we're already having trouble doing literary biographical work. Were used to looking at hand-written manuscripts, letters, edits of typewritten documents, it's all disappearing. Oh, the joy of finding a manuscript with erasures and cross outs, not to mention coffee stains and other spills. Shaky and hurried writing along with a switch to a pencil that looks as though something was written in anger is a researcher's dream."

Ray and Becky continued to stare.

Sidney shrugged again. "Sorry about that. Just finished an article for a national library publication dealing with the subject, so it's been on my mind. If I had only known about George and his photography, I would have used him as a resource. Well, thank you Becky," he said. "I really hope we haven't put you out. I'll send Geoffrey back as soon as I can."

"Tell him not to worry. I'll probably ask Bev to open up late tomorrow after the morning memorial service. Today is Wednesday, isn't it? Sidney, Ray, I do appreciate your thoughts and prayers, and tell Geoff not to worry about anything but getting better."

"We will."

"So, what do you think?" Sidney asked as they got back into the car.

"Curiouser and curiouser, as they say."

"Think there might be a connection?"

"Whether there is or there isn't, for my money there's more than enough circumstantial stuff floating around. This photography angle may just be the little push we need to get Hornig and Steele to reevaluate their original decision. The trouble is we still don't have any kind of a specific motive but then that will be Hornig's job to work out. We definitely have to get to them tomorrow, though."

❧❧❧

"Looks like it's gonna be a bad one," the FedEx driver said, coming out of the lobby entrance after delivering a package to the front desk and now seeing Warren in the doorway cautiously eyeing the darkening sky off to the south.

"Weather Channel doesn't think so," Warren answered, while continuing to look at the sky and not the driver.

"Well, all I know is what they say: 'Red sky in the morning, sailor take warning. Red sky at night, sailor's delight.' Don't know about you, but I don't see any red sky out there this afternoon. Take care."

Chapter 13

Susan eased the skiff into the channel, shut down the small engine, and tilted it up out of the water. She took the paddle that lay across the seat in front of her and began maneuvering toward Doyle's hole. Like everyone else who lived along the shoreline of the low-country, the Abbott's had a low draft skiff for moving about the hundreds of minor channels that made up the marshlands of the sea islands. She wore the uniform of the typical marsh wanderer: jeans, sweatshirt, and baseball cap.

The tide was coming in, just as it had on the day George Reed died. She timed her arrival just right. She and Geoff had worked out the exact location of Doyle's hole on the chart they obtained from the marina, which now sat on her lap as she made her way along in the skiff and down the fifteen foot wide channel. The water here had plenty of depth to it. The chart showed six feet. The grass along the edges stood about head high so she could just see over their tops. As she came upon the target area, she noticed that the grass and reeds became taller so that, to be seen from farther out into the river, you would have to stand up and certainly a small boat would never be noticed. She searched for what Daniel Doyle described to Sidney. Finally, she spotted the open area of the hole but found it separated from the minor channel by marsh grass growing almost completely out of the water. At this time in the tide cycle, Susan couldn't get her own flat bottomed boat over the lip and could readily see how Reed's large boat would not make it, even after the tide was fully in. There was no sound other than the quiet lapping of the water against the side of her boat.

She paddled slowly, searching the edge and then, following the instructions Daniel Doyle gave to Sidney and Tillie, she spotted the small channel that led to the entrance to the hole: a break in the lip where the water could slowly escape and continue to move for a while when the tide dropped. Doyle said the thick grass at high tide covered the entrance by no more than eight or ten inches of water. Even getting in at mid-tide would be a challenge but if you carefully watched the way the water moved, you'd see the entrance.

At this time of year the tall, thick grass wore a medium green color; the tips had some brown to them; and the base looked dark and seemingly impenetrable, especially in the mixed light of the threatening, late afternoon sky and the storm moving in from the Atlantic. As Susan continued up the minor channel, looking for the entrance, her route suddenly turned to the right. If anything drifted up the channel, it would either get caught in the grass or veer to the right and move farther inland. Doyle's hole was the kind of place you went intentionally, not by accident.

As she carefully eased in, she looked around the large oval expanse of water, about thirty yards long and twenty wide. She could see the water deepen as she made her way farther into the opening, then she stopped paddling and just sat there for a moment. "Now why would I want to be here?" she said quietly to herself. "If I was George

Reed, what would be here in the early afternoon that would interest me?"

She looked again at the space and began to focus on the marsh grass around the perimeter, searching for nesting birds or possibly another kind of nest disguised along the edge. Having learned of Reed's passion for wildlife photography, she made the assumption that something unique and connected to the natural life of the marshland would be the draw of the hole.

Moving slowly along the perimeter and peeking into the grass, sometimes using the end of her paddle to push it back, she found nothing. By the time she covered three quarters around the edge, she began to doubt her thesis. Suddenly, something swooped right above her head. The sound of the wings beating to gain height made her jump and instinctively duck. A great shadow followed, visible even with the sun tucked behind the clouds. It came so suddenly and quietly that she almost went overboard. The skiff tossed from side to side as she fell back against the small engine.

One hand went into the water where it landed on a submerged, slimy log making her pull back her hand immediately so that now she fell off her seat and landed in the bottom of the boat. Nervous and jumpy ever since entering Doyle's hole, she shuddered. It wasn't the first log she'd run into. There were lots of them caught in the grass and, as Mr. Daniel said, '*What's falls in that hole stays there. It can't get in or out on its own.*' Finally catching her balance, she looked to see what seemed to attack her but there was nothing there. Looking ahead, she saw some water boiling as though something jumped. She continued to look about her but could not figure out what produced the shadow.

The sun tilted toward the west and leaped into an opening in the clouds. She looked right at it, blinding her for a moment. The clouds were coming in from the east, from the ocean. She put her hand up to shield the sun and continued to look around above her. Pine trees covered the shoreline and reached out into the marsh as she directed her search along the tops of the trees. Then it came by again—the most magnificent bald eagle she had ever seen—and it flew close, right at the top of the tall marsh grass. She couldn't take her eyes from it and watched its smooth, effortless glide, weaving and turning as it again gained height above her. She continued to watch it rise, and then she saw something else in the top of a partially dead oak tree: a nest and there seemed to be something moving in it. *Oh, yes,* she thought, *if I was into photographing wildlife, and especially birds, you wouldn't be able to keep me away from this place.*

෭ఌ෭ఌ

"So," Geoff said, "was there anything missing?"

Sidney had just come in after being dropped off by Ray in front of the house and he seemed to be distracted. "Huh?"

"Was there anything missing? The Reeds'? The dark room at R and R?"

"Oh, I'm sorry, Geoffrey. Just trying to sort out some things. No, no. Becky said there was definitely nothing missing. All the cameras that were supposed to be there seemed to be in place when the police checked." Sidney came onto the porch and took the chair next to the sofa where Geoff sat with his feet up. "How are you doing?"

"Pretty good, actually. Headaches gone. Pain's gone. Of course that's the medication. I'm sure my head still hurts and is tender. How many stitches did they say they put in?"

"Eight."

"Great number, eight. Not sure yet as to whether I should consider it lucky or unlucky. So nothing was taken?"

Just then the front door opened and Tillie came out, carrying a pitcher of sweet iced tea and two glasses. "Oh, you're back. Let me get another glass." She put the tea down and returned to the house.

"Yes, I'm back and that looks good." Sidney then answered Geoff's question. "That's what she said and that's what she told the police. She also confirmed that, as far as she could tell, nothing was moved."

"Moved?" Geoff questioned. "Why would moved be of interest?"

"Might indicate how long they were there before you interrupted them. If they were looking for something they could convert to cash to buy drugs, they probably wouldn't be too neat about it, move things around, knock things over. Since the police took the cameras, lenses, and related equipment, we couldn't tell if they had been touched. Certainly everything on the shelves looked orderly and in place, but then maybe they never had the time to get started."

"I know your friend Ray Morton doesn't go for the blackmail routine but what if it wasn't drug related and the thief knew exactly what he was looking for?" Geoff sat up straight and was becoming more animated. "So he didn't have to move anything or certainly not much? It was not the catch-all drug stuff he was after but something else, something specific?"

"Okay, let's explore that line." Sidney also leaned forward. Tillie came back with another glass and Sidney motioned for her to sit down. "You're saying that it could have been a picture or, possibly, film that might be of interest and not the cameras and equipment."

"Right."

"So we forget about the drug angle and make the assumption that whoever was in that dark room came looking for something specific, and the most logical object would be a picture of something."

Geoff swung his legs around and sat straight up on the sofa. "A picture, if Reed took it a few days ago, and film, if he took it the day he was killed or shortly before."

"How 'bout some tea?" She filled glasses for both of them with ice tea. "There ain't never no pictures there unless they're hangin' up on the wire. He takes um home as soon as they're dry. Doesn't leave anything overnight.'

Sidney nodded. "That tells me our intruder didn't get the pictures, and I'd still be willing to bet that George Reed had no idea that the picture he took was of interest to someone else."

"Like maybe something in the background that he might not have realized was there?" Geoff asked, keeping the thought going.

"Possibly. Then, of course, we could be all wrong about the whole thing," Sidney said while reaching for a wine glass. "And there could be no tie into anything. You were hit because you walked in on someone trying to steal something of value they could turn into cash for drugs and just didn't have the time to accomplish anything else. In any event, the police have the cameras and, presumably, any film that was in them, which, one would hope, they develop. If, in the process, a potential motive shows up on the film, it just adds to what we've already found out. Of course, that will also assume the police know what they're looking at when they see it, which is why it's important that a good case is made to Chief Hornig, so that his people look at the film from the correct perspective.

"Or at least look at the film at all." Geoff's cell phone rang. "Hi, Susan," he said after seeing her name come up on the display. "How did you make out?" He listened to her tale of finding Doyle's hole and then she told him about the eagle. "So he could have been drawn, or better yet lured, to Doyle's hole." He listened again as she continued to give him an update of her findings and theories over the sound of the small motor pushing the skiff along the Morgan River. "Okay, you're heading back now? Good idea they say that storm coming in could be a bit nasty. You should make it in just before dark. Why don't you come over here when you get back and we'll have some dinner? Professor Lake won't mind."

Sidney nodded his head in agreement from the kitchen where he had just gathered up his glass of wine and Geoff's root beer.

"Okay, see you in about an hour." Geoff put his phone back on the table next to the sofa.

"She found something?" Sidney asked.

"Yeah, an eagle's nest, in a tree at the far end of the hole. Just the sort of thing someone like Mr. Reed would want to take a picture of."

Tillie leaned back in her chair. "Yeah, that sounds like Mr. Reed."

"So something else falls into place." Sidney took a sip of his tea. "But again, are the two incidents connected? If we make the assumption that George was killed because of an incriminating picture he took, then either the killer was able to learn where that picture was kept, while they searched for the eagle, or, based on the conversation at the time, learned that it was unprocessed film sitting in the dark room."

"I don't know, those are pretty big assumptions," Geoff said.

"Professor Lake, Miss Becky told Mr. Reed he couldn't work on his pictures in the office. The office was for business."

"Well, let's look at it this way. Our killer lays in wait off the sandbar until he sees George leave in the boat by himself, something Becky said he often does because he really doesn't like getting sun burned. He then gets intercepted by his friend who tells him about the eagle. He knows George's boat won't be able to make it into Doyle's hole, so he gets him to tie up outside the hole and transfer to the smaller boat. He knows George will bring a camera, presumably the same camera he used to take the pictures the friend was concerned about."

"You know, Professor Lake, and no offense meant, but if I had taken a picture of someone that didn't want their picture taken and that person was pretty clear about it, you'd be hard pressed to get me to go on a boat ride with him, especially if I knew he was pissed off about it. Sorry about that."

"Very good point." Sidney smiled. "But what if we're not really dealing with a case of blackmail or something exotic like that? As you know Ray Morton doesn't see that as a viable option or motive, so let's look at it another way. Suppose we go with the theory that George Reed didn't know he had taken the picture his killer was interested in? If he was focusing on object A and didn't realize he also caught object B and, in fact—" Geoff was about to butt in but Sidney raised the index finger of his right hand and stopped him. "—the murderer didn't know either, or at least didn't know for sure if he had been caught on film, and the joint boat ride was a fishing trip of a different kind?"

Geoff pursed his lips. "You mean if George Reed refused to change boats and go with the guy, it might be— excuse the expression—a dead giveaway? So the plan would be for Reed to get into the friend's boat and then the friend would have the opportunity to pump him to find out what Reed knew while they look for the eagle's nest."

"Precisely."

"If that was the case, it could also be possible that George had not developed the film yet, which is why he would not suspect his friend's motives and why someone was interested in the dark room and why I have a sore head."

"Exactly, because, according to Becky, the camera George kept on the power boat was a digital one with an instant image of the picture, which George would have reviewed and seen his friend in one of the images. Which would mean the digital one was not the camera that George had used to take the pictures that were a problem for our killer because he would only find that out by reviewing the images himself and realize he had the wrong camera. Which gives us not only the motive for the break-in but also the reason Reed had no reason to suspect his friend's motives."

Geoff leaned back against the sofa. "You realize we're reaching pretty good here."

Tillie nodded. "It sounds pretty good to me, though. I think we're on to sumptun."

"Yes, I do too but I also realize we could be way off the mark, which is why our main focus has to be getting the police back on the scene. The key, as I see it, is to provide possibilities to make them curious enough to invalidate their original conclusion. Some place in all of this is a motive for George Reed's death." Sidney suddenly stopped, seeing the sunlight disappear from the room. "What time is it?"

"Just past seven-thirty."

"I have to go," he said, putting his half-empty glass on the side table. "I promised General Brewster I'd try to sort some things out for him. You and Susan can work on the Shepard's pie that's in the refrigerator. Tillie, you're welcome as well."

"No thanks. I got to get goin'. I want to stop by and see Miss Ruth on the way home."

Geoff looked questioningly at Sidney.

"It's that book collection he inherited. He's trying to put together a police and insurance claim report. I don't think it will take too long. A good deal of the work has already been done. Keep the thought process going on the camera and film concept. I think it's a good one. There's something there we haven't picked up on, and I just don't have my finger on it yet."

☙☜☙

"I appreciate your coming over on short notice like this, Sidney," Brewster said, as he ushered Sidney into the hallway.

While Sidney lived in a seventy-five-year-old house among other similar houses on a side street and built on land split off from a larger property, the main house of which now served as a bed and breakfast facing the Morgan River, Brewster lived in one of the original houses on The Ridge. It sat on more than an acre, with a large circular driveway, originally designed for carriages more than 200 years ago. Because of its size and location along River Road, it once served as a hospital during the Civil War and had even been cut up into apartments for a portion of its life. The general and his wife bought it more than ten years ago, as they could see its potential, even in its state of disrepair, and embarked on a campaign to restore it to its original grandeur. The rear of the house backed up directly onto the marsh and had access to deep water.

"I suppose it's really not that critical, it's just that it's a puzzle and I suppose, if there is something of value missing, the sooner the police have the information, the easier it would be for them to act on it." The general ushered Sidney past the two open pocket doors to the library, just to the right as one entered, similar to the location of Lake's office at home but a world apart. "Besides, I need this all cleaned up for Saturday night and Helen said she doesn't expect Jarvis to be back in town until late Saturday afternoon."

"I can see your point, and I guess getting this out of the way is the right approach. A hot trail is better than a cold one for the police. Have you heard anything from them yet? Do they have any idea who broke in?"

"Haven't heard a word. That's their job not mine, especially as nothing seems to have been taken but that picture. Or at least we don't think anything else's gone. Hopefully, we'll know more over the next hour. However, if there is something missing, and I don't hear from them real soon, then we've got a different issue."

"You realize this room is an English professor's dream." Sidney now stood in a home library that actually had books in it, instead of the modern variety that had a few shelves and a big screen television set. "What a sight." Before him were floor-to-ceiling mahogany book shelves on all four walls. Directly opposite them was the small, original fireplace. An antique writing desk stood by the front window, and two reading areas were set up with wingback chairs, some with foot stools. A door on the wall opposite the window led to the great room, a recent renovation that included a new modern, yet period looking, kitchen.

The shelves were only half full in the area to the right of the fireplace and in the middle of the room were a mixture of boxes of books, some opened and others emptied with the contents stacked along the floor.

"How much of this is yours, and how much was your uncle's?"

All mine, except for what's on the floor. Had some knickknacks around for spacing on a lot of the shelves and just did some consolidating to make more room. You know I'm a history nut. Over a thirty-five-year military career, I'd spend as much time as I could learning about each country and region where I was stationed. In college, I was hooked on US Military history and just kept on going with it. Actually that's part of the problem, the stuff I got from Uncle Sherman is all fiction, and I don't do fiction."

"How much is there?"

"Seems to be between four to five hundred volumes, I'm not really sure," Brewster said, looking at the boxes in the middle of the room.

"And Jarvis Oliphant has been working on cataloging them?"

"Yeah. Jarvis has been going through everything. Of course, we were working on the assumption there was no inventory list and then a lawyer for Uncle Sherman named Springwood found a list in one of the computer files. I asked Jarvis to sort out what might be collectable or have some real value and those I would hang on to and he could have the rest for himself and the shop. Best I can tell he's been sorting by author and has them stacked alphabetically over there." Brewster pointed at the unboxed books in front of the empty shelves. "Had I known there was an inventory list, he could have just reviewed that instead of making up one of his own."

"Where is Jarvis, anyway?"

"Helen said he was at some book fair they hold up in Atlanta every year. He'll be back in time for the Garden Association party on Saturday. Helen, who's the gardener in the family, made him promise. I think she'd have his head if he didn't make it back in time. So they'll be here for the party. You too?"

"Wouldn't miss it."

"Good man." Sidney received a pat on the back.

"Okay, where are the lists?"

"Over here on the desk. Both lists are there: the one that Jarvis started and the one Springwood faxed to me." The general pointed to the writing desk that sat between the two front windows.

"I think the best way to approach this is for you to make a comparison of the two lists and note what's missing from the Jarvis list while I sort out by author what's still in the boxes, then we'll run your uncle's list against them. I think it's better that I do the crawling around on the floor rather than you. You may be in better shape," Sidney said, making note of the general's still-athletic-looking seventy-plus-year-old physique, "but you still have ten years on me. Besides, I'm built closer to the ground."

⌦⌦⌦

As the FedEx left the hotel parking lot, Warren wondered if he had just made a terrible mistake in having an idle conversation with the driver. Would he be remembered? But then the desk clerk would remember him, so why worry? No, at this point it made no difference. His life had become so out of control, it didn't matter. If he could just pull off this last forgery, he swore he would never do it again. It was just so innocent to begin with. A simple lie or rather a misrepresentation. No big deal. And then another one added to it. And then another more elaborate one to justify the previous one. If he could just get those pictures, he could make enough to stop, to retire, so he wouldn't have to mislead anyone again.

Chapter 14

As Sidney and Susan made the short, six-minute drive to Cal Prentice's, Susan continued to bring Sidney up to date on her and Geoff's ideas about the different cameras, as he concentrated on driving on the now wet and slick roadway. It stopped raining a few minutes ago, but from the lightening in the distance, the storm was just beginning and not ending.

When Sidney returned from Brewster's, Susan and Geoff outlined their theories and the three of them came to the same conclusion: whatever cameras were used by George Reed in the days before he died needed to be looked at with extreme care. Their assumptions were based on the mounting evidence that George Reed did not die an accidental death, that Reed knew his murderer, the break-in at R and R was related, and photography in some way was a key to everything that happened. So far, there seemed to be a number of cameras involved, and Sidney and Susan tried to sort them out as they rode. First, there was the ever present digital camera on the large boat George Reed used when he left the sandbar. Was it found on the boat? Where was it now? Next, what cameras were usually kept in the dark room? Were they all now with the police or were there others and where were they? Then there was the question of the film, prints, and digital images. Where were they usually kept?

Susan made notes on a pad provided by Sidney as they talked since Sidney wanted all of this sorted out before arriving at Cal's. During the earlier analysis in Sidney's living room, they pretty much decided that there was a strong possibility that the Reeds' house could be the next target of the person who broke into R and R. If the target of that break-in proved to be the camera and film used by George Reed during the previous couple of days, there could be a strong possibility that those cameras were in the Reeds' home where he worked on his pictures, making the robbery attempt at R and R definitely unsuccessful.

On returning from his project with General Brewster—and after speaking with Geoff and Susan—Sidney tried to call Ray Morton to find out if he had set up a meeting with Chief Hornig and to find out Ray's thoughts on the camera and risk to Becky Reed issues. No one answered. Next he called Becky Reed, with a request for a visit with her. Again, no answer. He left a message. Then he called Cal Prentice to see if he had Becky's cell phone number. He knew that Alice Ringfoot provided Cal with a periodic update of congregation members' information that was not usually in the published church directory, and it often included cell phone numbers and email addresses. Cal answered and said he would look but suggested Sidney just come over, since Becky and her daughter were due there any minute to drop off some photographs that George Reed had promised Caldwell Talbot for next week. Cal offered to get the pictures to Caldwell as Becky decided to go to her daughter's in Charlotte for a few days.

Geoff stayed behind while Sidney and Susan headed

for the Prentices', with instructions to field phone calls and, when Ray Morton returned Sidney's phone call, to let Ray know where he and Susan were going. Geoff promised to call Susan on her cell phone the moment he learned anything. Sidney still viewed his own cell phone as an emergency backup vehicle. Besides, not being the most technically proficient, he often pressed the button to end the call before he answered it and the call from Geoff he didn't want to miss.

Just past nine-thirty in the evening, they pulled up in front of the Prentices'. "It looks like Mrs. Reed is already here," Susan said, looking at the car in the driveway with the license plate holder reading: *I'd Rather be Gardening.* "And isn't that Tillie's car as well?"

"I think you're right."

The Prentices' place looked like a setting for a 1950s sit-com, complete with white picket fence, a neatly trimmed hedge, a line of rose bushes down the driveway, and a basketball backboard over the garage door, a picture postcard home for a Presbyterian minister and his family. "Are we going to tell Mrs. Reed everything?" Susan asked as Sidney parked at the curb rather than block the other cars.

"I think we have to. We'll let her come to her own conclusions. I just hope Ray gets back to me soon and tells us Chief Hornig has bought into all of this. It all makes everything a lot easier."

"Are you sure you want me along?" she asked, getting out of the car and waving a hand at the jeans, sweatshirt, and baseball cap she was still wearing from her excursion to Doyle's hole.. "I'm not exactly dressed to go visiting."

"Absolutely. The hat may not be necessary—"

She immediately took it off and placed it beside her on the seat.

"—but, under the circumstances, I don't see a problem

anywhere. Besides, at this point you know as much about this business as I do. So if I forget something, you can remind me. You've been to Doyle's hole and can add some credence to the fact that Becky's boat couldn't get in there. I'm also glad Tillie's here, as that'll add weight to the tide conversation"

Cal Prentice must have been standing in the hallway when Sidney rang the bell, as the door seemed to open before he had his finger off the buzzer. "Sidney, I thought it would be you."

"Hello, Cal, sorry about interrupting your evening. You know Susan Abbott, don't you?"

"Yes, of course. The church has all of its insurance with her father. Come in, both of you. We're all in the living room. I told Becky you would be stopping by."

Becky and her daughter sat on the sofa. Ruth Prentice, Cal's wife, was on one chair and Tillie the other. Cal moved a couple of chairs in from the dining room so everyone could gather around the coffee table, where a series of eight by ten photographs were spread out. Cal Prentice did the introductions all around, mainly for the benefit of Amanda Reed, Becky's daughter.

"We were just looking at the photographs Becky brought over," he said. "They're spectacular."

"Thank you, Cal," Becky said. "They really are, aren't they?"

"And these were asked for by Caldwell Talbot?" Sidney asked, while looking at her in such a way as to imply that the request seemed a bit unreasonable under the circumstances and, in view of the comments he made at the church office a few days ago, although the pictures of the raccoons were certainly worthy of a nature magazine.

"Yes, I know it seems a bit odd, but Caldwell is giving a presentation to the Marshland Wildlife Preservation Society of the Lowcountry next week on the topic of raccoons, and George's pictures were to be the centerpiece. In fact, the idea was to make a series of prints that could be sold to the tourists—Caldwell's idea—as a way of raising funds for the Society." Becky could see that both Sidney and Cal were somewhat surprised by the comment so she continued. "George and Caldwell were friends, as much as Caldwell could be a friend of someone born in Pennsylvania. But George…well, George was George. He liked Caldwell because Caldwell loved the marsh and everything about it and especially everything that lived in it. They had that in common. The fact that one of Caldwell's answers to marshland preservation was to recommend that all the Northerners who bought marsh front property be loaded on a barge and shipped back above the Mason-Dixon Line was a separate issue. George just got a laugh out of him and took most of what he had to say as pure bluster. It was Caldwell who told George where to take a lot of the pictures and even went out with him one night."

"When were the pictures taken?" Sidney asked.

"Over the last three weeks. He brought these home from R and R last Friday—"

Cal cut in. "Becky was dropping them off here tonight as she and Amanda are leaving tomorrow morning for Charlotte, and I promised to hold them in the church office for Caldwell."

"Can I offer any one something to drink?" Ruth Prentice asked, primarily directing the question to Sidney and Susan, since everyone else already had glasses of iced tea and lemonade, as did Ruth.

"No thank you, Ruth. I just needed to speak with Becky briefly and it has to do with George's death."

"Is something the matter?" Becky said, obviously startled, and with a hint of tenseness in her voice.

"I've come across some information that raises the

distinct possibility that George's death was not an accident." Silence. Then, as Becky was about to speak, Sidney raised his hand. "Let me explain."

For the next five minutes Sidney explained how he
became involved. He did not say that there were people
in town who thought she had something to do with
George's death. However, he did say that Tillie remarked
that her friend, Daniel Doyle, said it was a good thing
Becky took her nap during the rising tide because then
they would know for sure she didn't have anything to do
with George's death and that it was someone else who
did.

A number of times Becky tried to interrupt but Sidney
just held up his hand again and politely requested that he
be permitted to finish. When he got to the part about
Doyle's hole, he asked Susan to tell what she had found
and for Tillie to give some background about Daniel
Doyle and his tidal marsh knowledge. Finally, he connected the break in at R and R and raised the whole issue
of the cameras.

"I'm waiting for a call back from Ray Morton, who is
setting up a meeting with Chief Hornig as we speak. I
wanted Ray to do it because he has credibility with
Hornig, where I would probably just be brushed off. As
far as we know, they have officially closed the case and
Ray wanted Hornig to be the one to come up with the
suggestion it be reopened. My primary concern at this
point is your safety."

"My safety? I don't understand," Becky said.

Amanda sat straight up and her eyes widened.

Sidney tried to make his voice soothing. "Becky, if
I'm right and the break in at Roots and Rakes is tied to
George's death, and if the object of the search was not
found in the dark room, which both Ray and I are sure
was the primary target of the break-in, then it may be

somewhere in your home, either in a file drawer or on a computer."

"You mean someone was looking for pictures? What kind of pictures?"

"That's why the cameras are important. Whatever it is, I believe it happened in the few days before he died. While Susan and Tillie were talking, I had a chance to have a good look at these pictures on the table because I'm looking for something compromising in the background."

Clearly moved and upset, Becky held onto Amanda's hand. "I just—I don't—I mean—Are you sure about all of this? I can't believe someone would deliberately want to kill George. Oh, this is absurd. I can't believe this."

"Becky, I would not have given most of this a thought, except for Daniel Doyle's matter-of-fact assertion that George could not have been on your boat when he fell overboard because it was a simple fact of nature that the boat and George could not have ended up where they did on their own. That being the case, it then follows that George was in someone else's boat that afternoon and that someone was also with him when he died."

Becky and her daughter were both quiet, realizing the indisputable fact of someone being with George Reed when he died. "And you believe the break-in is connected?" Amanda said finally, breaking the silence.

"It's a very distinct possibility. My personal belief is that somehow your father may have inadvertently taken some pictures that could be embarrassing to someone he knew."

Susan cleared her throat. "Geoff mentioned that Mr. Reed always kept a digital camera in his boat, was that camera found and do you have it at home?"

"No," Becky said thoughtfully. "I presumed it went overboard with him and was lost in the marsh. Actually, the only camera at home is the thirty-five millimeter one he used on Saturday night. The police have the other large digital and another thirty-three millimeter from the darkroom."

Sidney blinked. "The night before he died?"

It looked as though light bulbs were going off in just about everyone's head.

"Yes. He must have been out there until two or three in the morning. The moon was almost full, and he was out in that skiff of his with the pole, roaming around the marsh. He always did that." Then she pointed to the raccoon photos. "He promised Caldwell he would get him some more pictures for his presentation, and Caldwell told him where he thought some raccoon nests were."

"And he didn't use a digital camera?"

"Oh, no. When he went on a 'real shoot,' as he called it, he used the thirty-five millimeter. He had all sorts of telephoto lenses for it. That little boat of his had everything all set up for a photo shoot. He had a series of tripods that he used to set up over the side so the camera would be stable, extra poles to stabilize the boat and, of course, lights. The police even chased him away one time when some people thought he was a peeping tom in the marsh and reported him."

"Would that camera normally be in the dark room at R and R?" Sidney said.

"Not usually. The film might be there but the camera would be at home in the den." She paused. "Oh, I see what you mean."

"Ummm," Sidney mused as he stopped and thought a moment. "Is there any way of knowing if any film is missing from the dark room?"

"I don't think so. No one ever really went in there, except George. If he was working on some film, it was either hanging up by clips from a wire that ran across the room, which, as you know, is really no larger than a closet, or he would have cut the film into strips of six images or negatives and those would be sandwiched between two pieces of clear plastic. There's a small work area on the right side of the room where he would work on those."

"So you have no way of knowing if the pictures he took on Saturday night are still in the dark room or not."

"Oh, I know they're not there," she said with great confidence as they all stared at her.

"They're not?" Sidney said.

"They're still in the camera, or I'm pretty sure they are. Depending on how many pictures he took, there may be two or three rolls in the den. That's where he would always leave them after being out on the marsh. He would then bring them into the dark room the following day. Depending on what his schedule was, it might be a few days before he got around to doing any developing."

Sidney looked puzzled and Becky continued. "As I said, he didn't get in until almost three and decided to sleep in. When I came home from church, he had just gotten up and was reading the paper and drinking a cup of coffee at the kitchen table. He hadn't shaved or changed yet."

"So he couldn't have gone over to Roots and Rakes to drop off the film."

"No. In fact, I packed us some lunch for the boat while he showered, and we headed out for the sandbar sometime after twelve-thirty. The camera, film, everything should still in the den where he left it."

"I wonder," Sidney said. "You know, it would be very interesting to see what is on that film. It also reinforces a suggestion I was going to make, which is that you and Amanda not spend the night at home. If the film that was shot last Saturday night is the key to everything and if that's what the break in at Roots and Rakes is all about,

then your house could very well be the next logical target. You're leaving for Charlotte tomorrow anyway, why
not leave a day early?"

"Better yet," Ruth Prentice interjected, "Please stay
here for the night. They say these storms are going to
continue all night, and driving to Charlotte would be awfully difficult with that wind and rain. Both Cal, Jr. and
Marion are away, and we'd love to have you. Please."

❧❧❧

The wind gusted and blew in all directions and the rain
came at him sideways as Warren stepped out of the skiff
and onto the already soaked shoreline. The back of
Reeds' house came to life just ahead of him with each
lightning flash. Floodlights around the attached garage,
which opened toward the street, kept the driveway and
walkway to the front door well lit but enhanced the depth
of the surrounding darkness at the rear. He made his way
toward the back door. He couldn't see anyone inside.
There seemed to be a nightlight in the den, another in the
front hall, and another in the master bedroom upstairs.
The bathrooms all seemed to have LED light sensors. It
was quiet—no one home. He would go through the patio
door to the kitchen.

Chapter 15

The rain downgraded to a drizzle as they started out, but the lightning continued all around them. The headlights from Sidney's car stretched long into the distance. The four of them—Sidney, Cal, Tillie, and Becky—were deep in thought about the death of George Reed and what they were now doing. The fifteen minutes' drive from Cal's house to Becky's seemed much longer in the deep, non-reflecting blackness created by the storm. The road was one big dark room.

Sidney did not tell Becky about the extent of Tillie's involvement and the rumors that Becky had something to do with George's death. That would be something for Tillie to explain. He danced around the issue and left it there. Once Becky became convinced that there was definitely something suspicious about George's drowning and the break in at R and R, she never pursued Sidney's motivation for helping her. She actually felt relieved, since she never really believed that George would just lose his footing. It wasn't like him. After some protesting, Cal finally convinced her that she and Amanda should stay the night in his guest room. Becky agreed but needed their bags, which were already packed in anticipation of an early departure, and some personal items from her home. Tillie volunteered to help. Becky and Amanda would leave directly from the Prentices' in the morning. Becky lived on one of the marsh islands just on the other side of the Morgan River, a recently developed community strung together by a series of causeways, and a mere five minutes from downtown.

It began to rain in earnest again, a few drops here and a few drops there, just enough for Sidney to switch the wipers from intermittent to the low setting. Water was a problem and a blessing in the lowcountry. The ocean had always been the lifeblood of the residents and, until recently, the primary source of income, with a seemingly endless supply of shrimp and oysters, but the canneries were gone now, and the shrimp boats seemed to be more of a tourist novelty than a way of life anymore. Now tourism was king, followed by real estate development. Every island that had a causeway or bridge seemed to be under development.

The old plantations were being broken up and sold off. Marsh front property that locals would have had difficulty getting rid of thirty years ago—because of its low-lying elevations, usually no more than five to fifteen feet above sea level, and filled with mosquitoes, no-see-ems, chiggers, and snakes—were being sold to Northerners for outrageous prices. The locals just shook their heads, knowing what the future held. Hugo was the last major hurricane to come close and that went north and hit Charleston, only giving the lowcountry to the south a glancing blow, with the winds coming off the land rather than the sea.

The last time the lowcountry received direct hits occurred in the late 1940s and the 1890s, following what seemed to be a fifty-year cycle. Back then, the residents tended to live on higher ground, which at least gave them some protection against the annual hurricane brushing. Everyone knew that, when big storms like the ones of fifty and a hundred years ago hit, there was no such thing as high ground.

There were no condos on the beach then, no resorts on Hilton Head, which everyone agreed would be under at least eight feet of water, even with a direct hit of a medium hurricane. Storms like the one Sidney was driving through were a common and expected event, even though trees would fall, power would go out, and trailers would be blown over. They were part of the charm of the lowcountry. However, they were also a curse, as, having survived one, many people had the feeling they could ride out and survive the next hurricane.

"Go all the way down to the end and make a left," Becky said. "Then about half way down on the right. Looks like the rain is really picking up. My goodness, it's dark. Usually you can see better than this." Suddenly a gust of wind hit and rain began falling in huge drops, which were being pushed in all directions. Sidney increased the wiper speed to high and leaned forward over the wheel to better see the road. He made a left turn down a road with no markings and had difficulty seeing where the edge of the road ended and the shoulder began.

"That's it on the right."

"Sidney," Cal said from the back seat, as he reached for the umbrella on the floor in front of him, "why don't you stay here? There's no point in all of us getting wet."

"Okay, let me pull into the driveway, and I'll keep the lights on the doorway for you."

"I'm sorry, Sidney, I usually leave the outside lights on. I must have forgotten. Didn't think I would be this late. Rain just makes it darker." Another gust of wind and a palm frond bounded off the windshield of the car making them all jump.

"Wow!" Cal exclaimed. "Hold on just a second, Becky, see if it eases up"

"Oh, look at that come down," Becky said.

"It's a good one." Tillie had her hand on the left rear door handle ready to move quickly. "Now you know why we don't put gutters on. There ain't no such thing as a gentle rain fall in the lowcountry. You can get two to three inches in no time an' none of it's gonna drip into a gutter."

"Okay, Becky, let's try it now," Cal said, opening the right front door. Becky opened her door as Cal tried to put up the umbrella, which he almost immediately lost to another gust, gave up, and just held the door to keep it from slamming on Becky. Tillie jumped out of her side, the oldest and spryest of them all.

Just then something caught Sidney's eye peripherally. As he watched Cal get out of the car and lean across the seat to catch the door and make sure it closed, Sidney thought he saw something in the left upstairs window. He turned his head but couldn't see anything as he squinted through the windshield. He moved his head a couple of times and realized that it must have been the frame of his glasses he saw as he moved his head. With all the rain, wind, and blowing debris, it was understandable.

They made a run for the front door. Becky, with the key in her hand. The umbrella proved useless as Cal almost lost it to another gust and finally closed it as Becky rushed to get the key into the lock. Finally they got the door opened and Sidney, following their progress from the car, could see the entry hall light go on. They seemed to stop in the hallway and then split up.

A light appeared in the window above the doorway, which lit up the staircase, and then the outside lights came on: two outdoor floods from the garage lighting the driveway and another the walkway to the front door. He turned off his car lights so they wouldn't blind them as they moved about inside.

A moment later, the lights came on in the downstairs room to the left of the entry door. He could see Cal move across the room to the far side. Sidney assumed it was George's den where the camera and the computer would be located. Cal, knowing Becky and George considerably better than Sidney, having been invited to dinner many times over the years, was familiar with George's den and knew where to look, as they had agreed that Cal would procure whatever film was lying about and the camera that should be on the right hand corner of the desk.

Sidney then spotted Becky and Tillie as they headed upstairs for the master bedroom, to the right at the top of the stairs, where the next light went on. Sidney again, could see a shape, more a shadow, move past the upstairs bedroom window. Becky was in pursuit of some items to put into an overnight bag and Tillie followed her into the master bath.

Sidney continued to watch the shadows moving about their respective rooms as the rain and wind continued to pound the car. He had reduced the speed of the wipers back to normal and listened to their rhythmic motion against the glass. Suddenly all the lights in and around the house began to flicker—once, then again, then total darkness in the entire neighborhood. A high-pitched sound suddenly pierced the thumping of the wipers. It startled him and then he heard it again. He peered through the rain streaked windshield. Lightning flashed, and he saw the shadow in the den move quickly toward the entry hall. Then he heard a definite shout.

He turned the headlights back on. The lights from the car picked out Cal starting up the stairway. Sidney pushed open his door. The rain and wind hit his face, and he struggled to get out of his seat. He still had his seat belt on. The door slammed back at him in another gust of wind. Finally getting unhooked and outside the car, he had difficulty seeing anything in front of him as he headed to the house, but he knew something was very wrong. The rain and the wind pounded him as he finally reached the front door and opened it. He stopped momentarily, surveying the scene in front of him.

Cal lay motionless at the foot of the stairs and Sidney saw Becky at the top, trying to pick herself up with the aid of Tillie. The contents of one of the overnight bags littered the stairway.

⸱⸲⸱

Warren dashed out the kitchen door into the darkness. He couldn't see the boat. *Where the fuck is it?"* He ran straight ahead, tripped over a planter on the patio, scrambled to his feet, and headed for the marsh. He fell again. This time into the marsh, his rain suit now soaking wet. The boat floated right next to him. He jumped in, grabbed the lanyard for the small motor, and yanked it hard. Again. Again. The engine caught. Another flash of lightning. He saw his way out.

Chapter 16

The blue, red, and white lights of the police cars and ambulance created dramatic shadows against the house and became even more amplified by the swirling wind and driving rain. The storm sent a pattern of sheets of rain in alternating pulses—first blowing one way and then the other. Debris was everywhere: tree limbs, branches, palm fronds, and a loose garbage can or two. The storm proved more severe than originally forecast. The sighting of tornadoes in the neighboring county and a considerable amount of local flooding added to its drama.

The lowcountry was aptly named. The water would eventually make its way to the marsh but the active development of the islands and the new and recently paved roads had changed many of the normal water absorption patterns, creating areas where more water would collect than the land could absorb. A few of the neighbors braved the weather to see if they could be of assistance. They stood by the Reeds' doorway, trying to ward off the wind and rain with umbrellas. A policeman spoke with them and advised going back to their homes, that everything was under control. Others were at their windows or standing in the protection of garages with their doors open.

The scene inside was one of controlled confusion. Becky sat on the sofa in the living room with Tillie next to her while being questioned by a city policeman. Sidney, across the room, sat in a wing chair going through the same process. In the hall, there were three paramedics working on Cal next to a gurney placed in its collapsed position. They were being very careful with his left arm and shoulder, as well as trying to keep his head and neck stabilized. Given the tumble he took down the stairs, they were not taking any chances.

Sidney explained all he knew to the officer interviewing him but did not volunteer any information about his concerns about Becky's security and the reason for the suggestion that she stay at Cal's, although the officer interviewing Becky would surely get that from her. Sidney figured he would cover all of that with Ray, who he called immediately after placing the nine-one-one call. After checking on Becky and Tillie to make sure they were unhurt, he also called Ruth Prentice and spoke with both her and Susan. He instructed Susan to notify Geoff and Robert James, Tillie's husband, of what happened and tell them that they were okay.

Becky and Tillie explained as much as they could remember—which were mostly disjointed comments, given how quickly it all happened—but first impressions were important. She and Tillie had gone upstairs to get the bags, which were already packed for the trip to Charlotte, and make up overnight bags for the stay with the Prentices. Becky explained that she planned to stay in Charlotte for a few days with Amanda so she could have some quiet time to sort things out since George's death. When she got upstairs, she went across the hall to retrieve Amanda's bag while Tillie stayed in the master bedroom putting some items into a separate container to go into the overnight bag. The lights went out just as Becky entered Amanda's old bedroom and then someone came out of the shadows at her. She screamed. He bumped into her. She grabbed at his jacket. It was dark and wet. He shoved and pushed at her, and she fell out of the room and into the hall. Everything was a blur. Tillie, hearing the commotion, came out of the bedroom but her eyes, surprised by the darkness, couldn't make out anything but a shadow.

Tillie remembered hearing Cal call to her as he came running up the stairs. The intruder jumped over Becky. Tillie, who was still holding an overnight bag, took a swing at the shadow, and then fell to the ground. She assumed the shadow crashed into Cal coming up the stairs. But she didn't know for sure as, being on the floor, she couldn't see very much. The officers continued asking questions as Ray Morton and Pete Hornig came through the front door.

One of the policemen, working with the paramedics, spotted the chief and came over to him. Ray surveyed the hall and did his best to make an initial analysis of the scene. He then saw Sidney and went over to him. He nodded to the policeman. "Keep going, I don't want to interrupt."

"I'm all done, Ray. It's okay." Then the officer turned to Sidney, "Thanks, Mr. Lake. We'll probably need to get a formal statement. In the meantime, if you think of anything else, please let us know." He then closed his book and headed out to the hall where his partner and the chief were still talking.

"You certainly know how to get yourself into the middle of things," Ray mused. "What in the world is going on, Sid?"

Sidney just shook his head, not even taking notice of

Ray's familiarity with his name, something he would normally have done. "I think there is a very frightened person out there, and I don't think it's your common burglar or experienced thief. This was really a risky move on his part."

"Did you get a look at him at all? Walk with me." Ray wanted to get away from Becky, make sure she couldn't overhear anything they would say.

Sidney got up and they headed for the entrance hall.

"No, he was gone by the time I got here. I was outside waiting in the car."

"You're sure there was just one?"

"No, as I said, I never saw him or anyone."

"What about the others?"

"No. I don't think anyone saw much either. From what I can tell he came at Becky too fast in the dark. Tillie hit at a shadow that plowed into Cal and knocked him head over heels down the stairs." A flash of light and an immediate crack of thunder shook the house. "Wow! That was close. I'll bet it hit in the marsh right out back."

"With any luck it will have hit your intruder hiding in the water."

"You think he's still out there?"

"Doubt it," Ray said as the rain began to pound again.

"You're probably right. When I came in and was checking everyone, I could swear I heard the motor of a boat above the rain."

"I think you're right about having a very frightened person on our hands. Your average druggie doesn't tool around in a boat, looking for victims. What I'm starting to get worried about is that he may now have the camera and film and be in the process of destroying them both or at least have them in his possession and begin to think he's in the clear, especially if no one can identify him. You tell everything to Lou?"

"Lou?"

"The kid who was just interviewing you." He turned and pointed to the policeman who was now talking to Hornig.

"Oh, yes. I didn't say anything about our concerns with regard to Becky's safety, though. I figured you can add that. Didn't want to get involved in explaining all the theories about George Reed's death."

"That's okay. What about Cal? Think it's at all possible he saw anything?"

They both looked over at the paramedics and the pastor who was now secure on the gurney about midway between the bottom of the stairs and the front door.

"Having run into him on the stairs, there's always a possibility, but I wouldn't count on it with the lights being out. He was out cold when I got to him. From the look of things, he may still be."

The paramedics had carefully raised the gurney up to traveling height in preparation for moving him out to the waiting ambulance.

"How's he doing?" Ray said to the female member of the team who was carrying some monitoring equipment past them to take it outside.

She stopped. "Hard to tell. He took it real bad to the head and shoulder coming down the stairs. That shoulder is in real bad shape,"

"Did he wake up at all yet?"

"Off and on."

A car's headlights flashed across the living room and then stopped in front of the house just as the lights came on. They had obviously been cleared by the police blockade up the road. Four people got out and came in the front door: Ruth Prentice, Amanda Reed, Susan, and Geoff. One of the policeman at the door recognized Ruth so he let them pass. Ruth spotted the gurney right away and headed directly to it but a paramedic stopped her, while Amanda called out for Becky and, hearing her reply, headed for the living room. Sidney reached over and took Ruth by the arm as the paramedics tried to make Cal as comfortable as possible in the new position.

"They have everything under control, Ruth."

"Oh, Sidney. What happened?"

"Took a fall down the stairs." No further explanation was needed at this point.

Just then Cal moaned and opened his eyes briefly, probably hearing his wife's voice. Ruth reached out to him and touched the side of the blanket that was covering him. "Oh, Cal," she said.

Cal, bleary eyed, looked in her direction "Someone else who didn't like one of my sermons, I guess."

"Oh, Cal," she said again, seeing he was trying to smile and put her at ease—the instincts of the pastoral minister always coming through.

"Mam?" said the paramedic. "We've really got to get him to emergency."

"He's going to be all right?" she said, looking straight into his eyes.

"His being awake is a good sign. We just want to get him to the doctors. They'll take good care of him. Do you have a ride?" he asked, meaning did she have a way to the hospital.

Ruth first looked at Sidney and then Susan spoke up. "Don't worry, Mrs. Prentice, I'll get you there."

Sidney put his arm around Ruth. "He'll be just fine. We'll all be praying for him. Don't you worry." He pulled her close. "The whole town will be praying for him. He'll be on every prayer list in every church in Morgan."

At this point, Pete Hornig came over and motioned Sidney and Ray to the side.

The paramedics started moving Cal again and Susan took Sidney's place on Ruth's arm. Sidney gave Ruth a kiss on the cheek. "I'll see you at the hospital in a few minutes."

"You okay, Professor Lake?" Hornig asked, as Sidney turned Ruth over to Susan and then walked over to the chief.

"Yes, but I think I like reading about crime scenes a good deal better than being in the middle of one."

"Tell everything to the officer?"

"Yes, he had good questions."

Hornig smiled. "Good to hear that." He then took Sidney by the elbow and led him over to the doorway to the den while the paramedics moved Cal out of the hallway on the way to the ambulance. Ray followed Hornig's lead. "Ray here has been telling me some interesting theories you two have developed. My initial reaction was to discount most of it, although I think, under the circumstances, I'll have one of my island guys have a chat with your friend Doyle and explore his tide theories. Obviously, tonight doesn't make me feel too comfortable. Don't want to say you're on to something, but—"

"We're on to something," Ray finished. "You heard about the boat out back?"

"Yeah, I got two people outside looking around. Not going to find anything in this storm."

"Your boat coming?"

"Yeah, they'll search the area from the water side with their lights. Who knows, with this storm he could have fallen overboard, and we could get lucky. So what do you think he was looking for?" The question was addressed to Sidney.

"Cameras, film, pictures. Same thing he was looking for at Roots and Rakes."

"Any more thoughts on why they're important? Ray gave me a pretty good rundown on your theories on the way over here," Hornig said, speaking in a low tone so as not to be over heard.

"That's the missing link. Although I think someone has the answer to that question but doesn't know it."

Both Hornig and Ray looked at Sidney, as though to say *keep going*, so he did.

"I have a nagging suspicion that keeps bringing me back to the idea that George Reed may have inadvertently taken a picture of something that someone is very concerned about. What makes it all very difficult is that George Reed, at the time he died, may not have had any idea why someone would want to get his hands on his camera much less try to kill him. From what I can tell now, that picture was probably taken on Saturday night and George was killed before he ever had a chance to see the images that he captured."

"You don't think he took the picture on purpose?" Hornig looked hard at Sidney, peered into him, challenged him to defend his view. It was a look that only a career police officer could do.

"The blackmail theory? No, I don't buy it. As I told Ray, I didn't really know George Reed that well, but I've learned a lot this week, and I think it's way out of character. He didn't need money."

"Everybody needs money. It's power. It's control," Ray said.

"Maybe so but it wasn't a focus of George Reed's. Roots and Rakes is an extremely lucrative business. He was a happy guy. Everyone who knew him said so. He drank a little too much but stayed out of trouble."

"Tough to do," Hornig said. "You drink too much, trouble finds you—eventually. Ever hear of him with a lady friend?'

"Chief, to be perfectly honest, as I said, until a couple of days ago, I didn't know much of anything about George Reed. We were casual friends. I saw George and Becky at church sometimes. Even sat with them at a Wednesday night supper, which is a bit inaccurate as George usually spent most of the time flitting from table to table. Whatever I know about him personally comes from general hearsay information I picked up since Tillie got me involved in all of this. I had some general impressions beforehand but I haven't run into anyone who spoke badly of him." Sidney stopped. "Well, maybe that isn't entirely true," he said, and then he recounted the story of his encounter with Caldwell Talbot in the church office on Monday.

"Caldwell, hah," Hornig said.

"Now, in all fairness, Chief, I'm not sure Caldwell's outburst was so much against Reed as it was Yankees in general. Besides, I understand they were supposed to be friends. In fact, they were apparently working on a project together that had to do with marsh raccoons. Earlier in the evening, we were looking at pictures George had taken for Caldwell."

"All of what you say may be true, but I intend to consider everything."

"So," Ray said, "you think you've got a murder on your hands?"

"As I said, I'm putting everything back on the table."

"What about Steele?" Ray asked.

Hornig now dropped his voice even lower. "Ray, to be honest, I told him he was moving too fast but he wouldn't have it. It was a pure and simple accident to him, and he argued that it would be better to focus scarce resources on real crimes rather than disrupt a bunch of innocent townspeople who were trying to deal with a tragedy. In truth, I had nothing to go on. I mean, everything was straight forward: the drinking, the falling off the boat, the past experience—it all added up. Except for something that I couldn't put my finger on. It may be what your guy Doyle spotted right away: the body was in a place it couldn't get to on its own."

Sidney cleared his throat. "Chief, back when all this started, I became aware of some gossip about Steele and Becky Reed, which I tossed off as just that—gossip—is that also on the table?"

Hornig looked long and hard at Sidney. "As I said, I've got to keep everything on the table, although, I must admit that's a reach. I've known Steele Wilcox for more than twenty-five years. I know his wife, Rose, and the kids. I know his parents. We've worked on and off for a long time. We go to the same Baptist church. Yeah, it's on the table but just barely and will probably be the first thing to come off. You've been Mr. Detective, what do you think of all this?"

"I tend to agree with you on Steele Wilcox. What started as bad gossip is destined to end the same way. But then, who knows? I would expect stranger things have happened. Unfortunately, as Ray has often reminded me, one of the most difficult things for a truly innocent man to do is to defend himself against a maliciously false charge. Good alibis for the innocent can, sometimes, be hard to find. But I still keep coming back to George Reed's photography as the primary connection to everything that has gone on. We could be dealing with a very casual acquaintance that just got in over his head."

"You still think he took a picture of someone doing something he shouldn't have?" Ray asked.

"Yes, I really do."

"Well, we intend to take a very close look at every camera he owned and every piece of film we can get our hands on, including everything he has in his computer.

And yes, I will bring SLED in, as much as I dislike bringing the state into anything."

"What about the county sheriff?" Ray said.

Hornig returned a look that was a clear answer.

Just then the siren from the ambulance was activated as it pulled out of the driveway, interrupting the conversation. "I've got to talk to my guys here a bit," Hornig said, excusing himself.

Following the ambulance were the lights of Ruth Prentice's car with Susan at the wheel. The rain had eased a bit and the space between the lightning flashes and the sounds of thunder were becoming farther apart, but the wind was still gusting.

"Ray, Tillie and I are going to take Becky and Amanda over to the emergency room. I think she's going to have a few bruises where the intruder grabbed and pushed her. The paramedics probably gave her something to calm her down, I don't know. They want her to be checked over."

"No problem. I'm going to stick with Pete and grab a ride when he's done." Ray then paused and looked at Sidney. "Sidney, you've got a funny kind of look on your face, you okay?"

"Yes," he said, coming out of his fog.

"You got an idea about something, don't you?"

"Possibly."

"And you're not going to tell me, are you."

"No, no, I don't think I am. Tillie and I have a little research to do first."

࿇

As soon as he made it to one of the marsh channels Warren turned off the engine. No sense in attracting attention. Even though he was sure no one saw him or heard him, he didn't want some public spirited citizen calling nine-one-one to report some fool out running around the marsh in the storm. He grabbed the paddle that was in the bottom of the boat and headed in the general direction of where he left the car. The boat he would leave nearby, anchored and tied up in the marsh grass, where no one could see it.

As he calmed down, he began to think about what just happened. *This is stupid. If they haven't found the pictures by now, it doesn't matter. Stop panicking. Get real. They don't know what their looking for and, even if they find it, they still won't know what they're looking at. Maybe they won't even recognize me. Might just be better to come up with a reason I was walking around Brewster's house at two in the morning. They'll never figure out in a million years what I was really doing there. Okay, that's it. Let the shit fall. All I can hope is that I didn't kill anyone else tonight. No. Time to just play dumb. I got what I wanted from Brewster, but he'll never know what's missing because I won't tell him, and he has no other way of finding out. No more forgeries. No, sir. I'm done.*

Chapter 17

Ray cautioned Sidney to go easy when meeting with Pete Hornig and Steele Wilcox. Hornig did not have any firsthand experience with Sidney's methodical, self-assured approach to solving problems, so Ray made a point of reminding him that he was the outsider. They, on the other hand, were the professionals. Sidney promised that he would do his best to keep Ray's advice in mind, as Ray knocked on the door to Hornig's office. They were called in immediately and found Hornig alone sitting behind his desk. Hornig and Morton had a multilevel bond, since they both had backgrounds in the Marine Corps. Hornig did two tours in Vietnam after Parris Island and eventually settled in Morgan, where he took a job as a police officer. Police work and local politics became his life and Morgan his home. Ray, on the other hand, stayed in the Marine Corps for twenty-two years before retiring his six stripes and trading them in for three with the sheriff's department, where he spent another eight years.

Hornig convinced him to change jobs and join him when it became apparent that the local Morgan department's detective unit needed upgrading—a result of the

influx of Northern retirees—which would allow the department to do more on its own before asking for help
from outside agencies like the county sheriff and the state
law enforcement division or SLED. Ray worked for
Hornig until Marie forced retirement on him a few years
ago.

"What's the latest on Cal Prentice?" Hornig directed
the question to them both as they sat directly in front of
him, the general niceties about the storm, weather in general, and superfluous chit chat having been dispensed
with. The chief's office was simple and straight forward
with Hornig's desk the focal point. It was a mirror image
of the chief: simple, straight forward, and a desire to be
the center of attention. Sidney and Ray occupied the two
wooden arm chairs directly in front and a third had been
brought in and awaited the coroner.

"Broken shoulder, broken wrist, concussion but
awake, alert and doing very well," Sidney answered.
"Everything seems manageable but the trauma, although
knowing Cal he'll find some way to put that aside and
give the entire incident a positive presentation. Still finding it all very difficult to believe, even if we did think
there might be a possibility of it happening. The problem
was that we, of course, didn't really think it would."

"How's Becky Reed?"

"Really shaken up. She and Amanda are staying with
Ruth Prentice for the weekend."

"Going to need to talk with her again but it will keep
for the moment. May work something out for later this
afternoon."

They were interrupted by a short knock on the door
and Steele Wilcox let himself in. Appropriately dressed
for work with the dark suit and tie and white shirt, Wilcox fit the expected image of the local funeral director
when he needed to and a good ole boy when it was neces-

sary. With the current mayor having announced his retirement, Wilcox had his eye clearly on the office. "Sorry I'm late," he apologized. "Couldn't get off the phone."

"Have a seat," Hornig said, indicating the empty chair next to Ray Morton.

"Sidney, Ray," Wilcox said in acknowledgment of the other two visitors.

"Sidney was just filling us in on Cal Prentice. Pretty beat up but seems okay."

"Good to hear. That must have been just awful last night."

"Yes, it was," Sidney agreed.

"Okay," Hornig said, staying in character and not wanting to let the little gathering linger any longer than necessary. "We need to get a few things straightened out. First, I've got one of Cunningham's people from *The Times* sitting out front, and they want this on the front page for tomorrow. Everything happened too late last night for this morning. So they expect some real detail. They won't interview either Cal or Becky, Cunningham doesn't work that way—doesn't believe in beating up on the victim—but he needs to be able to feed some information to Charleston and Savannah if they want to carry something. So, I want them to have a factual story, but I'd like it to be a positive one—one that shows we have everything under control. I also want it clear that the attack was focused and not random so we don't have a bunch of people thinking we have a crime wave on our hands. I don't want everyone in town thinking they're a potential target and need to have a loaded gun on their night stand."

"Pete," Ray said, "you going to formally tie all this into George Reed's death, the M word?"

"I can't do that."

"But it was," Sidney snapped.

Hornig gave Sidney a look that said *Here we go* and Ray rolled his eyes as if to say *I told you to take it easy.*

"Sidney, I know you're personally involved in all of this now but, without a motive, I'm not willing to go there yet. Just wait." Hornig held up his hand to stop Sidney from saying anything further. "I know all the arguments. Ray laid them all out for me last night. Yes, we did talk to your Mr. Doyle. One of my boys is a local who speaks Gullah and gets along with the Gullah community as well as anyone, and, yes, we did run some tests with the state first thing this morning. They were here at the crack of dawn working on the rising tide theory, and it looks like Doyle was right, but I don't want to go public with this yet, and I would appreciate it if you didn't either. Trying to keep it quiet that the state is fooling around where Reed's body was found will be virtually impossible in the Gullah community—they don't miss much, too much history, so they stay quiet and just watch—but not a problem for the rest of the town, as long as it doesn't show up in *The Times*. This is now a formal murder investigation with regard to George Reed but I want it to stay low key for the time being."

"So how do you explain last night?" Sidney had moved forward in his chair and he and Hornig were holding eye contact, as though there was no one else in the room.

The chief remained calm but firm. He'd spent a good part of his career walking the fine line between the local black community and the long-time white residents, and he knew an awful lot had to do with the way things were presented to both. "The way I'm going to initially approach this is as a drug-motivated, sick, opportunistic burglary. It's not uncommon, unfortunately. Someone spots an obituary in the paper. They see a business closed and empty and a house the same way. George Reed's death stays just as it is until we have someone to tie it to. My job is to direct public condemnation toward a lone, sick, individual who is an outsider in all communities."

Sidney knew the look on his face probably said he wasn't buying it, but he kept quiet. He knew only too well that there would be a segment of the town that would immediately assume that the person who broke into Becky Reed's house was black. He also knew they were predisposed toward that conclusion and would think that of just about every crime that occurred unless another race was specifically mentioned or a picture of the intruder clearly showed the person to be white. Becky couldn't confirm the attacker's race and Cal couldn't be interviewed last night. Hornig didn't really want to talk with the *Times* people until he had something from Cal so, for the moment, Sidney decided to defer to the chief's approach.

"Cal wasn't any help, I guess?" Ray said.

"No, it looks like the guy's back was to Cal. Becky caught his jacket and swung him around and Tillie hit him with a bag. When he broke free, he turned with his head down and barreled right into Cal at the top of the stairs. We have general size and build stuff from Becky but nothing really from Cal yet. He was in a daze when he was awake last night so we couldn't really get much from him. Can he recognize him? We have no idea. Don't even know if he saw his face. Although one of the paramedics seemed to think he said something about a man hit him in response to a question that was asked one time when he was awake briefly. Hopefully, he might recall something else but the initial interview was pretty inconclusive. We'll get back to him a little later today as well."

"As far as George's death is concerned," Wilcox said, getting his two cents in, "it stays as it is for the time being. No public tie in between the two incidents. The state lab is doing tests on some of the logs that were trapped in Doyle's hole and will run them against what I have from the bump on his head."

Sidney gave Wilcox a hard, steady stare. He had no doubt the coroner already orchestrated a press statement of his own that would show he suspected foul play all along.

Hornig tapped his desk bringing the attention back to him. "At this point—now, this is just among us folks in this room—I'm pretty convinced that the three incidents are connected but I don't want *any*, I repeat, *any* inferences by anyone that they are. I want whoever was with George Reed at the time of his death to feel we have not made any connections and that we're still looking at Reed's death as an accident."

"Another question," Sidney said. "What about the cameras and the film? Has anything been found yet?"

"Still being looked at. There didn't seem to be anything suspicious with regard to what we picked up at Roots and Rakes and the camera at the Reed's was empty. Everything is still being looked over real close. We've got people everywhere as does the state."

Ray now moved forward in his chair. "Okay, so in other words, we're out of it, it's completely in your hands?"

"Right. I appreciate what you've done so far," Hornig said, looking directly at Sidney. "And I know you like puzzles, but we've got it now and we know what we're doing. This is not to say we don't value your help, I'd just appreciate it if you didn't try to do anything further on your own—either of you." He turned to Ray. "If I need more help, I won't be shy in asking."

"Not a problem. We didn't go looking for this, it came looking for us. Even if last night hadn't happened, we had planned on being in here anyway."

"I know that," Hornig said, "and I don't mean to say I'm shutting you out. Sidney, I've learned a bit about how your mind works from Ray here and the sheriff over in Beaufort County had some good things to say about you. I truly believe you can be a valuable resource. I just don't want you going off on your own. If you've got an idea or a thought that could be helpful, my door is always open. Ray, you already know all this."

"Well, I think you've done a fine job," Wilcox said, suddenly in candidate mode. "Your motivations in trying to correct any idle gossip about Becky Reed is really appreciated and should be commended. I, for one, certainly appreciate it and I'm sure Becky will as well, once she becomes fully aware of your involvement. It's time to go forward now. With the chief and his staff and my expertise combined with the state lab, we should be able to show the community a unified effort in tying up all the loose ends and finding the person or persons who have done this terrible thing."

"Okay," Hornig said, "good point, no second guessing. Good reminder for us all around here," he added, now looking at Wilcox. "Keep personalities out of it, follow the procedures, and it will all work out."

"Pete—" Wilcox started to interrupt but the chief wasn't having any of it.

"Just let it ride, Steele. We go forward not backward. Everybody understand. Separate incidents, no known connections. No theories thrown out to the public. Okay?"

The tone was dismissive and the chief rose from his chair, followed by the other three. After some general comments among them, Wilcox left first.

"Silly-assed son of a bitch" Hornig said after the door closed. "Ray, I told that asshole to slow down. God, if there's any job that shouldn't be an elected one, it's coro-

ner." The chief's views on which town positions should
be filled by elections and which should be by professional appointment were well known to Ray. It was a topic
they discussed over and over again at their weekly get-
togethers at the City Hall Café. "I'm sorry, Sidney, don't
mean to get you in the middle of city hall politics. You
did good on this one, as usual. Looks like it's becoming a
habit. Anyway, now it's up to us to get to the bottom of
it, get the final answers to what's goin' on here. Unless,
of course, you already know them."

Sidney didn't respond.

❧❧❧

With the break-in and attack at Reeds', the authorities
came back to the investigation in full force, as hoped for
by Sidney and Ray, but life did not return to normal for
Sidney—too much had happened. He could not simply
say: *Good, now I can stop thinking about all of this and
get back to my literary projects.* No, he kept turning everything over and over in his mind. There were too many
events sitting out there that he believed went together; too
many conversations with undiscovered meaning, the sig-
nificance of which he was unable to determine; too many
observations which he knew he should see as critical. All
Friday afternoon he made notes, did research on the Internet, drew pictures of various locations relating to
Reed's death and the break-ins, and, above all, sat quietly
with his eyes closed, thinking, Mickey at his feet.

About midafternoon, Geoff came back from lunch
with Susan. She ended up staying the night at the Prentices'. Becky had a few bruises and a scratch or two from
where she hit the floor the previous evening. The emergency room doctor gave her a good check over and some
sedatives to calm her down. Susan drove them back to the

Prentices' while Ruth stayed on watching over Cal. Tillie also stayed behind, lining up her contacts with the nursing and cleaning staff to watch over Cal Prentice. Back at the house, Amanda put her mother to bed and then she and Susan sat down and had a long chat. Susan explained, in greater detail, about what prompted Sidney Lake to originally become involved, providing much more information than Sidney did earlier in the evening before they left for the Reeds'. She pretty much told her everything, which was her honesty trait coming through. Besides, under the circumstances, Susan felt that Amanda had better know everything. They both opened up as the evening wore on, partially because their adrenalin levels were still elevated. Susan learned a good deal about the relationship between George and Becky Reed and she, in turn, unloaded about her problems with Geoff and especially her parents' reaction to her dating a Northerner and their specific reaction to Geoff. It was a long night but a necessary one.

As Susan and Geoff came through the door, Sidney pounced on them and started outlining some of his thoughts and ideas The three of them then took off for the hospital to see Cal Prentice, who, although having awakened with a very sore head and an even more painful broken shoulder, smiled broadly as they came into the room. Ruth had a book in her lap for reading as Cal would periodically drop off to sleep from the medication. He told them the police interviewed him at great length and he admitted being surprised at some of the questions, as they seemed to deal with matters not related to the break-in, such as his relationship with the Reeds, what kind of church goers they were, what he knew about George Reed's photography excursions, if he knew of anyone who might hold a grudge against either of the Reeds or their business.

Sidney could see Hornig's approach of keeping the *M* word out of the equation and not, publicly, linking anything to George Reed's death but yet expanding the range of information gathering beyond what would be expected of a simple burglary with assault. Sidney then pressed him with questions of his own but Cal still had difficulty remembering it all, since everything happened so fast. When he first saw the image of a man, his back was to Cal, as Becky had partially spun him around by holding onto his jacket pocket. Tillie then hit him with a bag and, in the act of freeing himself, he turned and crashed into Cal's chest and knocked him back. As Cal reeled backward, the intruder gave him a shove, in order to get around him, and that sent Cal down the stairs. He remembered nothing else. His answers to both the police and Sidney were more revealing in what the attacker wasn't rather than what he was: Very tall? Couldn't tell. Very fat? No. Light colored hair? Don't think so. Black? Don't think so. Young? Don't think so. Jacket color? Not light. Markings? Not sure. Becky's descriptions were pretty similar, except that she had felt the jacket he wore and thought it was light weight, the kind that golfers wore when playing in the rain. The pants seemed to match and were of the same waterproof material. Sidney made notes of everything while Geoff talked to the nurses on the floor. Schmoozing was something he enjoyed and, in this instance, he recognized two of the nurses from a few days earlier when he occupied a bed of his own on the floor above. Sidney instructed him to see if he could uncover any information they might have picked up from the police or the paramedics that could be useful.

With Geoff out of the room, Susan then agreed to drive Ruth Prentice back to her house to change her clothes and freshen up, thus leaving Cal and Sidney alone to talk.

"Looks as though you're going to get a forced vacation," Sidney said.

"Not exactly what I had in mind."

"No, I don't imagine it is. Just don't push too hard around here. They expect you to rest for a day or two, not go searching out members of the congregation down the hall so you can make other people feel better. You're the one who's the patient this time. Besides, you're probably going to remember something about last night that you didn't realize you knew. This time you're going to have to remember it when it pops into your head, which is why you're probably going to get another visit from Hornig's people before the day is out."

"You think so?"

"Count on it. And let me know if you think of anything as well."

"It's still pretty much a blur."

"I'm sure it is." Sidney then changed the subject, knowing that the best way to have memories triggered was to focus on something else. "So what are you going to do with all this free time?"

"Ah, the concept of the opportunity," Cal said with a smile.

"What opportunity?" Although Sidney knew pretty much where Cal was headed, he decided to prod him on.

"Everything is an opportunity. A good many people would look at me lying here and say how awful it is, what a terrible thing has happened, and would dwell on the negative aspects of being all broken up and out of commission."

"It certainly sounds reasonable to me. You're saying it's not bad? Recommending a fall down the stairs to lift one's spirits?"

"No, no, that's not the point. The point is that my being here changes the dynamic for me and those around me and presents opportunities not just for me but them as well. I see a bit of skepticism on that face, Sidney, so let me explain. Because I'm here I'll have the opportunity to interact even more with the hospital staff. They'll get to know me better and I them. Given that the hospital is no longer authorized to formally release information to third parties, such as churches, about people being admitted, the more personal relationships I can develop with the staff, the better I'll be able to help people without family in the area, and this is an opportunity to enhance that relationship. I'll also have quiet time to think and write, to work on meaningful themes for Sundays. When I leave here in a few days, the opportunities will continue, and not just for me. My replacement this Sunday will have the opportunity to give a sermon he may have longed to give but had no venue. Opportunities come from bad as well as good events. As terrible as George Reed's death was, look at the opportunities it has presented: for you with your investigation, for your relationship with Geoff, and his with you and Susan Abbott, not to mention Tillie who thrives on helping everybody. Opportunities are there to take or to leave but they're opportunities that didn't exist before. You pray for guidance to take the opportunity or to leave it, but it's there all the same. Each decision creates a new opportunity."

"Easy," Sidney said, seeing Cal begin to move about more than he probably should, "or you'll give yourself the opportunity of seeing your name posted on the door there a bit longer than you anticipated."

"The name!" Cal exclaimed.

"What name?"

"On the jacket. Last night. There was a name or logo or something like that on the jacket of the person who knocked me down."

"What was it?"

"A boat. I think it was a boat. An image of a boat and some lettering."

❧❧❧

The day shown clear and bright as it usually did in the lowcountry after a storm. The fresh smelling morning air induced Warren to open the pick-up truck's window as he headed out of Savanah and west toward I-95. No need to sneak around the back roads on his way back to Morgan, as he'd told everyone he would be back around noon. One thing about last night bothered him, aside from the sore shoulder, and that was the boat. He was sure no one recognized him, so that wouldn't be a problem, but the boat he really should move. There was nothing in it, but it did belong to him, although you didn't register skiffs like you would a power boat. They were pretty much treated like a kayak.

Might be a good idea to run by where I left it and throw it into the truck. No point in leaving loose ends around.

Chapter 18

After Geoff roamed around the hospital floor and reacquainted himself with the staff, he came back to Cal Prentice's room, only to find the pastor and Sidney in deep, serious conversation. Not wanting to interfere, he left a note taped to the door telling Sidney that he would be downstairs in the cafeteria. He then called Susan on her cell phone and told her where he would be.

Geoff hunkered down at a corner table at the back of the hospital cafeteria with a cup of coffee and thumbed through *The Morgan City Times* until he spotted Susan come in. "So how's Mrs. Prentice doing?"

Susan pulled up a chair and put the large Diet Coke in front of her. The room was about half full with a mixture of family members and friends of patients taking a much needed lunch break and a few tables of hospital staff lunching together. "She's fine, now that she knows Reverend Prentice is okay. It was tough last night, though. When they brought him into emergency, we had no idea what to expect. At least there wasn't a lot of blood like there was with you. He was more dazed from the hit on the head. It was the shoulder and wrist that concerned everyone. That was pretty scary last night. Where's Professor Lake?"

"He and Prentice looked pretty intense when I went by a little while ago so I decided not to interrupt and left him a note. What was it you started to tell me earlier about you and Amanda Reed?"

"Oh, last night. That was kind of interesting. She really opened up about her parents. I guess that's what happens. She really needed someone to talk with—and not the family. There are sometimes when a stranger is better to let things out to. You can say some things you couldn't say to a family member. You don't have to worry about hurting feelings."

"What in the world did you talk about?"

Susan paused for just a moment. "It was mainly about her father. She was recalling what a tough time he had when she was growing up. For a long time after the Viet Nam War, he was pretty bitter and it kind of spilled over into everything else. Up in Pennsylvania, they almost lost the business to Mr. Reed's drinking. Coming down here was kind of a last chance for them. Once they came to Morgan and got hooked on the lowcountry, photography turned everything around. Mr. Reed finally had something to focus on besides himself and Viet Nam, which he found not many people cared that much about down here, since so many of them are still fighting the Civil War. That was her comment, not mine, of course. Normally, I would have disagreed but, under the circumstances, I just let it go."

"Did she mention anything about George Reed's relationship with Caldwell Talbot?"

"Actually, that did come up. The pictures of the raccoons were still on the coffee table where we left them before the storm hit."

"Were they really friends?" Geoff still couldn't be-

lieve Talbot and Reed not only got along but also may
have liked one another. Talbot seemed to be so completely focused against anything and anyone from the North."

"Amanda really couldn't say but, in their own way,
she thought they were. She felt there was some sort of
grudging respect between them. Apparently, the Reeds
originally came from around York, Pennsylvania, which
is not far from Gettysburg, so George had an appreciation
of the kind of impact the Civil War had on the South,
since it's still serious business in that part of Pennsylvania. Both of them had read Shelby Foote. The anniversary
of the Battle of Gettysburg and re-enactments are a big
thing up there. Also, a lot of local people had relatives
that fought for the North and are buried locally. They still
take care of the graves. As to whether they were actually
close friends, all she knew was that his name came up
from time to time but nothing more than that. Do you
think Caldwell had something to do with Mr. Reed's
death? My family and the Talbot's have been friends for
generations, although my daddy was not that close to
Caldwell. His sister, Miss Betty, and my mother grew up
together and were best of friends."

"It's hard to say. I know Lake has mentioned him
from time to time, so I think he's one of the people on his
list."

"I thought the police had taken over everything?"

"Oh, they have but Lake will never let go. One thing
I've learned about him is that he never gives up. His mind
just won't shut down. He has to follow everything to the
end no matter where it leads."

"You've gotten to know him pretty well, haven't
you?" Susan was in her twenty question mode again.

"Well, sort of. I'm not sure how much anyone could
really know him. What I do know is that he questions
everything and he seems to be able to hone in on subjects

and really concentrate. He also likes to take opposite positions as a way of testing his own theories. Sometimes it's difficult to tell which side he's on since he makes such a good case for both. Most people seem to approach research by following A to B to C to D to E in pursuit of Z. He doesn't. He does A and B and gets a hint about E and then uses it to go back to come up with C and D. It's fascinating to watch because he seems to come at things from all different sides at once and you're never quite sure where he is until he gets to the end."

"Does he have any kind of a life other than the university?"

"He has his roses and Mrs. Micawber."

"Mrs. Micawber? He has a girlfriend?"

"Susan, Mrs. Micawber is Mickey—his dog—that's her real name."

"Oh, I didn't know. Although I guess that's in character for an English Professor to name his dog after a Dickens character. I suppose if he had a cat as well, it would be called Oliver for Oliver Twist."

"Hero."

"He has a cat named Hero? I didn't know he had a cat."

"He doesn't. Hero is for Herodotus. It was the dog before Mickey. Lake is also big on philosophy and history."

"Actually, those are great pet names."

"Yeah, I was thinking that if I had a dog I'd probably name him Mac for Machiavelli."

She reached out and touched his arm. "Oooh, I like that."

"Lately, I've been learning a lot about campus politics, especially with what's been going on around the college this past year, and I think an awful lot of people in administration have been studying him—Machiavelli, that is."

"No more than the school system, but back to Mr. Lake, does he have a girlfriend? I realize he's not the dashing type."

Geoff laughed. "You mean being short, fat, bald, and nearsighted."

"I didn't say that." She smiled and gave him a playful slap on the arm. "Looks aren't everything, you know. You mean you're only interested in the physical side of me?"

Geoff paused and then, smiling, spoke slowly. "That sounds like a no-win kind of question to answer but let me try." He cleared his throat. "If you didn't have brains and a caring nature, your beauty would not tempt me."

"Very good," she said, laughing. "You're really getting good. You must have some Southern gentleman genes hidden in your background somewhere"

"I think some of Lake's diplomacy training is starting to take hold."

"Hi, Jersey," said a voice from nearby.

Both Geoff and Susan quickly looked up to see a young woman with a tray filled with a sandwich, a bag of *Tostitos,* a drink of something in a plastic cup with a straw, and a manila envelope under her arm standing above them.

"Oh, hi." Geoff said. "Philly, isn't it?" he asked, realizing it was the receptionist from *The Morgan City Times.*

"That's me. How ya doin'? Hear you got wacked on the head."

"Okay. Hard head, I guess." Seeing Susan clearly wondering what was going on, he continued. "This is Susan Abbott. You know, I don't think I remember your real name."

"No problem, and it's Jill. Leaving a lasting impression is not part of the job description." She made an effort to hold the tray in one hand and reach out the other to shake Susan's hand. The envelope fell to the floor, almost followed by the tray, which she managed to hold on to. Susan seeing the tray wobbling above her made a move to get up, out of the way, and help her stabilize the tray, all at the same time. Geoff moved his chair back quickly as the envelope dropped at his feet. Jill then got everything under control. "Sorry 'bout that. Almost got you pretty good."

Geoff reached over, picked up the envelope, and held it for a moment while she got organized. "You dropped this," he said, holding it out to her.

"Just drop it on top of the tray."

As he positioned the envelope in a vertical position between the sandwich and the soft drink cup, Geoff turned to Susan. "She's the receptionist at *The Times* I mentioned." He then turned back to Jill. "Have you got it now?"

"All under control, thanks."

"Hope no one's ill or anything."

"The hospital? Oh, no. Just grabbing a late lunch. This is as good a place as any, and it's cheap. Had to pick up some advertising copy and photos from the marina down the road," she said, tapping to the envelope. "You know, the place that just changed hands a little while ago. That's what 'go-fors' go for. Bennett and I stop in here a lot." She made a motion with her head to her right at a young blond-haired male, who seemed to be of high school age, sitting at a table two aisles away. "They send us out in pairs. Like lemmings or something or whatever it is that is running around in pairs. Somehow, lemmings doesn't seem right. I think they're the ones that jump off cliffs when told to—well, maybe that isn't too far off. Anyway, didn't mean to interrupt. Glad you're okay. Good to see ya again. Nice meeting you, Susan. Sorry I almost dropped lunch on ya"

"Yes, you too," she said.

And off Jill went.

Susan smiled at her as she left. "My goodness, what a whirlwind. You said she was a bit different for Morgan."

"You agree?" he said, sitting down again.

"I think so. Where did she say she was coming from?"

"The Marina. Probably the one we got the maps from."

"The Fort."

"Yeah, the one with the new owner. The guy who knew your parents."

"That's right, I had forgotten about him—and the nutty cashier. They were both a little strange."

The two of them huddled together and laughed.

ꞓꞓꞓ

Sidney sat in the chair to the side of Cal's hospital bed, watching the pastor sleep. They had been chatting away when suddenly Cal's eyes closed. Sidney was not unfamiliar with such happenings, as they had been going on all day. He assumed there was pain medication mixed into the IV liquid dripping down the tube into Cal's veins. The pastor would probably sleep for a half hour or until one of the nurses came in to check his vital signs, whichever came first.

Sidney heard a noise and turned to see Ruth Prentice come into the room. Just behind her, peeking around the door, was Alice Ringfoot, who had come to see her injured pastor. Sidney got up quietly and made his way to the door. "He just dropped off. How are you?"

"Oh, I'm fine now," Ruth whispered.

Sidney motioned her into the hallway where they would be able to talk. "Hello, Alice."

Alice nodded as she backed away from the entrance.

"There's a note here for you," she said, pointing to the outside of the door. Sidney took it down.

"Has he been sleeping much?" Ruth said, now in a normal tone of voice.

"No, I'm afraid I've been keeping him awake with my chatter. I guess I just wore him out."

"You're a good friend, Sidney. I think he'll need the rest now that the word is out. All sorts of people will be dropping by."

"I told most of them to leave him be," Alice said, "but they won't. He's done so much for others. You don't get too many chances to pay back your minister for a kindness. If nothing else, I'm sure there are people cooking and baking from one end of town to the next."

ৎৎৎৎ

Sidney caught up with Geoff and Susan in the cafeteria and sat with them. He then began to work out more tasks for Geoff to undertake. By this time Susan, was half asleep from being up most of the night with Amanda Reed, and they both told her to go home and get some rest. She didn't argue and finally excused herself. Geoff offered to drive her home but she refused, saying she would be just fine it was only a five minute drive and that she would give Geoff a call later. After she left, Geoff, took the opportunity to tell Sidney that he would go back to his own apartment later in the afternoon. Feeling there was no reason to keep sponging off of Sidney, since he felt okay. Besides, Roots and Rakes would be open tomorrow. Bev told Becky not to worry, she would handle everything while she and Amanda were in Charlotte. George's parents decided they would go to Charlotte as well for a few days before heading back to Florida. Tomorrow being Saturday, a big day for plant sales, Geoff told Bev he would come in and help her in the office for a while.

"Yes, it's good to get back into a proper routine. Just don't try to do too much," said Sidney.

"Too much? After the past few days it'll be like a vacation." Geoff suddenly realized from his tone that he treated Sidney like an equal and Lake didn't take an exception to it. Their relationship had certainly grown over the past week.

"I suppose you're right. There's something else I would like you to do, though. Actually, I need two things."

"Okay."

"First, I want you to rack your brain, assuming all the pieces are now back in place, and see if you can recall ever seeing a logo that deals with a boat."

"Boat? What kind of a boat?"

"Let's not even call it a boat. Let's call it a nautical theme. Working for Roots and Rakes, you're in and out of every gated community and golf community in the region, and they all have little symbols that represent them: crossed golf clubs, flowers, birds, jumping dolphins, palm trees, you name it, and someone has adopted it as their own. What I'm looking for is a boat or sailboat or something like that and some lettering near it."

"What's this all about?"

"Something Reverend Prentice seems to remember."

"About last night? I thought we were out of it? I thought the police were in control?"

"They are, but if we can continue to be helpful, I'm sure they'll appreciate it."

"Okay," Geoff said. "I'll see what I can come up with. You interested just in Morgan?"

"No, not at all. If you recall seeing anything anywhere, jot it down."

Geoff nodded his head. "You said there were two things."

"Yes, I would like you to be at General Brewster's Garden Club party tomorrow evening."

"But I haven't been invited. Besides, I'm not a member and my specialty is weeding and watering. I wouldn't know one flower from another."

"I'll clear it with the general. You presence will be to assist me, not to give a lecture or demonstration, which I don't think is planned anyway."

"Is this part of the Reed thing again?"

"It may develop that way."

"At this point, I think I'm looking forward to literary research."

"By the way, did you find out anything of interest from the nurses upstairs?"

"Not really. Nothing you haven't already mentioned. I guess Reverend Prentice is out of the woods, though. Looks like all the tests came back okay. The big problem is going to be his shoulder. They said it would take a long time to mend. Turned out his wrist wasn't broken as was first thought but it's a really bad sprain, which, they said, can sometimes be more painful that a break. Also he's going to need some serious physical therapy for some time. One of them added, 'Not tennis.' I guess he's a tennis player?"

"Yes, he is, and quite a good one."

"Didn't know that. Anyway, it doesn't seem as though there's anything new from their end. A nautical logo, hah," Geoff mused and looked off into space. "The yacht club has a couple of lines that look like waves for a logo, and some lettering."

"That one I thought of."

Geoff looked past Sidney again but this time he was greeted with a wave from Jill, who obviously thought he was staring at her. He returned the wave and then focused on Sidney.

"Someone you know?"

"Jill from *The Times*, nothing important."

Sidney got up. "I'm going to make my way back upstairs for a few more minutes and then head home. You know you're welcome to stay longer if you wish." Sidney, who had been living alone for more than twenty years, found himself surprised at not wanting Geoff to leave. He wasn't quite sure what he felt. He had plenty of friends, acquaintances, and hosted at least one dinner a month, and there was Mickey and, of course, Tillie, but having someone actually living in the house. *Well*, he thought, *must be the novelty of it.*

"No, thanks, anyway, professor. I've disrupted you enough. Besides, I need my own stuff. Nothing personal."

"Oh, I understand. Just pleased I could help. I'll talk with you tomorrow morning about the logos and Brewsters. I believe your friend is waving to you again," Sidney said, nodding at Jill.

❧❧❧

When Sidney arrived back on the fourth floor, it was obvious that word had spread quickly. There were now four large floral arrangements at the nurses station, one of which Alice Ringfoot held in front of her as she spoke to the nurse. "Two more," she said, "he already has two in there. Mrs. Prentice thought you might be able to spread these around the floor a bit. Brighten up a few of the other rooms that could use them."

Sidney walked on by and made his way to Cal's, where he found Ruth and a man and woman he recognized as elders of the church. One of the problems many churches ran into when the average age of the congregation got to be a good deal above the national average was they found themselves suddenly catering to the needs of retirees and the elderly. The result was they started to lose the young adults with growing families, which represented the church's future. Cal had been trying to have more elders and deacons with school age children so that the church's programs would better reflect the needs of members like themselves. It was a tough battle since that age group had the most time-challenged schedules, while the retirees were always looking to fill their days. The elders speaking to him now were both in their late seventies and while the group as a whole—the session, of which there were twelve members—now contained two members under the age of forty, Cal still had a lot of work to do.

Sidney, come in," said Cal. "You know Marvin Randolph and Emma Kelly, don't you?"

"Yes, I certainly do."

They all shook hands.

"We were just working out some details for Sunday. Martin Gainey has agreed to sub for me on Sunday. Martin was the pastor of First Presbyterian Church in Roanoke, Virginia and now lives out at Fripp Island. Have you met him?"

"No, I don't believe I have."

"Excellent speaker. A great biblical scholar. He's a great choice."

"Cal, we have to get back and finish the arrangements for Sunday," said Emma Kelly. "We're so pleased you're all right and we'll talk again tomorrow about some of the other matters that are pending." She leaned over and gave Cal a gentle kiss on the cheek.

"Thank you so much for your help," Cal said.

"I'll walk out with you," said Ruth. They then exchanged good-byes with Sidney and left the room.

"Doesn't look like you're going to get that rest and time to think you mentioned earlier," Sidney said, still in a low voice.

Cal just smiled. "Oh, yes, I will. All I have to do is close that door, pull the curtain, and dim the lights. It works wonders. I've already worked it out with one of the nurses. Besides, don't forget, I've got all night. Nobody sleeps in hospitals, they wake you every hour or so to check your pulse and take your blood pressure. Get lots of quiet time trying to get back to sleep after that. That's why they send you home to get some rest. Oh, by the way, Chief Hornig called and said he and one of his people are coming over in a little while."

"Good, make sure you tell him everything. A quick point: that logo wasn't the yacht club insignia was it?'

"No, I'd recognize that right away. I am trying to remember it though. The letter 'O' comes to mind but I don't know why."

"Keep at it. You'll probably recognize it when you see it." Sidney then changed the subject. "Cal, I'm not going to stay. I've monopolized more of your time than I should. I just feel guilty, I guess, for getting you involved. I'm sorry about that."

"Sidney, don't be silly. If we hadn't been there, Becky and Amanda might have been the ones seriously hurt, or worse. Remember, opportunities are being presented for everyone. It's one of the ways the world works and God uses us for His purposes.

"Okay, but I'm still sorry."

❦❦❦

The pick-up truck slowed to a crawl as it reached the closest point to the march possible without leaving the dirt road. Getting out, Warren looked around the secluded spot. Seeing no one, he made his way down a barely visible path that led to the water and an area of tall marsh grass ten yards away. He remembered shoving the skiff into an area of thick grass so he wasn't surprised at not seeing it right away,

Reaching the location where he was positive the boat should be—he found nothing. *Where is it? I know this is the place. I've left it here before.* He stepped to the edge of the water and pushed the tall grass aside first one way then the other. No boat. He looked for his anchor stone: a cinder block with a long rope tied to it. He looked and looked. Then about twenty feet away he saw a piece of the rope floating in the water. He rushed toward it, stepping ankle deep into the water and grabbed at the rope. It was still attached to the cinder block, which, underwater, had become snagged in some tree roots. He pulled on the rope and the end came to him frayed and broken. He looked around the marsh toward the channel thirty yards away. *Where the hell is the boat?*

Chapter 19

The Thursday *Morgan City Times* ended up not carrying the Reed home invasion story, as the publication deadline had already passed before Hornig could give the editor a statement. Jim Cunningham didn't press the point, since he had his hands full with every available reporter covering the storm. The general public of Morgan had no idea of the break-in at the Reeds' until Friday morning when the paper arrived on their doorsteps. That was not to say word of mouth had not carried the story around town, as it most surely did, but Friday's edition was eagerly awaited by many interested parties looking for a confirmation of what they heard at the supermarket, the hair salon, the local café. *The Times* carried a pretty straight forward account, as Chief Hornig had hoped: the break-in during the storm, the injury to Reverend Prentice, the attack on Becky Reed. The break-in at Roots and Rakes and the landscape business appeared only as a reference, as background, showing the business as being owned by Becky Reed and her recently deceased husband George. In a quote, Chief Hornig laid out the motive with his theory of a targeted attack based on the obituary of George Reed, who died the previous weekend in a boating accident, whereby the perpetrator assumed the house would be empty. No tie-ins and no commentary about anything else, although, having had the opportunity to interview Cal Prentice a second time before the paper came out, Hornig was able to state they were interested in speaking with anyone who believes they saw a white male of medium height in the neighborhood where the Reeds lived on the night of the attack. Cunningham of the *Times* and Chief Hornig made it a point of working together wherever possible, and controlling questionable speculation was part of their arrangement. However, the story ended up being buried on page six as the front page presented the results of the Wednesday night storm: all the trees that were knocked down, local flooding, and power outages across the lowcountry. Two color pictures dominated page one with lots of others on the inside that focused on the clean-up effort showing marine recruits from Paris Island clearing trees and debris from a trailer park in Port Royal, South Carolina, where a small tornado had been reported touching down briefly.

The Friday edition also included the *Out and About* insert section which prominently displayed the announcement of the Morgan Garden Association annual get together hosted by the current president, General Lawrence Brewster. Being one of the primary social events of the summer season, it always received major event coverage. Sidney, as a member of the MGA, responded to a call for help from General Brewster only two weeks ago after the caterer for this evening's cocktail party and the general had a disagreement, not an unusual occurrence for Brewster. The event was in jeopardy. The caterer quit and Sidney came to Brewster's rescue by enlisting the help of Tillie, who arranged for a local restaurant on Dear Island—that just happened to be owned by a

cousin—to provide the food and drink and Tillie personally took care of providing the set-up, serving and clean-
up staff. Tillie could always come up with experienced
people from the islands who needed the work and she
would guaranty their performance. In preparation for the
party Sidney agreed to lunch with Brewster at the City
Hall Café on Main Street at twelve-thirty on Friday. The
general wanted it earlier but agreed to the later time
which allowed Sidney to spend a considerable amount of
time on the phone with Hattie Ryan. The five-hour time
difference to the United Kingdom allowed Hattie to do an
extensive amount of research for Sidney. And he had a
lot of questions for her.

The Hattie Ryan, Sidney Lake relationship seemed an
interesting one for the twenty-first century, as the two of
them were so firmly rooted in the nineteenth. The subject
matter they taught—Sidney, the Victorian novel and
Hattie, English poetry with an emphasis on the Lake District School of Poets through Tennyson—brought them
together but their approach to life created the bond. They
actually tried to champion the three Cs—common sense,
common decency, and common courtesy—all three of
which they agreed were on the verge of extinction in
America of late. Keeping to character, they refused to
give in, regardless of the lost cause nature of their advo-
cacy, which drove them even closer together. Hattie, although a Catholic, actively supported the etiquette and
courtesy classes sponsored by the Bay View Presbyterian
Church and attended as many of their events as possible.
The South may be one of the few places in the country
where such a class could not only be held but also have
attendance by an equal number of boys and girls of junior
high school age. Just before the spring term ended, she
watched a group of young men being taught dining table
courtesy and being instructed on how to properly stand

and conduct oneself when a guest or other person approached the table.

Hattie watched from the doorway of the church hall
one day when the father of one of the male participants
came in and stood beside her. After a moment, she turned
and introduced herself, as he had not offered to do so.
After another moment, he then said to her: "This is certainly a real waste of time in this day and age, isn't it?"

Hattie merely looked him up and down in a very obvious manner and, seeing the jeans, T-shirt—with an adver-
tisement for a Mexican beer—and a baseball cap firmly
implanted on his head while standing in the church hall,
replied, "Actually, I think it's needed more than ever."

No one ever accused her of being the shy, retiring type
and taking prisoners was not known to be her strong
point, especially when the kill option proved more effective.

Sidney had long come to rely on Hattie's judgment
and friendship and believed her research skills second to
none. The trip to the Lake District was her third in the
last four years. Ever since her daughter graduated from
Georgetown University five years ago and was now off
on her own, Hattie spent part of her summer in England
doing research on not only Wordsworth, Coleridge and
Southey but also recently added William Hazlitt, who
coined the "Lake School" in 1817. So when Sidney needed something validated for the research he was doing,
Hattie, being in the Lake District and staying at a bed and
breakfast in Keswick, proved to be an opportunity too
good to pass up. While her drive to the Yorkshire dales
took her all morning, she had what Sidney hoped for by
the time they spoke on Friday.

The City Hall Café, a local hangout for the powers
that be in Morgan, purposely presented itself as somewhat dark and dingy and just unkempt enough to keep

most of the tourists away, not to mention the gated community types who tended to stay behind their gates for lunch anyway. At the Café, everyone pretty much knew everyone else and the owner and waitresses spent more time chatting with the patrons than serving them. Brewster, suggested the lunch to Sidney in an effort to explore contingencies for this evening as he would a military campaign. Try to examine all possible problems and their solutions and have not just a Plan B but possibly a C and D as well. As president of the Morgan Garden Association, a post his late wife held before him, the general had the responsibility for hosting the summer end of season cocktail party. During the spring, the group sponsored a variety of local garden tours and demonstrations, the proceeds of which went to the non-profit Morgan Restoration Society. He planned to have everything outside on the grounds of the Brewster home and to that end tents were currently being set up on the lawn between the house and the marsh and serving tables were set up on the back porch and the rear deck. The storms of Thursday evening forced some of the general's contingency plans to go into effect due to the extremely wet grounds. The result demanded the necessity to plan for more activities to occur in the house itself in the event the grass did not properly dry out and it became too muddy for people to slosh around between the house and the marsh. Also, the forecast called for more "pop-up" thunder storms for later in the afternoon.

The general and Sidney were bantering with Hal McGraw, the Café's owner when Dennis Carson, in his mandatory Bermuda shorts and golf logo shirt came up to the table and joined in. "This must be the gardener's table. Does the spouse of a gardener qualify?" Then he turned to Brewster: "Hope you're not having this guy cater tonight." He put his arm around McGraw. "I can't take his food more than once in a day."

"Saving him for when you come for dinner?" the general said.

"Is that an invitation?"

"No, that's a warning."

"Oh, you guys are a lot of help," said McGraw. "I see Caldwell in the corner over there maybe I'll go over and be abused by him for a while. Nobody's called me a Yankee for at least twenty-four hours."

One of the interesting facts of life around Morgan was that so many of the local business were owned and operated by non-Morganers—many of them from the North—which, of course, made some of the local people unhappy. However, it was not lost on the proprietors of the businesses that they were paying rent to the local gentry of Morgan, who, very shrewdly, kept control of the real estate, recognizing that while rents may be paid in currency with the pictures of Lincoln and Franklin, it was easily converted into Southern funds with Washington, Jackson and Jefferson properly represented.

"Didn't mean to chase you away," Carson said in an apologetic manner.

"Not a bad idea, though." McGraw simply headed for the back of the room.

Carson took one of the empty chairs and sat himself down. "Say, Sidney, didn't I see that fella who works for you the other day at the Fort? Van something or other. He was with the Abbott girl."

"Possibly."

"Yeah, they were lookin' for charts of the river. Apparently all they had was one of those tourist maps of the area. Won't get very far with one of those. Little funny, though, I would of thought Ed Abbott had plenty of charts."

"The chart could have been for Geoff," Sidney suggested. "He's a bright guy. I'm serving as a resource for his masters. But his boating experience is about as good as mine."

"That bad, eh?"

"Yeah, he said he was working on something…let me see…ah, I remember, Meredith, George Meredith."

"Meredith," Brewster said, "why is that name familiar?"

"It's one of the names on the list. Your uncle had a copy of *The Adventures of Harry Richmond*. It's one of the novels Meredith wrote in the early 1870s, just before he wrote *The Egoist*, the novel Geoff's working on."

"Is it any good?"

Sidney looked over his glasses at the general.

"Come on, Sidney, is it any good?" Brewster said, sitting back in his chair and gesturing with his hands.

"Of course it is. I find Meredith very amusing."

"You mean funny?"

"I didn't say that. He writes what would be called a comic style in the true sense of the word. There's an amusing and satirical nature to his work."

"General, I get the feeling you won't find too many belly laughs in it," Carson said.

"Is he right, Professor?"

"There might be a Victorian belly laugh or two."

"Sounds like this might go on the list for Jarvis to sell."

"You going to sell some of the stuff you got from your uncle?" Carson asked, taking an immediate interest in the topic.

"I've only got so much space. Some of its got to go. As Sidney here knows, I'm not much of a fiction fan. I doubt if I'll keep more than a hundred of the books I received."

"How about giving me a crack at some of it before Jarvis gets it?" Carson leaned forward, put both elbows on the table, and talked directly to the general, as if Sidney wasn't even there. "It's not that I'm in competition with him but I am trying to build up my used book section in the marina store. It's turned out to be a real money maker. Besides, Jarvis's clientele is not a lot different from mine. Not all my folks are just interested in used books they can get cheaply and throw away when they finish it or sell it back to me on their way back up the intercostal. I'm actually doing pretty good with it. Some of the big boat guys are looking for old undiscovered stuff."

"Sure, I have no problem with that. You too, Sidney. If there's something there you think you'd like, just say so. It's the least I can do for your help."

"Oops," Carson exclaimed, jumping up from the chair, "what am I doing here? I'm supposed to be meeting the wife at the *Palmetto* for lunch. God, she'll kill me. I'm outta here. Gotta play through. See you both tonight." And he was gone.

"Nice guy but there's something I'm not sure of. By the way, Sidney, I meant what I said about having first crack at the books I intend to get rid of. That also reminds me, did you ever find anything missing when you did that list comparison?"

"Actually, that's something I wanted to talk to you about. With all that happened with the Reeds and Cal Prentice the other night, I didn't get a chance to go over anything with you. I think there are three volumes missing. They seem to be by an author by the name of Bell. That list you have is a very simple inventory, in that it just has an author name, the number of volumes, and a comment if necessary. In this case, it just says 'first edition autographed.' For instance, in the case of that Meredith book I mentioned earlier, it just shows the number one under volumes and no comment. I knew it was *The Adventures of Harry Richmond* because I had seen it when I was unloading one of the boxes and remembered because of the Meredith name and Geoff's current project. Is that list all you received from your uncle's attorney? There wasn't anything more detailed?"

"That list was put together by the attorneys when they were getting ready to value the estate. Springwood, that's the attorney, said that he believed Uncle Sherman also had some sort of a bibliography list which showed when he bought a volume, who he bought it from, some background on the author, the publisher. He said there were like five lines on every book. He just hasn't come up with it yet."

"Interesting. I'd love to see that. In the meantime, I think you should probably notify the insurance company and the police that you suspect that something of value may well be missing. Hornig will want to file a report with the FBI's art theft program, depending on the value of the books that are missing. The insurance company may want to do the same."

At this point, they were interrupted with the delivery of lunch. The waitress, Greta, apologized for taking so long and put the blame on McGraw for letting one of the cooks take some time off. "It comes," she said, "but I seen ketchup moving faster outta a new bottle." For a change, she didn't stay around to chat but headed right back to the kitchen. She was also relatively new to the Café and not from Morgan.

"How do you eat that stuff?' Brewster said, frowning at Sidney's liverwurst on rye sandwich.

"I happen to like it. I'll take it over the nutritional value of that bacon, mushroom burger any day." Quickly changing the subject back, Sidney continued: "About tonight, as long as we were on the topic, you asked if I would say few things about your uncle's book collection. I have a pretty good idea of what's there and some of it's pretty interesting. If you think we're going to be stuck inside because of the weather, I'd be happy to help out. I'm sure it will be a good way to get people to circulate around from the kitchen to the great room to the library and the porch."

"Hey, Sidney, that would be great. If we do get stuck having this thing in-doors for the whole evening that would really take the pressure off."

☙☙☙

On returning home, Sidney went to his office, closed the door, and remained alone for more than an hour. Upon coming out, he found Geoff in the kitchen with the refrigerator door open.

"Professor Lake," he said, surprised. "Stopped in to pick up the rest of my things." Geoff held up a can of soda. "Hope you don't mind."

"No, go right ahead. I bought it for you. I certainly don't drink it. I arranged everything for you with regard to the garden cocktail party at General Brewster's."

"You're sure I'm invited?"

"Yes, you are. The general just invited you. Susan is expected to be there as well, along with her parents."

"So I'm a guest? No one expects me to clean up tables or mix drinks?"

"That is correct. You are a guest."

"You have something up your sleeve, don't you?"

"Possibly, if things fall together."

"Wanna give me a hint?"

"No. It may not be anything. We'll see."

"What do I wear?"

"This is the South, Geoffrey. You are going to a recently restored home and gardens in the Ridge circa 1827. You will be associating with many of the old families that live in the Ridge, as well as elsewhere in town. The mayor and possibly other elected officials will be there as will some local business people and some retired military. Think of yourself as representing Roots and Rakes at a gardening event. The Reeds will, for obvious reasons, not be there. I assume somewhere in your closet you have some slacks and a sport coat. A nice shirt would also be appropriate, as well as a tie, although the latter would be optional. This will not be a retirement community event where the formerly buttoned down Northerners show up in a golf shirt, shorts, and docksiders, although that is not to say that someone won't show up dressed that way."

"I get the picture. You know, I didn't even know you were in there, it was so quiet," Geoff said, jerking his chin toward Sidney's office. "I should have known, though, as Mickey wasn't here to greet me."

"I was on the phone with Professor Ryan earlier today. She's been in the Lake District doing some research on Wordsworth. Went on an errand for me in Yorkshire today and developed some very interesting information. We're about five hours earlier so it's getting a bit late for her and I needed to have some matters clarified."

"More literary research?"

"No, another project. As long as she was in the area, it worked out very well."

"Anything I should know?"

Geoff knew that trying to get information out of Sidney Lake, when he didn't want to give it, was a lost cause. So he changed subjects. "Susan tells me that Reverend Prentice's doing pretty well. I guess that left side of his is going to be out of commission for some time. What will they do for a replacement over at Bay View Presbyterian? He doesn't have an assistant, does he?"

"No, but that's not a problem. You would be amazed at the number of retired ministers who live between Savannah and Charleston. They'll be plenty of coverage for a few weeks."

"But it'll be months not weeks."

"I don't think so. Presbyterian services are much simpler than the Catholic ones you're more familiar with. A Sunday service is not quite as rigorous. The liturgy is simple, not complex and elaborate. The focus on Sunday is the teaching from the pulpit not the Sacrament of the Eucharist. Communion for us is once a month on the first Sunday and is distributed by the elders. All Cal has to do is sit and watch. These next few weeks will give him the opportunity to write some of the best sermons of his life. Minimum interruptions, no visiting the hospitals, no visiting the nursing homes and assisted living facilities, meeting's with elders and deacons kept to a minimum and, above all, no committees. No, this could be a very productive time for him and, if I know Ruth, she'll keep Cal and his visitor traffic under control."

"Well, when it comes to religions, they're all a mystery to me. I just show up at mass now and again to keep my hand in. My parents always took me when I was younger. I never really paid much attention to it all."

"You probably will when you get a little older. It's amazing how Pascalian we all seem to become as we age. Now, I think we should talk about this evening and what I have planned for you to do. By the way, how did you make out in your search for nautical logos?"

"Not too good. In fact, I couldn't find one boat on a logo anywhere. When I was over at R and R this morning, I even went through the files. We keep a file on each of our regular or repeat customers and have copies of their stationary from correspondence we had for one reason or another. I still couldn't find anything. Checked the yellow pages for advertisements—still no luck." Geoff suddenly stopped. "Wait a minute! Do you remember yesterday, in the cafeteria, that girl?"

"What girl?"

"The one that waved to me."

"The one that you said was from *The Times*. Yes, I remember. You seemed a bit embarrassed by it."

"Never mind that. She stopped by earlier and chatted with Susan and me. She said she had just come from the marina down the road where she picked up some advertising copy and some photos. While she was talking, she dropped the envelope they were in. There was a logo on it, one I hadn't seen before."

"Dennis Carson's new place. Actually, it's not new, it's been there for years."

"Right. Well, I think he just changed the logo. On the envelope was a fort tower. You know, like the rook in a chess set, and it had crossed oars on it."

"Very interesting, Geoff. Yes, you're right. I think just saw that logo at lunch. Very interesting."

ೞೞೞ

With any luck the boat is at the bottom of a channel someplace. I can't find it anywhere.

Boats disappearing during a tropical storm in the lowcountry was a pretty common event. Warren was sure the boat contained nothing that would link it to him, so he wasn't the least bit worried. He was just sorry about losing it. He mainly kept it around for his grandchildren to use when they came for a visit. No, he felt comfortable it would not be a problem. Just another irritating loose end.

While Warren continued toward the City Café to pick up the lunch he ordered earlier, two of Hornig's marine police spotted a skiff hung up in some deep and tangled marsh grass. They shut down their engine and drifted toward it.

Chapter 20

S idney stood in front of his desk as he spoke on the phone. "Geoff, Lake here. I know we just left one another less than an hour ago but I'm arranging a meeting for before the party tonight and I need you to be there."

"How soon before and where?"

"Five o'clock at General Brewster's."

"That's like an hour from now. Yeah, I can make it but will I have time to come back here to change my clothes before everything starts?"

"Good point. No. Why don't you get dressed so you can just stay after the meeting? I'll plan to do the same and recommend it to the others."

"How many others are there?"

"We will be five: you, Ray Morton, Susan, and Tillie, and me, of course."

A pause. Then Geoff sighed. "What's this all about, Professor?"

"Let's just say I think I've found the motive for the murder of George Reed, but I'm not quite sure who killed him. I'd like to flush some things out before the evening gets started."

"Okay. Whatever you say, Professor."

After finishing with Geoff, Sidney had the same conversation with Susan. She originally planned to go with her parents but could get around that without too much of a problem.

Next on his list he called Ray Morton. Tillie was already at Brewster's, having shown up around noon to help with the set-up, specifically the kitchen arrangement and staging for the distribution of the food and drinks. There would also be a bar—manned by her nephew—in either the dining room on the deck out back, depending on the weather.

❧❧❧

Geoff's social world revolved around the university, which ruled out most local residents and confined him to cocktail parties hosted by professors or sponsored by the university or one of its departments. Receptions for University events such as art shows, guest lecturers, classical concerts and other special entertainment events would also be prominent on his calendar. He could not remember ever being inside a house on The Ridge. He worked on plenty of lawns, repaired sprinkler systems and delivered mulch and spread it around gardens but be invited inside as a guest? No, not ever.

Even though Geoffrey came from a middle class family in Wheaton, New Jersey—his father worked as a manager at the glass works—and felt comfortable within the town's social structure, the inner workings of Morgan mystified him. Wheaton, a small town not unlike Morgan, sat within the Washington, Philadelphia, New York, Boston corridor and realized its place in the overall society around it. One could not ignore events and activities within the region as they appeared on the front page of every local newspaper and the television feed came from

Philadelphia or Wilmington, Delaware. In Wheaton, no
matter how affluent you were, you always knew you were
still a small fish in a large pond. Morgan, however, exist-
ed in its own pond. Washington was a world away. Even
Atlanta and Columbia were places that did not have a daily impact on the way the city worked. Since the founding
of the original settlement in 1680, the residents have always been in control of their own destiny and the important families knew they were just that: important. Not
much had changed until recently but even that occurred at
a slower pace than other places.

Brown vs. The Board of Education changed everything, then came the Civil Rights legislation of the 1960s.
The development of Hilton Head and Myrtle Beach provided the impetus for the second Northern invasion and
then cable television brought the rest of the world into the
residents daily lives. But for all the change that came in a
rush of legislation and technology, old ways adapted
slowly. Morgan's first families continued to swim in and
control their small pond, although the pond grew larger
and many began to notice new, even larger fish swimming in once restricted waters.

While the jacket fit comfortably, the white dress shirt
just didn't feel right. His mother bought it for him when
he attended college in New Jersey. She told him that if
someone in the family died, she didn't want him showing
up in a black tee shirt. Although his weight had not
changed in the last four years, his body structure had,
making the shirt a bit tighter under the arms and around
the neck. He realized that, even if he wanted to, he could
never have managed to put on one of his old ties. The end
result was a white shirt open at the neck, no tie and a blue
blazer. Susan offered to take him on a shopping excursion
next week to correct his wardrobe deficiencies. While
there were things about Sidney Lake that drove Geoffrey

up the wall, he had to admit he always looked presentable, nice, neat, and maybe that wasn't too bad.

Geoff parked his truck about two blocks away and walked to Brewster's. Upon entering the walkway to the house, he saw two of the set-up crew looking down and commenting on the surface. The old bricks and stones appeared very uneven in both color and size and he could understand why the previous owner paved them over in order to achieve a uniform smooth surface. It was when the general did some repair work on some of the broken concrete that covered the walk that he found the bricks and cobble stones underneath it. Mrs. Brewster did some research and found that the original walkway came from ballast carried by sailing ships that, at one time, regularly came to Morgan and slave labor, most likely, constructed it. She ordered the concrete completely removed and the walkway restored for historical accuracy as a tribute to the history of Morgan and the craftsmanship of the slaves who so perfectly fitted the mix of stones together without the benefit of modern day mortar. The people walking in front of Geoff made a point of commenting on the walkway but also watched their step on the stones, something he made sure to do as well. The stones had been hand cut and made and, while carefully placed, did not have the evenness the modern foot was used to. Geoff continued on, actively looking for Susan, since he did not see anyone he knew.

The Morgan Garden Association, known locally as the MGA, was one of many such groups in the greater Morgan area. Each gated community had its own garden group, and a Deer Island group, made up exclusively of black members, started a club very similar to the MGA. Churches also had their garden clubs and the University sponsored a few as well. There were also quite a few people who belonged to more than one group but the

MGA stood above the rest. You had to be invited to be a member and reside in the downtown historic area. Over the years, managing its size proved to be a challenge as the region grew, since there was no way they could exclude residents such as the General and Sidney Lake, and they finally became racially integrated when a former executive vice president of Citibank in New York bought the largest home in the Ridge, planted the most elaborate native plant landscape in town and applied for membership. The object, subsequently, became keeping the Association exclusively one of local residents within a specific geographical area, which meant, for the most part, longtime residents. There were always exceptions to the "longtime" rule, of course, such as a few adventurous Northerners who chose to live in town and renovate an existing historical residence rather than opt for new construction and possibly a gate, and out of area Southerners, like Sidney Lake, who adopted Morgan as their home and were accepted as such. Membership then became one of social acceptability, heritage and economic standing rather than race, which is why Jenny and Louis Craig—of African-Caribbean ancestry—quickly became the most recent members of the garden club and fit the new member profile perfectly—especially as he was a retired partner of a major Chicago law firm.

Community involvement also played a major role in how outsiders were treated. The Northern invasion broke down invisible barriers simply because the newcomers didn't see them. Retirees in and around town were adopting local public schools, whose students were mostly black—the private Christian schools set up after segregation became illegal were still predominately populated by white students. There were mentoring programs everywhere and tutoring by retired school teachers who had taught in school systems from New Jersey to Illinois, seemed the norm. The new residents also became involved in Habitat for Humanity and set up competitions to see which gated community could build the most houses the fastest. For the new residents, joining MGA fit naturally into the new and emerging demographics of the town but not all the old members embraced the trend and some even felt threatened.

"Geoff" Susan called from the rear porch. "We're in here."

"Oh, good. I was hoping you were here already." Geoff walked over to the new deck at the rear of the house and greeted her with a kiss. "You look nice."

"Thank you. One thing we Southern girls know how to do is dress for a garden party." She did a quick twirl for him, which expanded the skirt of her blue and white flower print dress. "Come on in. Everyone's waiting."

"Ah, you're here," Sidney said as they entered. "I wanted to talk with everyone before General Brewster came back. We have about twenty minutes." The door from the deck opened into the kitchen and Sidney positioned himself on the inside lane of the island while Tillie, and Ray stood on the opposite side with their backs to the French doors that opened to the deck. Geoff and Susan joined them. Tillie and Ray acknowledged their presence with a wave and a smile.

"I wanted to speak with all of you before the guests arrived as I have a few specific tasks for each of you," Sidney continued. "As I mentioned on the phone, I believe I have uncovered the reason for George Reed's death. My problem is I'm not convinced that I actually know who killed him—"

"Sidney," Ray interrupted, "you know what we promised the Chief."

"Yes, I do, and everything we learn will be made available to him before the evening is out. Both he and his wife will be here. So let me explain what I need you all to do. The general has asked me to give a talk on the collection of books he inherited from his uncle. As you know, I have been helping him determine the value of the collection and to make sure none of them were stolen during the break-in that occurred one week ago today. My intention is to do that but to also make some controversial remarks relating to the connection between the theft of the painting from here last week and the death of George Reed on the following day."

Ray looked hard at Sidney, rolled his eyes, and shook his head.

Sidney ignored him. "What I would like each of you to do is to monitor a specific person and watch their reactions to the points I make, if you agree to do so. If you feel uncomfortable in any way, please say so. I'm not asking you to do anything, just let us know what the person's reaction is and especially if they don't react to something that everyone else in the room does. That's all I'm looking for. The local police don't have enough evidence to even put together comprehensive list of suspects, but I think I do. The trouble is it's all instinct and what I want to do is to give Chief Hornig a reason to focus in a specific direction."

"Miss Becky isn't on your list is she? 'Cause if she is, I got a problem."

"No Tillie, she's not."

Tillie relaxed her position that had stiffened as Sidney talked.

"Is everyone on board?" he asked

They all looked at one another and nodded their heads in agreement. "Long as I don't have to tackle anybody, sounds okay to me." Tillie chimed in, getting smiles all around.

"Ray?"

"I'll go along as long as you promise the chief is told everything before he leaves."

"That's my plan."

"Okay, but I still have my doubts."

"Understood. Now, before we run out of time, this is what I think will work. Tillie, I would like you to stay close to Caldwell Talbot and watch his reactions. I know you work for the Talbot's so I figured that would be a good match. Besides, you're a loyal South Carolinian so you're automatically on his good list."

"That's fine. Mr. Talbot can be a little strange at times but Miss Edith is a good lady, a nice lady. You think Mr. Talbot did something to Mr. Reed?"

"I didn't say that and please don't make any assumptions. Just let me know how he reacts when I make my comments."

"Okay."

"Susan. I'd like you to keep tabs on Jarvis Oliphant. Again, there's the South Carolina connection so small talk would be a normal thing to do. Geoff, I'd like you to hang around Denis Carson. I know you met him the other day over at the marina, so, again, there should be a comfort factor. Ray, if you could do *two* people for me: General Brewster and Chief Hornig. Like the others I need you to watch the general as I open up a can of worms and, as far as the chief is concerned, try to keep him under control and not let him interrupt what I'm doing. As I mentioned, he'll know everything I do in a short amount of time."

Ray still had the questioning look of earlier. "Sidney, remember that dinner you promised when you first got me involved? Well, there better be more than one. In fact, I can see a month's worth of them at this point."

"I'm serious," Sidney said.

"Who are all these people?" Geoff asked, looking over his shoulder.

There were now almost fifty people milling about the house, with most of them being inside.

"Geoff, I'll introduce you as we go along. You'll recognize some of them. Let's go inside, it looks like it might rain again," Susan said as she guided him through the open French doors that went into the great room from the deck

"This place is really something else," Geoff said on entering. While the exterior of Brewster's kept to its 1837 heritage, as dictated by the Historical Review Board of the City Architectural Department, the inside had been completely remodeled and updated to look like something out of *Southern Living* magazine. "I hadn't expected this."

"Lots of the houses in town have been redone inside." She walked toward the large fireplace in the middle of the wall as they entered.

"No," Geoff said, stopping. "Professor Lake said he wanted me near a door that exited the great room and onto the wrap around porch. He said it was near the entrance to the library."

"Oh, I guess he meant the door over there." She pointed to an area on the far side of the fireplace. The door filled the area between the window next to the fireplace and the corner wall. "The library is on the other side of the wall—the next room over. Did Professor Lake say what he wanted you to do?"

"He said he wanted me to take up the space in front of the door until I spotted Carson and then let him know."

"And that's it?"

"No, he also said something about possibly my running an errand later and then he would take over Carson."

Geoffrey purposely lowered his voice as two couples moved over to the fireplace near them.

"Do you have any idea what he's doing?" Susan now also spoke in a low tone.

"Not really, but I think it has something to do with Professor Ryan in England. Have you seen Lake recently?" Geoff surveyed the room and had difficulty seeing past the first ten feet in front of him as people moved back and forth, greeting one another.

"I saw him earlier in the kitchen. He was speaking with Chief Hornig."

"So Hornig is here."

"His wife is the treasurer of MGA. She was president a few years ago. They always come to MGA events, as do the Talbots. They're in the kitchen now. Look, there's Ray and his wife with my father."

"Oh, yeah." Geoff moved his head to get a better view. "But I don't see Lake. It sure looks like everyone else is here, though."

"I know he's here."

"Hey, isn't that the guy from the marina, Carson, the one I'm looking for?"

"Where?"

"See where the bar is set up on the counter that angles out from the wall, he's standing with a black couple."

Susan moved to her left to look around some guests, more and more of which were coming into the house as the sky suddenly began to darken and a soft rain began to fall. "I think you're right. I don't remember seeing him at one of these events before. Although that doesn't really mean anything, as with most couples, his wife is probably the member. Even if he's the main gardener in the family, he'll still make sure his wife is the primary name on the roster."

"Do they have things like this all the time?"

"A couple of times a year, aside from the flower shows and educational meetings. A good many of the members are Master Gardeners. I suppose there are some people who just belong for the social side of things."

"So I guess anybody who is anybody shows up?"

"And this time there will probably be a full turnout, except for anyone away on vacation for the summer. Lots of people have places in New England. Getting to see the inside of Brewster's is a big draw too. It hasn't been on the Fall house tour since Mrs. Brewster died. A lot of people haven't seen it since the restoration and renovation. Oh, look there, it's Professor Lake." Susan spotted him coming in the kitchen door from the back porch. The rear of the house had two exits: one from the kitchen, in the center of the back wall, and the other the French doors in the middle between the kitchen door and the right rear corner of the building. The breakfast room area was usually set up inside the French doors but the table and chairs had been removed to facilitate the traffic flow.

"I see him. Who's that he's with?"

"Looks like the people from a few doors down, the Gregory's, I think."

"Okay, do me a favor and hang around this door for me. I don't have the faintest idea why but I think it's time to find out."

"Okay."

"Thanks. Be back in a minute." He headed in the direction of Lake.

Susan stood where Geoff suggested for a few minutes and then then began looking for Jarvis Oliphant and his wife Helen. Along the way she stopped to say hello to Tillie who stood with Edith Talbot near the bar that was run by Tillie's nephew. There was another bar—run by her son-in-law—in the kitchen. The caterers set up the staging area in the butler's pantry—which contained a refrigerator, sink and oven and microwave—and Tillie would routinely rotate around the three points of the kitchen, butler's pantry and the great room to make sure everything ran smoothly, while always keeping either Miss Edith or Talbot in view.

General Lawrence Brewster stepped in front of the great room fireplace and faced the overflowing room of guests, many of whom were standing near the open French doors that led to the rear porch and deck. The soft rain stopped but very few guests ventured outside again. The general raised his glass and began tapping it with a spoon.

"Could I have your attention please?"

A few people in front stopped and faced him but others, especially near the doors, continued their chatter.

"Excuse me. Just a moment."

More success but still a good deal of chatter.

Then suddenly from the crowd came a booming voice: "LISTEN UP!" and the chatter stopped.

"Thank you," Brewster said, "and thank you, Colonel Santulli," he added, acknowledging the owner of the booming voice.

A few snickers and some good natured chuckling followed.

"We don't really have a formal program this evening, since this is just a thank you get together for having made this past season such a successful one, but the weather has forced us to make a few adjustments to my original plans. As most of you have already figured out, the liquid refreshments can be found in the kitchen as well as in here." A few more chuckles. "And a couple of Tillie's people are making the rounds with some rather interesting things to eat," Brewster continued. "I know that most of you are used to the food provided by Mandy Stone Catering, since she and her people have been fixtures at the

MGA gatherings for the past few years, but due to my error in scheduling, I didn't get her locked into for tonight in time, and she was booked for this weekend.

"However, Tillie James came to the rescue and, if you've tasted those little stuffed mushroom things, you'll know why we're not suffering much. However, if the weather continues to improve, we'll move out onto the deck as best we can." Brewster pointed. "Also, that tent or canopy—or whatever they call those things now days—isn't much use to us on the wet grass but Colonel Santulli, who, if you didn't know before, you probably do now—"

A few more chuckles and turning of heads.

"—has offered to arrange to move the tent so that it covers a good portion of the deck. That way I can have the food, which was supposed to be under the tent and now have planned to move under the cover of the porch, which is a little tight, moved off the porch and onto the deck when it's covered." Brewster cleared his throat. "Now, since we have a few minutes, and I would like to avoid having our good mayor and police chief—"

Heads turned toward the French doors where Peter Hornig was standing with a fairly short, rotund, red headed woman.

"—report us to the fire department for violating the occupancy laws, I've asked Professor Sidney Lake to help me out. You all know Sidney here." Brewster waved at the professor standing off to his right. "He's the one who grows those roses we all envy."

Some murmuring.

"As most of you know, a few weeks ago I inherited my uncle's collection of books. Uncle Sherman was an avid reader and collector of fiction, something I am not, being a student of history, and particularly military history," Brewster said with a bit of a smile, looking straight at Caldwell Talbot in the back of the room.

Tillie stood a few feet away near a table with empty glasses and plates on it. Caldwell, in return smiled back at Brewster and nodded his head in true gentlemanly fashion,

"And I've had both Jarvis Oliphant over there—" Brewster smiled, gesturing to the proprietor of The Previous Page and his wife standing near the entrance to the kitchen. Susan had been quietly speaking with Helen and stood a few paces behind her.

"—and Professor Lake here—" Brewster nodded to Sidney who stood beside him. "—take a look at what I've inherited. They have both told me that Uncle Sherman had very good taste. Well, Sidney has agreed to provide an overview of the collection and to make some comments on the authors, for those who are interested. What we'll do initially, is split up a bit so that those who would like to hear Sidney's take on the additions to my collection can move into the library with him as a way of thinning out the crowd in here."

More murmuring followed, with a number of interested parties walking ahead of Sidney as he began to move toward the Library.

"Anyone who would like to stay in here or, as the rain seems to have eased up a bit, would like to wander around the grounds and the garden," Brewster said, "you're welcome to do so. After all, this is supposed to be a garden party."

When Sidney looked over the people as they entered the library, he did not see any unexpected faces. He knew the members of the MGA who were the readers, chatted with them as they came in, and waved to others who were already there. Caldwell Talbot and his wife entered in the first group. Then came the Elliots, avid members of the Life Long Learning Program at USCB. Susan's parents, the Abbotts entered with the Oliphants, Jarvis and Helen. Dennis Carson, of the new marina, and his wife were followed by the Cunninghams of *The Times*. In all, at least twenty-five people quickly assembled and began milling about the library. In the great room, milling about also dominated the activity, when suddenly there was a tinkling of a glass again.

"One more thing." It was the general again. He'd managed to move over to the doorway to the library. "A number of people have been asking about Reverend Prentice and how he was doing, and I thought it would be easier if Ruth gave us an update so we wouldn't be pestering her all evening with questions. The fact that Ruth is here would certainly testify to things going well, but, Ruth, why don't you just come over here so the people in both rooms can hear?"

He motioned for her to stand where he was, which she did, and he then moved to the side. There were more people in the library now than in the great room so she moved herself fully into the room but tried to position herself close to the doorway in order to deal with both rooms. Some of the people in the library moved over to the door to listen, which made everything more congested.

"Thank you, Larry. I don't mean to make a big thing out of this. You've all been so kind. I just wanted you all to know that Cal is coming along very well. He has been heavily sedated and is now on some heavy pain medication but, finally, seems to be getting back to his old self and, no, thankfully, he wasn't really in a coma as some had feared."

The local rumor mill had been off and running again.

"He's awake off and on since the fall, thanks to the pain medication which makes him drop off from time to time."

A number of people were whispering to one another to the effect of "*What happened*?"

"But yesterday morning, the doctors felt he was out of the woods, as they say. His head is banged up a bit, his shoulder is broken, and he has a sprained wris, but it looks as though they're all going to be okay as well. Interestingly, he said that, during the time he was knocked out, he remembered dreaming about his sermons."

"Maybe that's why he slept so long," exclaimed a voice with a strong Southern accent from the crowd in the library, causing a burst of laughter and bringing a smile to Ruth's face.

"Ruth, what exactly happened?" came another voice, this one from the region of the library doorway.

"It's rather complicated, and I really don't know the full story, other than it appears that while Cal was accompanying Becky Reed home, they ran into an intruder in the house and, during his escape, he knocked Cal down the stairs."

The room grew quiet, followed by low murmuring again as everyone started talking to one another. Ruth looked around nervously. The time seemed endless but no more than five seconds passed.

"Oh, how terrible, did you know about this?" Helen Oliphant whispered to Susan.

Susan nodded her head and mouthed the word "Yes."

"Did you say Cal was pushed down some stairs?" one of the people in the doorway asked.

"That's what I was told, yes. I wasn't there."

"And you say he's all right?"

"Yes." Ruth paused and motioned to the library group to stay where they were. "Oh, don't press closer, I'll speak up." She raised her voice. "Both Sidney Lake and Allen Cunningham know the whole story, and I'm sure they can tell you what happened. I just wanted to thank you all for your prayers and your expressions of comfort and caring."

At this point, a number of people came forward and started talking quietly to Ruth. Sidney, seeing the opportunity to grab back the Library room's attention, spoke up from his position by the door. "Perhaps I'd better explain. I thought this would come at some point in the evening, and I suppose now is as good a time as any."

Allan Cunningham, editor of *The Morgan Times* also took the opportunity to chime in. "For those of you who did not read the paper this morning, we did cover the break-in and did have a story about it. Sidney, since you were there, why don't you explain what happened, provide us with a firsthand account?"

"Please do, Sidney. You probably know as much about this as anyone," a voice in the small crowd suggested.

"Yes, it's true I was at the Reeds' on Thursday evening. Reverend Prentice and I were there, during that awful storm, to keep Becky company while she picked up overnight bags. Becky and her daughter Amanda had decided to spend the night with the Prentices. Based on some information that Ray Morton and I had uncovered, we had convinced her that it would not be advisable to stay at home that evening, as there was the possibility that George Reed's murderer might do exactly what he did, only we had anticipated that he would wait until Ruth and Amanda had gone away—"

"Just a moment, Sidney," Cunningham interrupted. "I don't recall any police report indicating that George Reed was murdered. In fact, I still haven't seen one." He looked around for the police chief as he spoke, but Hornig remained in the other room with Ray Morton at his side. "As far as I know," Cunningham continued, "I don't believe there has been an official report issued about the intruder at Reeds' on Thursday night. Cal Prentice's fall was never formally listed as an attack. Isn't George Reed's death still listed as an accident?"

Everyone in both rooms tried to hear every word being said and kept moving closer.

"I don't think so."

"Might I ask who told you otherwise?"

Dead silence in the room now.

"I believe that the true nature of the investigation has finally come out. I spoke with Chief Hornig here earlier. I'm quite sure he's still here somewhere."

Susan knew, for sure, that something was going on, since she had seen Lake and Hornig talking earlier. She also now realized that she had lost contact with Geoff, who disappeared after a brief meeting with Professor Lake, and she hadn't seen him standing in his assigned position by the door to the side porch when she came into the library.

The slight murmur in the crowd grew louder.

"Do they know who did it?" asked an unidentified voice from the crowd.

Sidney shook his head. "If they do, they have not said so."

"Sidney, why do I have the feeling you know something?" Cunningham asked. "How did you get involved in all of this?"

"In answer to the first part of your question, yes, you could say I know something. In answer to the second part, I've had my suspicions that something wasn't right ever since I learned about the nature of the tidal effects in the area where George Reed was found."

"So what happened?"

❧❧❧

Shit, they did put it together. Warren, standing next to

his wife, moved slightly away from her. *But why haven't they approached me? It has to mean they know something happened but they still haven't a clue who they're looking for. They're expecting whoever did it will try to make a run for it. Got to stay cool. They don't have anything on me.*

Ray stood next to Chief Hornig. "I guess Sidney's not on your 'good' list at the moment?" he whispered.

"I told him to open the can of worms," Hornig whispered back. "We found a skiff with bits of blood and hair imbedded in the wood. Expect it will be Reeds'. Also running the serial number on the small engine. Don't want to officially say anything yet. Someone in the room probably has some answers for us. Have some uniforms outside on the excuse of traffic control."

"Motive? And who?"

"Not yet, but soon. Cover for me. I need to become invisible for a little while."

Chapter 21

"Yes, go ahead, Sidney,. The chief and I will have a chat later," Cunningham said, the implication being that Hornig had broken the agreement of openness between the two, in that the chief was supposed to trust the editor and they would work together in deciding what would be appropriate to be published in *The Times* with regard to a sensitive, ongoing investigation.

"Go ahead, tell us what happened, Sidney," another voice chimed in.

"Keep talkin', Sidney. Might make for an interestin' story," Caldwell Talbot called out from his position at the entrance to the library from the front hall.

As everyone moved closer to Sidney at the entrance to the library from the great room, Caldwell went in the other direction where there was much more room to spread out. Miss Edith followed him and Tillie made as though she would head for the kitchen through the front hall and then stopped at the front door.

Sidney, seeing that Caldwell changed positions decided that it would be good for him to do so as well. "I think Caldwell has the right idea. Let's all shift into the library, as we've already moved a good deal of the furniture out so I could give my book talk. It should give us some more room and relieve some of the crowding pressure." He made his way through the guests that had gathered around the doorway and positioned himself behind some of the remaining furniture in the room—one of a pair of wing chairs, separated by a small table—and watched his audience assemble.

He waited for everyone to adjust and settle down in the room. He also checked on the locations of Tillie and Susan and made sure he knew where Dennis Carson stood and with whom. He knew Ray had Hornig under control and the general continued to stand by the door with Ruth Prentice.

Sidney then began again. "It is an interesting story, Caldwell, most interesting. So how did I get involved? Well, I have a friend, who will be nameless, who disliked the unfair gossip that developed after the report of the death of George Reed. You may recall that George Reed's death was declared an accidental drowning and the general inference taken from *The Times* story—" He looked directly at Cunningham as he spoke and placed his hands on the top of the back of the chair., "—was that a) George was alone, b) he had been drinking—that was not specifically mentioned but it is a fact that it is something that he, unfortunately, was noted for—and c) he simply lost his footing and fell overboard, hitting his head in some manner and drowning, a simple but tragic accident that no one really seemed to question. The truth, however, seems to have been quite different, as both Chief Hornig and Steele Wilcox will attest." He continued to look at Cunningham who did not object to the analysis, although the editor clearly ran the report through his head and tried to remember exactly what his paper reported and what it didn't.

"Our gossip problem begins," Sidney continued, "and

keep in mind there is no basis for any of it other than being pure malicious speculation. Our coroner, Steele Wilcox, is a close friend of the Reeds and the words *cover up* unjustly came into play. Also, George and Becky, on occasion, had somewhat public arguments over his, what we might call, inappropriate use of alcoholic beverages."

A side comment or two was made from the assembled listeners.

"There were even a few unfounded suggestions that George Reed lost his footing in the boat during a heated interchange with his wife and just fell overboard and she left him to fend for himself, while she returned to the sandbar in the boat."

More murmuring.

"I feel quite comfortable mentioning all of this as there is no basis in fact for any of it and it's definitely not what happened that afternoon on the Morgan River. As many people can attest, Rebecca Reed is a good woman of strong and impeccable character. My friend, having heard some of these comments that I have just outlined, asked if I would inquire through my contacts at city hall what the actual details of the accident were, the newspaper story being somewhat limited. My friend was particularly interested in obtaining irrefutable proof that an accident did occur and that her friend, Mrs. Reed, could not possibly have been involved."

At this point Tillie stood straight and tall in the front hallway and gave her head a small affirmative nod.

"Confident of the outcome, it seemed a relatively simple task, and I agreed to find out the information on her behalf."

The reactions of a number of people listening to Sidney's explanation confirmed that the gossip was well known to them. Susan continued to stay close to Helen and Jarvis Oliphant, although now she had two people between her and Miss Helen, but she could still see them clearly.

"The problem I ran into, however, is a simple one," Sidney continued. "The job of the police is to pursue and find the presumed guilty and not to spend their time confirming anyone's innocence. In other words, they are not in the business of proving that someone did not do something evil or illegal but the very opposite. As a result, I didn't come away with much more than the original story reported in *The Times*. But suddenly, my friend, who had started me down my inquiry road, advised me that *she* had obtained irrefutable proof that her friend, who is obviously Mrs. Reed, could not have been involved.

"Now having been dragged into this, where I ran into one dead end after another, and the authorities had no evidence to say that any particular person was not involved, I wanted to know what irrefutable evidence she had obtained. And so I was introduced to a Mr. Daniel Doyle. You must understand I am not a boater, as many of you know."

A few snickers and comments were made to one another. When taking a ride in a friend or colleague's boat, everyone knew Sidney usually held on for dear life when getting on or off and then positioned his chair, in which he sat immediately, so that he could not see the wake or feel any of the spray. One might wonder why he would bother to go out on the water at all but Sidney, although he could be a royal pain from time to time, enjoyed a day out with his friends and colleagues, except for the racing around in the boat part, and they in turn enjoyed him.

"The water is all very nice to look at. When the tide is in, it looks as though we all live on a large lake and, when it is out, we are on a large grouping of small streams. It's all very pretty but that's about as far as my interest goes. Mr. Doyle, however, has spent all of his eighty-plus years boating and fishing every inch of the lowcountry. I've been advised that there isn't a spot around Morgan that he doesn't know intimately, and there is no one more knowledgeable of how the tide moves and shapes every inch of the marshland. Mr. Doyle was very pleased to explain to me that, given the location of the sandbar from which Mrs. Reed was rescued from the rising tide, the location where they found the empty boat in which George Reed took his afternoon ride, and the location to where the body of George Reed drifted, the possibility of Mrs. Reed returning to the sandbar without her husband and just letting the Reed's boat drift away from the sandbar, just couldn't happen, as the rising tide would have pushed it in the opposite direction."

A woman's voice could be heard saying, "I knew it. I told you so." She stared directly at her husband and had a look of vindication on her face.

Sidney paused briefly. "Also, there is no possibility that she could have left the boat out in the channel and then swam to the sandbar, since she would have been going against the tide during its strongest movement of the day. In effect, completely clearing Mrs. Reed of any and all malicious gossip concerning her involvement, which was why my friend no longer needed my assistance.

"I should say that I found Mr. Doyle to be a delightful gentleman and spent some additional time with him discussing his understanding of various aspects of the tides and their history of continually changing the dynamics of the different parts of the marsh. Then, just as I was about to leave, he made the remarkable statement that George Reed didn't fall from *his* boat at the location where he was found. In fact, Reed's boat couldn't have made it into the location because it drew more than twelve inches and Reed's body could not have drifted in to that same location because the water mainly comes into that area through a spot in deep reeds and grass. The only way George Reed could have arrived, in what we have begun to call Doyle's hole, was in a flat bottomed boat that drew no more than three or four inches."

Some heads were seen nodding and Sidney, in the absence of Geoff, kept an eye on Dennis Carson whose head nodded with the others.

"If he was alone in that small boat, it would have been there when he was found, as it would have been impossible for it to drift out on its own. If someone was with him, then that someone watched him drown and then left."

Some people began talking to one another. Susan kept trying to secretly watch Jarvis, and Tillie made a point of going in front of Caldwell toward a large tray with empty glasses on it.

"My understanding is that the police did suspect something but decided not to make it public." The latter statement was made at the suggestion of Ray Morton and Chief Hornig when they conferenced with Sidney an hour earlier and Cunningham could be seen making a mental note of the fact to include in his discussion with the Chief later in the day.

"Why didn't Doyle tell someone? Let the police know? Why did he just go on letting people think it was an accident when he clearly knew it wasn't?" The aggressive question came from Martin Woods, a recent transplant from Harrisburg, Pennsylvania, who had retired last year from a forty year banking career and purchased a home on the golf course at Quail Hollow Estates.

"Good question, Martin. However, as I too am not originally from this area, the answer to that question, as to why a local black man might not be inclined to volunteer information to the police and why such an inaction would not be looked upon as being unusual in this part of the country, requires an historical as well as cultural explanation. If he would, the answer or explanation might best be provided by Allan Cunningham here of *The Morgan Times* who has lived his entire life in and around Morgan and, perhaps, could educate many of us on the subject." Again playing the political game, Sidney felt this would give Cunningham the opportunity to look like an insider, as though he too knew there was something amiss. Sidney had learned well the need for saving face in a small Southern town.

"Very interesting, Sidney. Yes, I suppose I could make a comment to that effect, although I know that many of you already know the answer but for the benefit of some of our more recent residents, I can see where it might be a little puzzling," Cunningham began. "Actually, it's both easy and difficult to understand. Most of the people of the islands in the lowcountry trace their history back hundreds of years. Doyle's reaction is certainly understandable. He would have grown up here in the 'thirties and 'forties and learned very quickly that he was an inhabitant of two very different worlds, and to a large degree those worlds still exist, one white and one black. If a white man dies under any kind of suspicious circumstances, you don't voluntarily put a black face in the picture."

"Even today?"

"Martin," Allan continued, "you have to understand that there is not a black person born here who doesn't know of a relative or a friend that was either killed, beaten, or imprisoned simply because of the color of their skin. If a black man were to be walking down Main Street in the evening, and he saw a police car coming his way, his instincts are to make himself as inconspicuous as possible."

The Craigs, the only black couple in the room and one of three couples in the garden group who retired here to a gated community, were suddenly very visible.

"The truth is the slaves may have been given their freedom more than 150 years ago but they were never really freed. They were just no longer owned. Freedom didn't really begin here and, in most of the rural South, until the 1960s and, in most of the smaller towns, it's still a work in progress. For many of us who have lived here all our lives and have worked very hard to be inclusive in everything that goes on in this area, it can be a very frustrating process. We have black churches and white churches, not because any church door is closed to a member of any race. There isn't a preacher from a white church in town—or black for that matter—that wouldn't be absolutely overjoyed at having local members in their congregation of a different race.

"Although some of the white churches do have black members, they were probably not born and raised here. The black members of the local Episcopal, Baptist, Presbyterian, Catholic, Methodist, you name it, were members of those churches elsewhere. We have a Greater Morgan Chamber of Commerce—that does have a few black members—but we also have a Deer Island Chamber of Commerce that is made up of black business people. We have the Morgan Art Guild that is mainly made up of white artists but we also have the Island Artist Association which is exclusively black. Even with the college, where we've made great strides at the undergraduate level with the younger generation but in the continuing education and especially the lifelong learning program, where mature adults are involved, there is a history of exclusion, both voluntary and involuntary, that's difficult to overcome.

"There are no official restrictions that would stop anyone in Morgan from belonging to any mainstream organization and, believe me, the organizations and clubs have tried over and over to expand but with very little success. All of this boils down to a trust issue. The black community knows from experience that everything and everyone is equal, until there's trouble. And then you're on your own.

"The social divisions here are not very different than they were forty years ago, except that they are voluntary—sort of—but that's a more delicate topic. We are doing our best to provide true equality but, for the most part, anyone in authority is not completely trusted and, given the history of the police with the island people, with good reason. For Doyle not to come forward voluntarily is not all that surprising. In all honesty, with the history he has experienced personally, I probably wouldn't either. So, no, George Reed's death is a white man's problem. Which brings me back to Sidney here, I assume the police are aware of Doyle's comments?"

The room was completely quiet. No comments now. Not even the shaking of heads.

Sidney nodded. "Yes they are. Everything I've said so far has been told to them by either me or Ray Morton or they have uncovered it on their own, and my understanding is they have now brought their investigation completely out into the open, so that all of the four crimes that are now linked with the death of George Reed are now under full investigation as one incident."

"Four crimes?" a tall dark haired man, whom Sidney did not know, asked.

"Yes, four. The murder of George Reed was number two. The reason for the murder was crime number one, and I'll get to that in a minute. Number three was the break-in at Roots and Rakes, the Reed's gardening business, on the day of his funeral—which many of you are familiar with—and included the attack on Geoffrey Van Horst, who works for Roots and Rakes and is also attending USCB. The fourth, of course, is the break-in at the Reed home where both Reverend Prentice and Mrs. Reed were injured.

"Why break into a landscape business like Roots and Rakes?" Sidney asked rhetorically. "A good question. There certainly isn't much there to steal and since George Reed's death, at the time, was certified as an accident, there was no reason to believe there was a connection. The police initially put it down to a drug-related break in of a business that was closed. A very logical conclusion. However, there was something there that would be of great interest to explore by the murderer of George Reed."

He paused and looked over the room. He had everyone's attention. General Brewster, Chief Hornig, and Ray Morton were also now in the room standing by the entrance coming from the great room.

"You're right about there not being much to steal," Woods finally said to break the silence. "Although—" Attention turned to him. "—he did have that dark room in there. He showed it to me once. He had cameras and stuff in there."

"Exactly," Sidney agreed. "As many of you may know, George's first love was nature photography. He maintained a dark room at Roots and Rakes and, as best Geoff and the police can determine, Geoff was attacked by someone who was hiding in that room."

"But what were they looking for?" inquired Woods again.

"Let me come back to that also, but first let's move on to crime number four, the attack at the Reed's home." Sidney looked at Woods, raised the index finger of his right hand, and shook it ever so slightly, an act that Geoff knew well, as he had seen him do it on numerous occasions in a classroom setting, when Sidney wanted to stay on a particular subject and take his thought process to its conclusion. "This is the interruption of the murderer that Ruth Prentice referred to a few moments ago. Becky Reed and Cal Prentice were attacked at the Reed's home on Wednesday evening during that terrible storm that came roaring through town. I was sitting in the car outside waiting for them. Where is our connection here? First of all, it was determined that George Reed's computer, that is located in his den, had been turned on and the intruder was apparently searching for something when we drove up. You will recall that the storm had made the evening particularly dark. Seeing our lights, he ran upstairs and hid in an empty bedroom. But why would he be interested in George Reed's computer? I have since learned that the main use of that computer was for the editing of the digital photos that George Reed took and it contained a complete catalogue of his work—"

"Mr. Lake," the tall dark man interrupted again, "are you saying that George Reed's photography had something to do with his death?"

"I'm saying it is the primary reason for the four crimes. You'll have to forgive me but I'm afraid I don't know your name."

General Brewster stepped forward from off to the left of where the professor was standing. "Sidney, this is Howard Springwood, a good friend of the family from Charlotte."

"Of Springwood and Reynolds?" Sidney said, "Yes, we've spoken on the phone."

"Yes," Howard said.

"Ah, but let me get back to your question. Yes, photography is the key. Whoever killed George Reed did it because of some photographs George had taken. It is believed George Reed was lured to what we now call Doyle's hole by someone he knew; that he transferred to that person's boat, a flat bottomed one; and was murdered while he was taking pictures of an eagle's nest located above that location. I don't know if the murder was accidental or intentional as, quite frankly, that's irrelevant to the late George Reed. I am, however, reasonably certain that George Reed had no idea why he was attacked."

The room now buzzed with a low volume of conversation and comments. Martin Woods spoke up again. "But how is that possible?"

"To answer that we must go back to crime number one."

ↇↃↇↃ

Warren listened attentively as Sidney spoke in the library. He didn't panic but his heart raced as the events of the past five days were peeled back like the leaves of an artichoke in an effort to get to the center. The bit about the tide stumped him. He had no idea there was a hole where George died. He just assumed everyone would think the body drifted in there when the tide went out. He then rationalized that it really didn't make any difference, anyway, as there was still no way to connect him to anything.

And they still didn't have the pictures. The skiff was empty. There was nothing in it to connect to him and, even if there was, the storm would have washed everything clean. As long as the pictures and camera never showed up, they had nothing to even remotely connect him to anything.

With a hint of a smile now on his face, he moved back next to his wife and continued to listen to Sidney. Out of the corner of his eye, he spotted Chief Hornig, Ray Morton, and Steel Wilcox quietly and seriously talking together. *I'd love to know what they're talking about.*

Chapter 22

Interestingly enough," Sidney continued, "crime number one occurred here in this house."

Brewster, who'd dropped back into the great room to speak with Tillie's nephew, as he wanted to see about setting up an additional bar area in the library, moved back to the entrance of the library just as Sidney finished his last comment. He leaned into the room. "Here? You mean the break in last Saturday?"

"The very same."

Almost everyone had questions written on their faces and seemed mystified. They spoke among themselves while trying to get a glimpse of General Brewster, who was now fully in the room. The local paper never carried a report of the theft, and many of the people in the room knew nothing of the robbery.

Cunningham did not appear happy and the tone in his voice showed it. "But what do they have to do with one another? Why in the world would someone break into this house and a landscape business and what in the world does it all have to do with George Reed?"

The room quieted down, although some movement continued around the doorway. The editor had just asked the question they were all trying to formulate,

"A most appropriate question, Allen, and the very crux of the puzzle. If you recall the sequence of events last Sunday, when George Reed died, some of you who were at the eleven o'clock service at Bay View Presbyterian may remember that Becky Reed came to church by herself, without George, and why? After the service, while much of the congestion stood around the refreshment table under the magnolia tree, she apologized for her missing husband by explaining that he had been out until three in the morning on one of his midnight photographic expeditions in the marsh. Becky knew it was three because that was when she awoke to his fumbling around in the dark, and then she had difficulty getting back to sleep, which prompted her nap on the sandbar. George, on the other hand, slept until after eleven on Sunday morning and was not the least bit tired Sunday afternoon, hence the ride in his boat while his wife slept."

"Of course!" Martin Woods exclaimed, becoming obviously excited. "Reed was taking pictures in the dark Saturday night and got a picture of Brewster's thief with the painting, which is why he dropped it. Reed spooked him and he ran."

"Yes, that's it," said another.

"He got a picture of the thief," came another voice.

"What painting?" an elderly gentleman in a dark blue suit said to his wife.

She sat next to him on a sofa perpendicular to the wing chairs where Sidney held court. "The painting that was stolen from here." She patted his hand. "Don't worry, I'll tell you all about it later."

"So we're back to the drug addicts again," Cunningham said. He stood with his wife, who was the Morgan Garden Association member in the family, just to the right of the sofa and near the fireplace.

"Well, they weren't art collectors," Brewster said, with a laugh. "That painting wasn't worth more than a couple of hundred dollars. Fact is, the frame is probably worth more than the picture."

Suddenly three or four separate conversations erupted in the room, with people commenting with their immediate neighbors on Sidney's theory of George Reed's death. A number of people started talking about the drug problem in town.

Some others made comments about "…those kind of people."

Finally, Mary Cunningham, the editor's wife said to Sidney, "So do the police have any idea who might have done it?"

"Have they figured all this out like you have?" another guest inquired.

Sidney stood quietly for a moment, letting the multiple of speculative conversations go on, and then he began again but ignored the last question. "There are a few problems with the conclusions I've heard a number of you make. First: I believe George Reed knew his killer, which would negate the theory of the random break-in being done by local drug addicts." He hoped Susan and Tillie were still in contact with Talbot and Oliphant as, in all the confusion and, with the side comments being made, he lost Dennis Carson, didn't see him anywhere. "You see, George died in a place in the marsh where his boat could not reach because of its size. He had to transfer to another smaller one provided by someone he knew. That someone also knew there was an eagle's nest in that location that George would be anxious to see. This was the bait for George to bring along his camera. Also, the murderer knew from Becky that morning after church, as the congregation mingled under that magnolia tree, that she and George would be on that sandbar Sunday afternoon. That may also indicate that our murderer may be a member of Bay View Presbyterian Church."

A few gasps were heard.

"Secondly, it is extremely likely that George Reed had no idea that he had taken a picture of our thief since he was focusing on the wildlife that would be in the foreground. Our thief may also have realized this same fact when they met in the marsh last Sunday and George made no mention of the previous evening."

"So your saying George Reed not only knew his murderer but that person may also have been a friend?" questioned the editor.

"Oh, my," exclaimed the woman on the sofa.

"What was that?" said her husband.

"I'm afraid so, Allen" Sidney agreed.

Just then Ray Morton peeked into the room and waved to Sidney. "There isn't much more I can say at the moment," Sidney continued. "This is where the authorities are in their investigation, although I understand they have some strong leads and—as they currently say—persons of interest. I'm sure our good editor here will have an update in the *Times* tomorrow and I'm sure all of this will be sorted out and come to a conclusion quite soon." He wanted to close out his talk and find out what was going on in the adjourning room but people kept posing questions to him as he tried to get to the door. "I'm sure *The Times* will have much more information in tomorrow's edition."

Allen Cunningham now had his phone to his ear and talked quietly over in a corner by the front window.

When Sidney finally reached the doorway, Ray leaned over and whispered, "Hornig's got Carson cornered in the kitchen. You might want to get his ear. They identified the motor on that skiff as possibly belonging to him. It's recorded in the marina's service log. "

While the library now buzzed with activity punctuated by speculation driven conversation, the great room continued it's socializing around the food and drinks. Sidney and Ray made their way through the milling crowd until they saw Chief Hornig and another man in serious conversation with Dennis Carson. Spotting Sidney, Hornig immediately came over to him.

"Thanks, Sidney, your planned string of revelations spooked three people in the library in addition to Carson here, but we're following all of them."

"Glad I could be of help. You know, I'm becoming convinced that our thief was not really interested in murder. George Reed's death may have been an unintended outcome of the thief's desire to get the camera that could hold the incriminating evidence." Sidney then went back over in more detail what Susan Abbott had discovered at Doyle's hole and described it more fully. He placed great emphasis on how the murderer would have enticed George Reed to the spot where he could take pictures of the recently hatched eaglets. "I believe the object here was to, in some way, get possession of Reed's camera or accidentally destroy it. It is very possible that our thief's original plan was to *accidentally* push George Reed out of the boat while he was holding the camera, since I'm willing to give our thief friend the benefit of the doubt. However, I believe the plan went terribly wrong when Reed's sure-footed-ness made it clear to him the intentions of his friend. Reed's fall from the boat then became tragic when he hit his head on something made of wood, presumably a submerged log, an event confirmed by the coroner."

"Not so sure about that, Sid, I think the murdered knew he was in a corner and felt he had no choice," Ray said, while also checking the expression on the chief's face.

"Possibly, but I still think our thief now panicked, quickly left the scene, and headed back to the Reed's boat, where it was anchored, retrieved the anchor, and set it adrift, never realizing the unique nature of the place he killed Reed."

"But, Sidney," Brewster, who followed them to the kitchen, declared, "if our thief destroyed the camera Reed was using, why the other break-ins?"

"Good point. I believe that when George Reed went overboard, being the professional photographer, his first instinct would be to save the camera, which he probably tossed into the boat. The problem, as our thief later learned, is that the camera is the digital one that George always kept on the boat for taking *opportunity* pictures, such as an eagle flying by. The camera he used at night and for many of his wildlife studies is a thirty-five millimeter one. At first, our thief thought he was in the clear but when he reviewed the images on the digital camera's memory stick—he had taken from the camera that George threw into the boat—there were no pictures of the night before. In fact, there were no night photography pictures at all. So, either he had the wrong camera or the memory stick had been changed."

"So are there pictures or not?" said Hornig, whose phone buzzed continually as he talked.

"Oh, there are pictures, all right. Just before I began my little talk, Geoff called Susan to tell her he had to go on an urgent errand for Becky Reed—I tried to find you both but you were not in the room and Ruth Prentice just handed everything over to me unexpectedly. You see, George had actually shot three rolls of thirty-six pictures each on Saturday night. He intended to go to the dark room at Roots and Rakes on late Sunday afternoon after he and Becky returned from the sandbar. He had the film with him but not on him. The undeveloped film that he shot the night before he died, I just found out, is in Becky Reed's beach bag that she kept with her on the sandbar."

"Is it still there? said Hornig."

"Possibly. I'm waiting for Geoff to call back. When he got the call from Becky Reed—his number was the only one of ours she had on her cell phone—Geoff couldn't find me so he took off on his own for the Reeds' and called Susan from his truck."

Just then Susan came rushing over to Sidney with her cell phone extended. "It's Geoff."

"Geoff. It's Lake."

"I've got them and I'm on my way to police headquarters. Won't take me more than five minutes."

Sidney relayed the message to the chief and Ray. "He said he found the film and he's on his way to the police station."

"Let me talk to him." The phone changed hands.

"Geoff, Chief Hornig, hand them directly to Captain Schwartz. He'll be waiting for you. There'll also be a car heading in your direction from here to give you an escort if you need it. Don't stop for anything. What are you driving?"

"Blue Ford pick-up with a Roots and Rakes sign on the door." As Geoff answered Ray wrote the information down and waved to the detective standing next to Carson.

"Thanks, Geoff. Don't stop for anyone on the way in, even if you know them."

"Agreed."

Hornig handed the phone back to Susan.

"I'll tell Millar," Ray said, meaning the detective with Carson.

Hornig then turned to Sidney. "So when did all this happen?"

"Just a few minutes ago. Becky's in Charlotte and would have called you direct but didn't have a Morgan police number with her but did have Geoff's since he worked for her. Said she realized the film never left her bag on Sunday. With all the confusion, she merely dropped the bag in the garage where she usually left it. When she talked to Geoff, she also gave him the access code for the garage, told him where to find the bag, and he just went in, picked it up, and took off. This will, of course, come as a surprise to our thief who took those two rolls of undeveloped film he found in Reeds' den, which will have pictures of raccoons on them."

The chief nodded. "The problem is that, unlike digital pictures, the film has to be developed, which I assume the crook wouldn't do in town, for fear of being detected. He may still not know he took the wrong film."

"Just as a curiosity, Chief, where will you develop the film? I assume you don't have a photo lab anymore." As Sidney spoke, Tillie's nephew suddenly appeared at his elbow and just stood there.

"Never had one. Always used the county's but theirs got the budget axe so we either send it off to the state lab if we need something, or if we're in a real rush we go to a local professional photographer. Actually, in this case— being Saturday—Captain Schwartz will take it over to Walgreens down the street, and the manager will run them through their equipment and make up a disk for us. Won't take more than ten or fifteen minutes."

"So it's just a matter of time then," General Brewster said. "Good. But you know there's something that doesn't make sense about all this and that's the stealing of one of my paintings by someone who was supposed to be a friend of George Reed, or at least someone who was acquainted with him. I mean, as far as I know, George didn't hang around with drug addicts—unless the con- gregation at Bay View Presbyterian has changed recent- ly—but then we seem to have discounted the drug connection anyway, so how does he know the thief?"

"Excuse me, just a minute, General. Chief, you said three people left the library in the confusion and you're watching them, who are they?"

"Talbot, Woods, and Oliphant.

"What about Carson?"

"He's right over—Where the hell is he? Where's Millar?"

"I think he headed out to meet Geoff," Ray said. "Come on, Chief, I'll check the grounds."

"Okay, I'll do the parking area." They both took off in different directions. The chief frantically dialing again.

"Mr. Lake," said the young man next to him. "Aunt Tillie told me to stay close to you, just in case you needed someone to help with anything. I won't get in the way but I wanted you to know I was here."

Sidney gave him a quick look and noticed he had taken off his apron. He stood just under six feet and appeared extremely physically fit. Tillie had mentioned in passing earlier that he was the one with the football scholarship to Clemson. At that moment, Tillie made her way into the room from the library and headed for him.

"Professor Lake, Susan said to tell you that Mr. Oliphant seemed to receive a phone call just as you finished, said something to his wife, and then left in a hurry."

"What do you mean *seemed to* receive a phone call?"

"Susan said she was standing right behind him and she never heard anything ring or buzz."

"What the hell's going on?" Brewster said.

"If you'd like to drive, I'd be more than happy to explain it all on the way."

"You're on."

"You're not leaving me here," Susan said. "Geoff said where you go I go."

"Bobby goin' too," Tillie said. "You may need him."

"Okay. But let's get going."

Chapter 23

Hornig made one call after the next as he made his way along Brewster's driveway.

"Hey, Chief, there's Carson." Ray called from behind him.

"Where?" he said, looking up from his phone."

"In front of you."

Carson, seeing the Chief, gave a wave and immediately came toward him, to the Chief's as well as Ray's, surprise.

Hornig quickly shut down his phone and put it away. "Dennis, where'd you go?"

"Left my phone in the car, just went out to get it. What's up?"

Ray arrived at his side. "We still had a couple of questions for you."

"Oh, sorry. When Millar left, I thought you were all through. No problem, what else do you need to know?"

"Your logo. You put it on some rain suits?"

"Yeah, great advertising, real practical for using on a boat too—mix two of my passions: golf and boating."

"Well, it was identified as being on the rain suit the attacker wore at Reeds'."

"You're kidding, somebody was wearing one of my rain suits?" Carson paused while Ray and the Chief both looked at him and didn't speak. Carson held up his hands. "Hey, don't look at me. I just sell the damn things. I don't push people down the stairs in them."

"How many *have* you sold?" Ray said, moving from in front of Carson to his side.

"Gee, I don't know, just got them in a couple of weeks ago. Maybe three—maybe four."

"Know who bought them?"

"I could easily look it up."

"Is there any other way someone could get one of them?" Hornig asked.

"Gave some of them to the workers at the marina."

"You use one?"

"Sure, of course."

"Anyone else you can think of?"

"Lemme think." Carson paused. Now nervous, he spoke quickly. "Wait a minute, Rotary. Made an announcement at Rotary. Gave a little talk about buying Bubba's marina and changing the name. Told them how I was going to do things different, told them about my new Book Buy or Trade program for boaters going up and down the coast. Raffled off five of them for Rotary. Proceeds to go to their 'End Polio' fund. Hey, these suits are a great idea. Great for working on a boat in the rain down here. They're lightweight, easy to move your arms and walk around, easy to get on and off. Everybody with a boat should have one."

"Okay, I'm sold. I'll make sure I get one from you," Hornig said, "but is there a record of the people who received rain suits?"

They were all momentarily distracted as a large SUV cut across the nearby lawn. Ray recognized it as Brewster's and watched it as it made its way to the street.

"Pretty sure Rotary knows," Carson continued. "I can think of a couple off hand: Martin Woods for one, and I'm pretty sure Father Jon, you know the retired Episcopal priest, won one." He nervously thought for another moment as the SUV disappeared from sight. "And Jarvis, yeah, I'm pretty sure Jarvis Oliphant got one."

"Jarvis?' Are you sure?"

"Yeah, definitely Jarvis. He does some fishing now and again in that little skiff of his."

"I thought he didn't like the water," Ray said.

"Maybe so, but he sure likes fresh fish."

Ray's phone chimed. He gave it a quick look and read the text from Susan. He then gave Hornig a look and pulled him aside. "Sidney went after Jarvis. That was them in Brewster's car"

"Shit!"

෴

Brewster maneuvered the car down his driveway and onto River Road. Sidney sat up front with Susan and Bobby in the back of the Lincoln Navigator.

"Where to and what's going on?"

"Oliphant's store. If Ray and the chief don't find Carson around the house and grounds, I'm sure they'll be on their way to the marina. I'm pretty sure those were the instructions I heard the chief giving on his phone as they left."

"The store is about ten blocks from here. So explain."

The primary shopping and tourist street—Main Street—stood directly between the Ridge and Oliphant's store.

"Okay. The stealing of the painting was a cover-up for the theft of something else, something of value you had no idea you had, and therefore wouldn't miss. The thief had purposely taken a painting of little value to reinforce the idea of a petty theft. In reality, he was carefully placing it at the edge of the marsh, between your house and the Rollins' next door when he spotted George Reed taking pictures directly in front of him. He did his best to hide but George just kept taking pictures. He was absolutely certain that when they were developed, or reviewed, if they were digital, they would clearly show him in the background."

"So the thief was reasonably sure that George didn't actually see him or even know he was there in any way?" Brewster said, while he maneuvered the SUV across the neighboring lawn, his own driveway being blocked with guests' cars.

"That seems to be the case, since when he told Becky of the great success he had in filming the night before, he made no mention to her of having met someone in the middle of the night in the marsh."

"But what of mine was stolen?" The general took out a neighbor's bush as he finally hit the pavement and turned toward Main Street. Sidney held on as best he could while Bobby hit his head on the ceiling of the car, and Susan bounced against him.

"Some books you received from your uncle."

"Books? But we didn't even know what was there."

"Correct. One of the problems you had was that lack of an inventory list."

"Right. That's why I asked Jarvis to help me go through everything, catalogue what was there so I could keep the valuable stuff, and he could then buy the rest. He found some and so did you when you looked the other day. But the books with any value are all accounted for." The light turned red just as Brewster approached the intersection that defined the shopping area and he slammed on the breaks. "You see anything coming after those two cars. I've got one on this side."

"No, it's clear."

As Brewster continued across the intersection Sidney continued his explanation. "So we thought. You will recall that Jarvis was working without the benefit of the list, but I had one. One of the reasons I recognized Mr. Springwood's name a little while ago was because, as you know, Springwood and Reynolds were your late uncle's attorneys, and they came up with an inventory list. However, the list we received was somewhat abbreviated, as it provided the author's last name—and sometimes their first—and the number of volumes of their work that your uncle had in his collection. As a result, I telephoned Mr. Springwood and asked him if he was ever able to come up with the suspected more comprehensive list or was this the best he could do? He confirmed my suspicions that a comprehensive list was found among your uncle's papers. A list that was part of an extremely comprehensive data base your uncle maintained on his computer."

Brewster slammed on the brakes again, this time to avoid hitting a group of shoppers crossing in front of him. "So the original list we had to work with was an abbreviated one of this data base?"

"Yes. Springwood also confirmed that Sherman Brewster updated it two days before his death and there were 659 volumes in the collection."

Brewster started up again. They were still four blocks away. "And what was your final count?"

"It was six fifty-six."

"So if we're looking for Oliphant, why is Hornig looking for Carson?"

"Because he's the logo," Susan said.

"The what?"

"When Reverend Prentice was knocked down the stairs he spotted a logo on the rain suit the attacker wore: the new logo for the Old Fort Marina."

Sidney took over again. "Chief Hornig also did some background checking with the Jacksonville Police and found out Carson's bookstore down there was involved in selling signed and inscribed first editions that were forgeries. They were first editions of best sellers that someone signed the author's name to without authorization. He told the authorities he bought them in good faith and just resold them for a profit. The police were not entirely convinced but couldn't prove anything."

Brewster pulled into the Coast Bank parking lot a block away from The Previous Page and stopped. "So why are we chasing Oliphant while Hornig chases Carson?"

"Because," Sidney stated, "I'm convinced Oliphant is our thief and murderer and I don't want him to have the chance to destroy those books. Susan, call Geoff and have him tell everyone where we are."

"I don't think Jarvis is here yet," Brewster said as he got out of the car. "I spotted his car still parked in front of my house. It was pretty well blocked in. Have to assume he's on foot and we're here first."

"If he's walking," Bobby said, "he probably won't come the way we did. From where his car is parked it's easier to head over to Castle Street and come down the street parallel to Market. My bet is he goes past the store and comes down Harrison—no lights there—and back-tracks on Market to the store."

"Is there a back entrance?" Brewster said.

"Yeah. But it's all lit up for safety with cameras put in by the store two down from the Page. If he doesn't want to be seen he's better off going in the front door."

"If you don't mind my asking," Brewster said, "how do you know all this?"

Bobby smiled. "My father owns a plumbing supply business in a strip mall on Deer Island. We put in the same lights and security system, as that store has, and came down and talked with Mr. Givens, the owner before we had everything installed. Aunt Tillie arrange it all."

"Should have known your aunt would be involved with it somehow," Sidney said with a chuckle.

"Do you think he's armed?" Brewster asked.

Sidney shook his head. "I don't think so. People usually don't bring their guns to MGA garden parties but I'll bet there's at least one in the store. If we can delay his getting in, the guy tailing him should show up along with Geoff and the Calvary. How you doing, Susan?"

She held up her hand, indicating she had Geoff on the phone. After getting out of the car, she walked away from them while speaking softly. Sidney gave her a wave and then he and Brewster walked quietly across the street to the corner of the nearest building and looked down the sidewalk. The Previous Page stood at the end of the business section and the only real activity came from The Fresh Catch, a seafood restaurant and bar a half a block away farther down on the other side of the street.

As they peered around the corner, Sidney realized that Bobby wasn't with them. He looked around. "Where's Bobby?"

"He's with you. Isn't he?"

"No."

Suddenly they spotted movement across the street from them. Bobby could be seen casually walking along toward the restaurant, as though he didn't have a care in the world. Looking back down the street toward the store, Sidney saw Jarvis Oliphant come around the corner just as Bobby predicted.

"Why don't we just follow Bobby's lead and just casually make our way down the street?" Brewster suggested.

"Okay. Susan, you stay here and give Ray another call. Let him know what's going on."

Susan nodded and moved back toward the car.

"You have a plan, General?" Sidney asked.

"Just want to keep him from getting into the store. Let's try the insurance form angle. Come on." The general stepped out onto the sidewalk with Sidney a half step behind. They walked at a steady pace. They didn't want to appear rushed, just comfortably walking down the street. Bobby, across the way appeared to be about twenty yards ahead of them and almost across from Jarvis. They managed to cover about ten yards when Jarvis spotted them.

"Sidney, General, what you doin' down here?" he said to the two men coming toward him. He seemed nervous and surprised.

"Helen said you would be here. Said you had a call about the front door being left open or something like that," Brewster said as they kept walking toward him. "Wanted to get hold of you before you left to finish off those insurance forms. Sidney here has been helping me to document what was stolen last week. You know, those insurance and police reports I have to fill out."

Jarvis stayed where he'd stopped, in front of the front window just before the entrance to the store, while Brewster moved forward at a casual pace.

"Sidney tells me there seem to be a couple of books missing," Brewster continued. "Since I didn't get a chance to speak with you earlier, I thought I'd try to catch you before the night is over. Have to get that damn report in, and I was hoping the three of us could compare notes and we'd give you a ride back to my place."

Jarvis took a step backward. "Didn't find anything missing when I was goin' over stuff."

"Oh, that's right. You didn't know there was a complete inventory list, did you? Received it from my uncle's attorney while you were out of town. Sidney, what's the name of that writer whose books are missing?" Brewster kept his eyes fixed on Jarvis, who took another step backward.

Sidney took a step behind the general and slightly to his left. "Bell. Three volumes."

Jarvis broke. He turned and started running down the street toward The Fresh Catch. Brewster made a move to go after him and Sidney grabbed his arm as he spotted Bobby come across the street at a run. Jarvis took a quick look over his shoulder to see if Brewster was coming after him and never saw Bobby."

"Grab him, Bob!" the general yelled. "Stop him!"

Jarvis never knew what hit him. Bobby blindsided him with a body block that slammed him against the wall of the store next to his. The air could be heard being forced out of his lungs as he bounced back into Bobby's arms. Bobby grabbed hold of him and kept him from hitting the ground. The general then sprang forward to help Bobby keep him under control, although Jarvis wasn't struggling very much. Sidney stayed in place and watched everything play out in front of him.

"Hold him," Sidney said, seeing Detective Millar and a uniformed policeman get out of an unmarked police vehicle that just stopped across the street in front of the restaurant. "I don't think he's going far."

Bobby and Brewster held on to the now-struggling Jarvis and waited for the policemen coming in their direction. Jarvis also saw the uniform approaching. He stopped struggling and looked back and then forward again. "What's goin' on?" he said.

Trapped, he put his hands in his pockets and shrugged his shoulders. Millar, seeing where the hands went, lifted open the front of her pants suit jacket, revealing the holster on her belt, and, Jarvis, seeing the movement, immediately removed his hands and kept them in front of him. The uniformed officer then took hold of him, and Bobby and Brewster let go.

"Mr. Oliphant," Millar said, "I think we need to talk."

Hornig told her not to arrest Jarvis but to hold him for questioning while they tried to find the missing books that would pin the theft on him. They also needed time to get the film developed, which Walgreens already had in their developer.

A car came down the street from the opposite direction and stopped in front of The Previous Page while a patrol car rolled to a stop around the corner on the street which Jarvis originally came from. Neither had their lights flashing. Hornig and Ray Morton jumped out in front of the store.

"Let's all move around the corner," Hornig said as he ushered Sidney and Brewster over to where the other patrol car parked. "I don't want a bunch of tourists from the restaurant milling about."

They all moved down the side street about ten yards and then Millar, the uniformed officer, and Jarvis joined them.

"If there's anything you'd like to say voluntarily, Jarvis, this would be as good a time as any," Hornig said. "Everything's still pretty informal at this point."

Jarvis looked like a deer caught in a car's headlights as he surveyed being surrounded by four police officers, Sidney, Bobby, and General Brewster. "I think I better not. I think I better talk with Randy Brendan first."

"That's fine. Officer Hunsichar," the chief said, gesturing to the uniformed officer who drove the police car, "will give you a seat in his car over here and explain your rights. By the way, Fred, you have those papers for me from Judge Collins?"

"On the front seat, Chief, all three of them," Hunsichar said.

Hornig then turned to Jarvis. "We have a search warrant for the store, might make it easier if we had the key."

"Okay."

"After you have your chat with Fred, you're welcome to join us inside and help us out if you like."

Jarvis handed over the key. "Still think I'd best talk with Randy."

"That's fine, Jarvis, not a problem."

Hornig handed the key to Millar. "Let's do the back door and stay low profile. Folks across the street will just think it's a routine drunk stop. Don't want the tourists to get antsy."

The four of them went down the alley nearby, entered the store through Jarvis's office area, and assembled just beyond it in the main room. The front window and sales area lights were kept off but the rest were turned on.

"We'll wait just a minute or two while Fred sees if he can convince Jarvis to cooperate. Sidney, just what is it we're looking for? I wouldn't have thought three books of fiction would be that important, enough to kill someone over, but I take it they are."

"Killing over I'm not so sure but, yes, quite important and significant. You see, the three volumes were written by an author by the name of Bell and they were actually one book."

Millar began taking notes as Sidney talked.

"According to the database listing that was obtained from Sherman Brewster's computer, it was published in June of 1848 by the firm of T. C. Newby. Additionally, and this was scanned into the data base, there is a short note inside the front cover of volume one by the author to a person referred to as 'Nell.' In the note, the author is apologizing for the condition of the volumes, as she had made pencil notations in them correcting portions of the text. The author further advises that the volumes were her own personal copies. They were received from the publisher and she was sending them to 'Nell,' as the author's sister, Charlotte, had received a note from Nell, who we are quite sure is Ellen Nussey, indicating her disappointment in not being able to obtain a copy on her own, since they were sold out everywhere. The note is signed simply AB."

"Who the devil is Bell?" Brewster said. "Is it really worth anything? I mean, is it really worth stealing and all the cover up and everything that's gone along with it?"

"Oh, my God!" The exclamation came from Liz Millar. All heads turned in the detective's direction. "Sorry."

"Ah, Detective Millar, you've figured it out." Sidney smiled. "You must have checked the reading list I gave to your daughter in preparation for the Victorian Literature course she signed up for this Fall. For the rest of you who have not figured it out, the books are actually the original three-volume set of *The Tenant of Wildfell Hall* by Acton Bell, which is the pen name used by Anne Brontë, Charlotte Brontë's youngest sister. In answer to the second part of your question, the original three volumes would be of great value on their own.

"However, one clearly identified as being the author's own copy, with pencil notations by the author, combined with that note to Ellen Nussey…well, I think most people would be hard pressed to put a price on it. From a research standpoint alone, Brontë scholars would be lined up around the block to get a look at her comments on her own work."

At this point, Officer Fred Hunischar came in with a

now very nervous and clearly agitated Jarvis leading the way.

"You're still welcome to help out, Jarvis," Hornig said.

The bookseller merely shook his head in response.

"Well, why don't you and Fred just have a seat over there by the front door? Sidney, you're the expert. What do you think?"

"I don't think they'll be out here in the main room for fear of being damaged by a browser, although there's a closed case in the back of the room where Jarvis keeps rare and collectible books. It's not locked but being behind glass doors keeps casual browsers away."

"Where else?"

"First of all, I don't think you need to worry about checking the house for the books. If they're anywhere they're here, although the stolen film could be there. The office here is where he does his cataloging and reference work. Everything is pretty jumbled in there. It looks as though it's in complete disarray, but it's not. I'd say this is the primary place to look. However, as we all know, the best place to hide something is out in the open, and when looking for a book the best place is with other books, especially in a book store."

Horning nodded. "Okay, Liz, take a look at those shelves near the office door. I'll check everything on, in, and around the desk. Sidney, I'd appreciate you not touching anything. I don't have a problem with your making suggestions, but I only want experienced investigators doing the actual searching. Ray, take a peek at that cabinet with the glass doors."

As the three searchers split off to their assigned tasks, Sidney stood by the doorway. "Chief, just a thought. That desk looks a lot like mine at home. There should be a shelf down below in the back. I usually put printer paper and other supplies on it. It's not really visible since the chair is in the way and, being under the desk, it's dark and out of the way."

"Liz, you're younger than I am, take a look down there."

"Sure."

As she got down on her hands and knees, Hornig's phone rang. "Hornig...You got the pictures...Good...All taken that night in Brewster's marsh?"

A loud noise came from the main room behind him. Sidney turned to see Jarvis opening the front door and Fred falling to the floor.

The chief pushed Sidney out of the way and yelled, "Jarvis!" but the now-panicked bookseller rushed out the door. He fell head over heels from tripping over Bobby's outstretched foot beside the parked car in front of him. Bobby kept talking on the phone with Tillie—giving her an update on everything that happened—while another uniformed officer appeared from around the corner and pounced on Jarvis.

"Get away from me!" Jarvis yelled. "It was an accident! Ah didn't mean to hurt anyone. Ah didn't! He just fell overboard. It was an accident!"

Everyone now assembled outside the bookstore while Jarvis was handcuffed and led to the police car around the corner.

"I guess looking under the desk spooked him," Hornig said. "What did you find?"

"Haven't really looked yet," Millar said. "Although I didn't see a shelf."

"Let's look again."

Inside, Millar crawled back under the desk.

"There's definitely no shelf here." She continued to poke around. "Wait a minute. There seems to be something funny about the back here. Yeah, the shelf Professor Lake mentioned has been covered over with a panel of some kind. Yeah, there it is."

They heard something pop as she removed the false back to the underside of the desk.

"Got them, the three Bell books and it looks like five others."

Chapter 24

"S idney, that was quite a performance," Brewster said.

Although the guests had left, the lights still glowed fully, throughout the downstairs. Brewster invited a few friends back to unwind and satisfy his curiosity while Tillie's people cleaned the rest of the house. Colonel and Grace Santulli, Sidney Lake, Ray Morton, Susan Abbott, and Tillie James sat comfortably in the center of the library. Bobby popped in and out as he helped straighten up the room and move the furniture back to where it should be. Susan stayed behind when Geoff went off to police headquarters with Hornig's people to file a formal statement about the film found in Becky Reed's beach bag. At Brewster's request Bobby moved the drinks in from the bar in the kitchen, as well as a few extra chairs, and the seven of them were now sitting and discussing the events of the evening.

"Chief Hornig asked me if I would do it. We had a long conversation before the party began and I laid out as much as I could for him. He agreed that I put together a pretty good circumstantial case against Jarvis and the others but he said he needed something more before he could act against anyone. Plus, he had no intention of moving against a member of one of Morgan's leading families without something concrete to go on, so I agreed to throw out some ideas that might make a few people uneasy and see who reacted."

Brewster held up his hand as a stop sign. "Funny you mentioned leading families, which, of course, the Oliphants are, but do you know what Caldwell said to me later after we came back and Jarvis was arrested? I kidded him a little bit and mentioned it was too bad Jarvis wasn't a Yankee, and he said breeding always tells in the end. The Oliphants came south in the 1870s after the war and Caldwell said they were always considered carpetbaggers anyway." Ray almost lost his drink. "He said it with that smile and twinkle he has and I can never tell whether he's serious or just pulling my leg," Brewster confessed with a chuckle. "Sorry, Sidney, I didn't mean to interrupt. Keep goin'."

Sidney looked at Ray. "Are you all right?" Ray just gave him a wave and signaled for him to go on while he blotted the drops of the scotch and water that splashed on his jacket. Sidney shook his head. "I suppose you can't really judge an entire family by one member but, well, I suppose we could digress on that all evening."

"Professor Lake, what finally got Chief Hornig to act?" Susan said.

"He was on the verge of moving but just couldn't bring himself to do it without something more concrete. While we were talking earlier, he received a call and stepped outside. Just then Geoffrey came over and said it was too bad that the thief managed to get the film the other night, referring to the two rolls of film that Becky knew had been on George's desk, and then he said '…unless it was the wrong film.' At that point, we began to explore some possibilities. Becky said it was George's plan to go to the dark room after the sandbar, which would mean the film could have been on the boat, in their car, or some other place. It was shortly after that Becky called Geoff from Charlotte—cell phones can be useful at times—and told him that George planned to go to the dark room at Roots and Rakes, after they were finished on the sandbar for the day. It wasn't unusual for them and he always put the film in her beach bag. 'And where is the bag now?' he asked her. She said it was on the shelf in the garage next to the entrance to the laundry room. Becky provided him with the key pad code to the garage doors and Geoffrey, unable to find me or the chief, took off on his own to see what he could find, since the Reeds' is no more than five minutes away from here. Sure enough, he found three rolls of undeveloped film and a note that said 'See WJO. May go out. G.' He called Susan who then told me, and I told Chief Hornig immediately. Just in case, he'd already arranged for search warrants for The Previous Page and the Old Fort Marina."

"Both places?' said Santulli, who leaned forward in his straight-backed chair.

"Who's WJO?" Ray asked.

"Mr. Oliphant," Tillie replied. "Full name Warren Jarvis Oliphant. Didn't use the name much except with some folks he didn't grow up with. Didn't use it as a rule, as it was his father's name, too. So he was W Jarvis Oliphant. Then they wouldn't be confused."

"Makes sense.'

Sidney cleared his throat, drawing their attention back to him. "Although I was pretty confident Jarvis took the books, the remote possibility did exist of it's being Carson, in view of the rain suit and his being a former bookstore owner in Jacksonville who might understand the value of the book. Hornig wanted to cover all the bases, as he put it. At that point, he asked me to put on my little show when the opportunity presented itself. Both Jarvis and Carson were in the room, and I was told not to mention either one of them, or for that matter, anyone—"

Just then Geoffrey peeked into the library with Mickey in tow. "Thought you would all still be here. Hope you don't mind my bringing Mickey."

"No, certainly not," Brewster said." Mickey and I are old friends."

Having been given the okay, Mickey came in first and made a direct line to the two people in the room she did not know: the Santullis. After much rubbing of ears and pats on the head, Mickey went over and settled down next to Sidney's chair. Geoffrey settled down on the arm of the oversized and overstuffed chair that Susan occupied.

Ray Morton, who sat on the sofa next to Susan's chair, took a sip of his scotch. "Sidney, what really convinced you it was Jarvis and not an outsider, such as maybe Springwood, who would have also have known about the books?"

"First off, it was Tillie here who was the catalyst for everything. She just knew there had to be something fishy going on—" Sidney chuckled. "—couldn't resist that one."

Ray groaned and rolled his eyes. "Okay, what about it, Tillie? What made you so sure all along that there was something else going on and why were you so sure Becky Reed couldn't be involved?

"Because of what my grandmother always told me."

"Which is?

"When you want to know what a person is really like, you got to imagin' them as what they would have been like as a seven or eight year old. That's the age just before they start to change, when they check their feelin's before speakin' an' doin'. Before that they're wide open an you see the clown, the sneak, the lover, the snitch, the helper, the good, and the bad. When they get older, they may hide it but the temptation will always will be there. Miss Becky is a good one, not in her nature to be bad."

"I'm going to have to remember that one. Just curious, but how do you see me and, say, Lake over there."

Tillie thought for a minute.

"I'm sorry, Tillie, I didn't mean to put you on the spot."

"No, no. It's okay. I was just lookin' at you both, an' I saw two of the biggest bizzy-body seven-year-olds I can imagine." The laughter resounded in the room, and Tillie had a great big smile on her face. "I ain't fired, am I?"

"No absolutely not," Sidney said, while laughing.

"Okay," Ray said. "I'm sorry for the interruption but it was worth it. Sidney continue with your story."

"I think I better. Well, you remember when I mentioned being in The Previous Page, looking for charts of the Morgan River? Well, I came across Jarvis's computer in his office while he stepped out. He later said he had been doing some research and sorting out new books he had recently acquired. What caught my eye was the computer screen: the Brontë Society web page was on it. It meant nothing to me at the time but, when I realized it was the Brontë books that were missing, it registered. As someone who taught Victorian literature for a lot of years, I have memberships in a couple of these societies: Dickens, Hardy, Thackeray—there are lots of them, and they all have web sites. From the Brontë site, I learned of a regional meeting of the American branch of their Society in Jacksonville, Florida, earlier this week. A quick call this afternoon to Robin Attwater, the regional representative for the Southeast United States, confirmed that Jarvis was there Tuesday evening—and not in Atlanta as he told Helen—and made lots of inquiries about Anne Brontë.

"Of course, we have to come back to Tillie again and her fried Daniel Doyle. Without him we would never have pursued anything. By the way, Geoffrey, how did the police make out with that film?" said Sidney, changing the subject a bit.

"Nothing firm yet." The response came from Pete Hornig, who'd just entered the room. "There's definitely something in the background of a couple of the shots but they're going to have to work on them a little more to see what level of clarity they can get. Be pretty sad if Jarvis did all this for nothing. I mean, if they really can't identify him from the pictures."

"Come on in, Pete. Grab yourself something and pull up a chair," Brewster said, waving one hand at the table with the liquor, ice, wine, and glasses all neatly arranged. "You could probably use something about now." As the chief headed for the table, Brewster shrugged. "Well, you at least have proof of the books being in his possession."

"I could use one of those," Hornig said, giving a nod to Colonel Santulli's scotch on the rocks.

Brewster chuckled. "Pete, how did you ever know exactly which editions of those old books you were looking for?"

"It was all Sidney's doing. He gave us a description we couldn't miss. How in the world did you know all that specific information about the books, Sidney?"

"Ah, we have Professor Ryan and the Brontë Society to thank for that."

"So that's what Professor Ryan was doing," Geoffrey said.

"Exactly. Once I knew we were dealing with *The Tenant of Wildfell Hall* by Anne Brontë and, since Professor Ryan was in England, a reasonable distance from Yorkshire where the Brontë Society and Museum are located in the town of Haworth, I asked her to do some research for me and she came up with this." Sidney took some pieces of paper from his pocket and placed them on the coffee table for all to see. "I typed this up based on the information Hattie, or Professor Ryan, gave me over the phone." The papers gave a complete description of the three volumes including their size and how the volumes were broken down by story content. "The people at the museum said that they have no record of any copies of the book having Anne Brontë's pencil notations in them. Such a book might have been part of the author's copies she received, although no copies of them have ever surfaced. They do know that her sister Charlotte received author's copies of her books, so they presume Anne did as well.

"Professor Ryan theorized that it could have been part of the Brontë material assembled by a one TJ Wise almost seventy-five years ago. Wise and his co-author JA Symington put together the first truly comprehensive documentation of Brontë materials. It was titled The Shakespeare Head Brontë and contained not just the novels but also letters as well as both published and unpublished materials written by members of the family. Today, Wise is generally considered to be one of the great swindlers of literary artifacts, as he talked members of the Brontë family, friends, and acquaintances into providing him with a great deal of original Brontë material, which he eventually sold off to collectors for his own profit.

"This probably accounts for so much original material being in both private and public collections outside of England. These volumes are just the sort of thing that Wise would have loved to get his hands on.

"I haven't seen the books yet but I can't wait to get my hands on them, as the general's uncle's database provided only a general comment about Anne Brontë's notations and no mention of the note she wrote to Ellen Nussey. You can be certain the museum would be interested in all of the material since there is no record of Anne Brontë ever having made comments about one of her books. Also, we have to consider that the note could very well be a forgery, given the reputation of TJ Wise. We also have to consider the possibility of Jarvis himself writing the note. There were some papers with it that indicated he was practicing Anne Bronte's handwriting."

"Well, I've looked at them, Sidney," Hornig said, "and, in addition to matching the physical description you provided, they're full of pencil notations that seem to be written in the same hand as is the note inside the front cover addressed to 'Nell,' who I guess is that Ellen Nussey you just mentioned? Just how valuable do you think they are? That may be an important part of the case."

"It's difficult to say. Probably a good guide is the recent auction of a three volume first edition of Emily Brontë's *Wuthering Heights*. It's not signed and it doesn't have personal notations but sold for over £160,000, which would be around $250,000, so I have to believe that Jarvis had early retirement on his mind."

"He sure is getting his dream," Ray added. "Let's hope he confesses to everything before he finds out what's on that film."

"You know," Susan said, directing her question to Sidney, "there's something I never quite understood." They all turned to look at her, including Mickey who had moved across the room and was now sitting at her feet. "What triggered you to make the connection between George Reed and the theft here?"

"Ah, that was not my doing, that was Mickey."

"Mickey?" both Ray and the general said in unison.

Mickey, hearing her name, sat up straight at the side of Susan's chair.

"Oh, yes. That day I went to meet Tillie at Gregory's—where she told me about Daniel Doyle and the problem with the tides—Tillie, Mickey, and I went over to the spot where the painting had been found. While there, Mickey decided to nose around the marsh nearby and found no less than three nests. Later, when we realized that someone was looking for Reed's camera or film, I began to wonder if this might have been the location that George Reed was photographing the night before he was killed. Actually, the general here confirmed that George was out there from time to time, and Caldwell was even with him, once in the area, looking for raccoons. So it fit."

"So it was Mickey who solved it all," Susan said, scratching Mickey behind her ears.

"Ah, yes," Sidney said, "it was Mickey who did it."

Just then Hornig's cell phone rang. He answered it as he walked away from the group and headed for the library door that led to the front entrance hall. Suddenly he was heard to say "*Shit!*" and then "God damn it!" He then continued talking quietly. The library remained quiet while the chief spoke on the phone. After a moment or so, Hornig came back in.

"That didn't sound too good," Ray said.

"Good news, bad news. Jarvis has confessed to everything, claims he didn't mean to do it. All he wanted to do is see what pictures were in the camera. Never really wanted to hurt him, but it all got out of hand when he tried to get George to fall out of the boat on his own, didn't mean to kill Reed. Yes, he did admit to stealing the books. Also seems he's made a practice of forging author's signatures and putting them in some of the books he was selling so he could charge a premium for them. Have a feeling some of what he has in that glass doored bookcase of his needs a second look."

"Okay, that's obviously the good news, what's the bad news?"

"You're never going to believe this. The books, the Anne Brontë three volumes, they're gone. Someone lifted them from the seat of one of the police cars."

END

About the Author

With a background in international banking, author Tim Holland's financial articles have appeared in banking and financial trade magazines. Book reviews and literary criticism have appeared in publications of The Recorder Publishing Co, New Jersey; The Brontë Society, Haworth, England; and political commentary and general interest in *ToTheCenter.com, Charleston Post* and *Courier, Summerville Journal Scene, The Beaufort Gazette, The State, The Fountain Hills Times, Arizona Republic*, and *Virginia Gazette*. He has given speeches and presentations in twenty-two states and twelve countries to large and small groups alike.

CPSIA information can be obtained
at www.ICGtesting.com
Printed in the USA
BVHW042209271019
562167BV00029B/782/P

9 781626 946736